Pixieland
Forest of Sighs

by

MaryBeth Hewes

Shadow Wolf Publishing
Bartlett, Tennessee

Pixieland: Forest of Sighs

Cover and chapter art and design by MaryBeth Hewes

Edited by Amanda H. Braswell for Spot On Editing
Contact at amandahbraswell@gmail.com

Book formatting by D.E. LaRiviere

Shadow Wolf
Publishing
www.shadowwolfpublishing.com

Dedicated to my wonderful husband, Newton Hewes. The last section title in this book is JOY. Newton is my best friend and the one who brings JOY into my life.

Acknowledgements

- I would like to thank my wonderful husband Newton for his encouragement and support.
- Thank you to my daughter, Susan Polk, for all that she does to help promote my books.
- Thank you to my beautiful family. I hope you will always enjoy these stories.
- A big thank you to all of my internet friends who read my stories daily. You know who you are. Thank you for taking the time to post comments and queries. And thank you for the many generous compliments as well as words of encouragement. This experience has been so much fun and I am pleased to have such great friends to share the journey with me.
- Thank you to my friends who provided inspiration for some of the new characters' names:

Laney Eaton	-Morella, the Morel faerie
Andrea Krochalis	-Skuba, the mountain elf
Aline and GB	-Aline, the forest faerie
Susan Polk	-Ernie the blue mouse and also Sandrea, the Dynast twin
Pam Stack	-Bridget, the young girl in the story
Summer Bailey	-Summer, the Dynast twin

- Mason the Shadow Dweller is inspired by Woodland Park's Atlas Shannon, the beautiful Dogue de Bordeaux belonging to our good friends Viola and Jim Shannon. Atlas' likeness appears as art in the book. Thank you, Viola and Jim.

- Thank you Pam and Bridget for the inspiration that led to the writing of Part One of this book, "The Faerie House". Although the story is entirely fiction, I hope that Bridget will be able to see something of herself in the young girl within these pages.
- I would like to thank my first grade teacher Pat Cavender for her unending patience with the little girl who struggled during those first two weeks of school. Her understanding helped me to adapt and grow.
- Thanks to Amanda Braswell of Spot On Editing for her professional edits of this manuscript.
- I would like to extend my thanks to Donna LaRiviere for her excellent work on the cover layout and for so beautifully incorporating my artwork into the book.
- Finally, a big thank you to publisher D. E. LaRiviere of Shadow Wolf Publishing for formatting my books and for all of his help and guidance.
- In memory of Joe Ann Rich. We lost a dear friend and online reader this year. We were all saddened by your passing and we miss you very much, Joe Ann. Our hearts go out to your family.

Prologue

The twin moons of Pixieland disappeared as if by magic as the first fingers of dawn reached across the rich woods, rolling hills and flowering meadows of this beautiful world. First light was accompanied by brilliant birdsong as feathered friends filled the air with their melodious greetings to the brand new day.

Newton the Crow had been dreaming. In his dream he was human once again and walked the pristine halls of the city's largest hospital. From somewhere a loudspeaker was blaring "Dr. Newton Bennett, you are urgently needed in surgery. Dr. Newton Bennett... "

Newton moved restlessly in his sleep as one hospital corridor led to another and then another. Newton's sense of panic matched the increasingly urgent tone of the repetitive voice from the loudspeaker. Try as he might, the good doctor could not find the location for the surgery and, as he walked faster, the voice from the loudspeaker grew louder. Newton clapped his hands over his ears to muffle the piercing sound. Wildly, he looked around in every direction, but he could not find his way. The hospital corridors had become an unfriendly maze with Newton trapped inside.

Newton the Crow woke with a start and immediately felt an overwhelming sense of relief. It had only been a dream. The portly crow stretched, fluffed his feathers and looked around. Pixieland was as lovely as ever and Newton appreciated the bright sounds that filled the early morning air. The crow breathed deeply. He could smell honeysuckle and roses as well as a hint of lavender. He just wanted to forget all about the disturbing dream.

Newton flapped away from the tree and flew around the meadow lost in thought. Today he would be leaving Pixieland and returning to Earth. The Pixielanders always referred to his home planet as Otherworld and the more time he spent here, the more planet Earth had begun to seem like Otherworld to him as well.

The crow wasn't sure why he had been called upon to help Pixieland. However, he knew what Victoria wanted him to do first and he hoped that he was equal to the task. As if his wings had a mind of their own, the crow turned and rose higher in the air beginning the long flight to the Forest of Sighs. He just wanted one more look at the Dark Wood. Maybe the dreaded forest would reveal some of its secrets in the early light of this new day.

As Newton drew nearer he could see the dark smudge against an otherwise flawless landscape. The crow landed in the grass as close to the trees as he dared and gazed into the impenetrable wood. He wondered how so many trees could have such black foliage and still be alive. There was not one spot of color. Everything about the tight clustering of trees was dark and dismal and sad. The sounds of woe were heartbreaking and Newton found himself wondering how such a dark place could have any reason whatsoever to be in a beautiful world like Pixieland.

Newton heard a twig snap and turned to see Victoria standing next to him. She was entirely covered with a simple brown hooded cloak. In a soft voice the Portal Keeper said, "I do this too, you know...stand here and try to understand."

Newton nodded. "This is the day we go back to Otherworld. Buddy and I are ready. Those who are going with us will meet under my tree later this morning just as you suggested."

Victoria smiled at the mention of the elf, Buddy. She knew that he was the first one Newton had met after arriving in Pixieland. Since then they had become the best of friends and were often seen together. Buddy had a love for adventure and Victoria doubted that the energetic elf would want Newton to participate in any future adventure without him alongside.

Newton had allowed Buddy to study the ancient elixir recipes from the mysterious Book of Crows and the young elf had mostly perfected the art of elixir making. His potions allowed one to change into another creature for a day. Victoria knew that this skill could prove handy, but she also knew that Newton was a shape shifter and did not need such a potion. However, there were rules that governed his abilities. Newton must only use his gift for good reason and only to benefit others. If the crow ever failed to follow these rules, Victoria knew that he would lose the ability to shift shape. But Victoria believed in Newton and she did not think that he would fail.

The crow and the Portal Keeper stood there in silence for some time. When Victoria turned to go she spoke. "Until later this morning then?"

Newton nodded and repeated, "Until later this morning."

As Newton stood and stared at the Forest of Sighs, it suddenly occurred to him why the dream of the previous night had bothered him. It had been the first bad dream he had ever had since living here in Pixieland. A shudder of dread ran down his spine. The Dark Wood had begun to spill over into the rest of Pixieland. A bad dream here, maybe a negative thought there…

Newton knew that it must be stopped. There was much at stake. All of Pixieland hung in the balance.

Chapter 1

The purple fog of morning had already begun its retreat from the rolling hills and lush valleys of Pixieland. The promise of another beautiful day hung in the air along with the damp smell of honeysuckle and cherryvine. Wildflower could hear the boys from inside her faerie home. She smiled and fondly shook her head at the sound of their voices. Those two were always up to something. Her toy dog Cookie and his friend JJ, the green parrot, had been inseparable ever since the time that Cookie had found the small bird lost in the woods. For reasons unknown, JJ had no memory of his past and when they found him, he couldn't even tell them why he wasn't able to fly. Fortunately, after a thorough inspection of his wings, Newton the Crow assured him that the condition was temporary—something to do with flight feathers. Newton also told JJ that he needed to exercise his wings to keep them nice and strong for the day when he would be able to fly again. JJ had devised a clever method for this. He would sit on Cookie's back, his tiny feet holding onto the fur as tightly as possible. When Cookie trotted along investigating first one thing and then another, JJ worked hard, flapping his wings rapidly. This felt almost like flying and worked well except for the occasional times when he lost his grip and landed in the dirt.   Cookie, being a busy dog with a keen sense of smell, was usually otherwise occupied and did not generally think to stop and give JJ a chance to regain his perch.

"Wait up, will ya!   When are you ever gonna learn some manners?" grouched JJ.

He had just lost his footing on Cookie's back again and taken another unplanned dust bath.   Shaking the dirt from his feathers, JJ wolf-whistled loudly in an effort to get the dog's attention.   Cookie heard him and looked back, tilting his head to one side.   JJ puckered up and whistled again to watch the little dog hold his head at precisely that angle and perk up his ears.   Cookie whimpered softly and JJ laughed.   "You crack me up, you know that?"   The green parrot started the slow climb up Cookie's leg, flapping his wings a little to help him along until he reached the animal's back and walked straight to his favorite spot right behind the dog's shoulders.   Cookie stood very still while JJ (otherwise known as Cookie's "feathers") regained position.   Then JJ yelled, "Ok, LET'S ROLL!"

Wildflower called to the boys as she watched them disappear over the hill, "You two come home early this evening.   Don't forget—we leave bright and early tomorrow morning."

She barely heard JJ's voice as it floated to her from a distance, "Right.   We'll be back before dark and that's a promise."

Wildflower's thoughts turned to the conversation that had taken place with two of her friends yesterday.   She had been flying around gathering bits of this and that in the woods when she heard their familiar laughter drifting down from the canopy above.   She followed the musical sound until it led to her friends Aline and Rosie. They had been discussing their upcoming trip with Newton and Buddy to Otherworld. Aline and Rosie could not wait to tell Wildflower all about their plans.

Wildflower nodded knowingly and said, "Guess what! Buddy came to see me earlier today. He asked if I wanted to go along too, so I will be joining you on that trip to Otherworld."

Rosie asked, "What about Cookie and JJ?"

Wildflower pulled a face and then grinned. "They are coming with us."

Rosie loved those little rascals, so she was very happy to hear that they would all be going on the trip together. "Don't worry, Wildflower. We know that Cookie can be a real handful so we will help you take care of him, right, Aline?"

"Of course," Aline replied.

Then the three of them put their heads together chatting happily about all of the fun things they might see and do in the other world.

Buddy whistled as he walked down the path to Okikki's garden. The elf had no intention of going to Otherworld without his favorite squirrel friend. As he entered the garden he found her busily digging up some tasty nuts. Buddy held up a platter of his famous pecan-berry delights. They were still warm and the delicious smell wound throughout her garden and tickled Okikki's nose. She twitched it a little, then turned and smiled, revealing a few tiny white teeth.

"Oh, yummy!" she proclaimed as she rolled her big brown eyes. "What do I smell?" She hugged her friend quickly, took the platter and tucked into the largest piece on the plate.

"Get packed, Okikki. We are going back to Otherworld! Victoria the Sentinel of the Main Portal will be sending us," Buddy said importantly. Then after a dramatic pause he continued. "Aline wants a tiger elixir for her birthday. Since there are no tigers here in Pixieland, we are going to Otherworld to search for one."

Okikki's voice sounded muffled behind a mouth full of Buddy's treats. "I don't know what a tiger is, but hopefully it will not mind if you borrow a couple of hairs for the elixir."

Buddy looked doubtful. "I have been reading about them in Newton's book of animals and from the description they sound rather dangerous."

Okikki swallowed the pecan-berry delight. She looked curious as she asked, "What does the Main Portal Keeper have to do with your elixirs? I mean, she doesn't normally open portals unless it's for an important reason. Your elixirs are very nice and all, but I don't understand why she would get involved in the making of them."

Buddy waved a hand dismissively as he explained, "It has something to do with Newton. Victoria is sending him to Otherworld for a different reason. But the really good news is that she has said it's fine for us to go along and search for the tiger at the same time."

Okikki considered all that the elf had told her while he waited for her response. She asked, "Do you think the trip will be safe enough for Tango?"

Buddy glanced at Okikki's son who was scampering up and down a nearby tree. The elf was pretty sure that the youngster could hear their conversation. He was not a tiny baby anymore and Buddy knew that the group of friends who were going on the trip could assist Okikki with the youngster. The elf answered honestly. "Finding the tiger will not be without risk." He clapped his friend on the back and remarked, "But when has a little risk ever bothered you? Unless I miss my guess, you won't want to stay behind. Wildflower, Cookie, JJ, Aline and Rosie are all coming along with us. You know that we will be happy to help you keep an eye on Tango."

Okikki had absentmindedly begun to nibble on another delight. She was thinking and chewing, thinking and chewing. Buddy waited patiently.

Tango, who had indeed been listening to the whole conversation from a distance, ran up to them and tugged on Okikki as he begged, "Please, Mama, can we go with Uncle Buddy to Otherworld? I want to see the tiger!"

Okikki looked from her son's eager face to Buddy's. It didn't take long for her to decide. In her heart, she longed for another adventure and this promised to be an exciting one. She didn't relish the thought of staying behind in Pixieland waiting for the others to return. Hugging Tango, she said, "I don't see how we could possibly turn it down. It will be fun to help you make Aline's wish come true. When do we leave?"

Buddy clapped his hands in delight and rewarded Okikki and Tango with his famous, fabulous smile.

Chapter 2

The next morning, Newton and Buddy stood waiting under Newton's favorite tree for the others to arrive. Before long they heard talking and laughter as Wildflower, Aline, and Rosie came fluttering down the path. Cookie trotted along in front with JJ on his back.

JJ wanted Newton to know that he had been working on his wing exercises, so when he noticed the crow watching their approach he flapped his wings as rapidly as possible. He quickly lost his balance and fell. As usual, Cookie paid no attention at all and kept moving. An exasperated JJ yelled, "WAIT UP, WOULD YA?"

Wildflower hid a smile and held out an arm to the irate green bird. "Hop aboard, JJ. I will give you a ride."

JJ climbed onto Wildflower's arm, muttering under his breath about the trials of dealing with ill-mannered canines.

When Cookie finally noticed that his feathers were gone, he ran back toward Wildflower. The papillon saw JJ sitting on the faerie's arm and the little dog jumped and barked as if to say, "Please return my feathers." Wildflower laughed as she sat the little bird down on Cookie's back.

Okikki and Tango came running along the tree branches

overhead to join the friends. Tango's face shone with excitement. "Hi, Uncle Buddy!" he called out enthusiastically as he caught sight of his favorite "uncle". Buddy smiled and waved at both Okikki and Tango.

Newton rasped in his crow voice, "Is everyone ready?"

They all nodded. Buddy turned just in time to see Moziac the Cat approaching the group.

Meanwhile in Otherworld, it was the last minute of the last hour of the last day of school before summer break. Bridget had been happy all day and now with the final bell about to ring for the very last time this year, her excitement was growing. A moment later when the bell sounded, she was the first one to emerge from the classroom. Her eyes scanned the throng of students filling the hallway. Bridget grinned from ear to ear as she noticed her best friend Brooke waving in her direction. The girls had been planning their summer vacation for weeks. Among other things, they were looking forward to sleepovers, playing computer games, and trips to the local skating rink. The two eight year old girls vowed that *this* summer they would put on those metal skates and somehow find the courage to actually join the other skaters on that slippery rink.

Bridget and Brooke looked at each other and giggled as they made their way down the hall and out the front door of the school where their mothers were waiting in the car line to collect them.

The next day, Bridget was in the kitchen baking cookies with her mother Pam when the phone call came that would change her entire summer. Pam answered the phone, then turned and handed the receiver to Bridget.

"Oh, hi, Brooke," Bridget began and then lapsed into silence as Brooke spoke on the other end of the line. In a weak voice Bridget said, "Oh, well, then, ok...have fun. See you later..." As she hung up the phone her face crumbled.

Pam took her daughter's hand and led her over to a chair at the kitchen table. She sat facing Bridget and softly asked. "What is it, honey?"

Bridget looked as if she might cry as she blurted out, "Brooke is going to be away for the *whole* summer."

Pam took one look at her child's sad face and said, "Oh, no, and you two had such big plans. Tell you what. I will find something very special for us to do this summer. We'll make our own fun, just the two of us, ok?" When Bridget nodded mutely, Pam wrapped her arms around her and gave her a big hug. Looking over Bridget's shoulder, Pam's eyes fell on the computer sitting in the corner of the living room. It gave her an idea.

Later that night after Bridget was fast asleep, Pam logged on to the internet and began to search. When she stumbled across a site about building faerie houses, she knew that it would appeal to Bridget's active imagination. As she scanned the information and the pictures of various faerie houses built by others, she spoke aloud, "The Faerie House." *That's it!* Pam's enthusiasm mounted as she thought to herself. *Bridget loves stories about faeries and elves and magical creatures. We'll drive to the mountains, rent a cabin in the woods and build our very own faerie house.* Pam could hardly wait until the next morning to tell Bridget about her idea. She knew her daughter would miss her best friend, but Pam hoped that what she had in store for Bridget would cheer her.

Moziac sat down, flicking her tail in true cat fashion. She looked at the group of Pixielanders before her with a seemingly indifferent air. Then she focused on JJ who was sitting on Cookie's back with his feet curled around two hunks of dog hair. As she gazed at him, he started to feel nervous (she was a cat after all). When JJ was nervous he whistled. First he belted out a wolf-whistle and then it turned into a rousing verse of "Row, Row, Row Your Boat". Cookie twisted around in an effort to see what the little bird was doing. The curious dog turned in a tight circle trying to see JJ who was whistling madly. Wildflower attempted to straighten Cookie. Buddy tried so hard not to laugh at the trio that his ears turned red and wiggled. Okikki had her hand firmly over Tango's mouth, but her son's shoulders were moving up and down suspiciously.

Moziac's eyes twinkled as she spoke loudly in order to be heard over the whistling JJ. "I will be opening the portal to Otherworld. Someone should hold Tango, JJ and Cookie during the transport."

Okikki took charge of Tango. Buddy picked up Cookie and in response the little dog made some rather odd noises under his breath.

Wildflower glanced at Buddy apologetically. "Please forgive Cookie if he growls just a little bit. He's *so* independent and he never, ever likes to be held." She cast a no-nonsense look at Cookie, then turned her attention to JJ, carefully cupping her hands around him for the transport.

Moziac gave further instructions. "Everyone gather closely together."

As the group tightened, they heard a sound like a great wind blowing. It started low, but built rapidly until it was a tremendous roar.

Everything around them began to break up and the last thing Newton remembered seeing was a tiny, white-haired lady standing right where Moziac had been just a moment before. Her arms were outstretched and her large eyes were gold with just a hint of green. She looked straight at Newton and smiled the same clever cat smile. In that last split second he mouthed *Victoria?* The crow wondered briefly if the others had seen the same thing. Then their world wavered and disappeared.

Pam and Bridget loved the little vacation cabin in the woods. The Blue Ridge Mountains were nothing short of breathtaking. Earlier that day they had spotted an overlook from which they could see the mountains spread out for miles. The nearer peaks were a deep purple and those further away ranged from dark blue to the palest of blues until they finally merged with the white of the cloud-covered sky.

Mother and daughter gazed in silence for a while, just taking it all in.   Then Bridget said, "Read it again, Mama!"

Pam smiled at her daughter as she removed several folded pieces of paper from her purse.   The papers included guidelines for the proper way to build a faerie house as well as examples.   "Now remember," Pam said, "we don't want to copy any of these houses. We want ours to be a Bridget original!"

"Ok, Mom, but they are all so pretty!" exclaimed Bridget.

"Yes and yours will be pretty too," encouraged Pam.   "It says that everything you use to build the faerie house should be natural—no man-made items.   We need to gather whatever we want to use from the woods."

Bridget brightened at the prospect.   "I know!   We can get some sticks and pine cones, some nice leaves and acorns.   And I brought those seashells and some sand from the beach last summer."

Pam nodded and smiled.   "That sounds good."   Then she added, "We also need to decide if we want a freestanding house or if we want to build it against something.   Maybe we could find a tree that has a hollow space down low near the roots so that we could use the inside of the tree as our walls.   Or maybe we could find a way to secure a freestanding house to a tree somehow."   Pam studied the pictures, thinking of different ways they could construct the house.

Bridget exclaimed, "I would really like to build it in a hollow tree if we can find one.   I think that would be the easiest and we could build a little front porch with a roof as well!"   As Bridget shared her thoughts, she became more and more animated.

Pam smiled as she watched her daughter's eager face and listened to her excited chatter. She gave Bridget a quick hug and suggested, "Let's get started."

Chapter 3

Not too far from the little cabin where Pam and Bridget were staying stood a house with a tin roof. Beyond the house there was a lovely garden that boasted a fine little pond with a waterfall. That the waterfall was man-made did nothing to stop the many frogs from hatching out on a regular basis. On any given day they sounded like an amphibian chorus vigorously performing to the music of the waterfall spilling into the pond. The garden was beautiful in every respect and a treat to the eyes. The atmosphere was relaxed and when one entered, it felt as if time stood still while birds sang, frogs erupted and crickets chirped. The occasional bunny could be seen hopping in the tall grasses that grew at the edge of the garden. It was a soothing place to sit and think or just daydream.

On this particular day while Pam and Bridget searched the woods, there was a disturbance beneath a generous pile of leaves that covered the ground around a certain mature oak of undetermined years. A pair of eyes peeked out from beneath the leaves, then an entire face. Then a young mountain elf named Skuba emerged and, after brushing leaf dust off of his clothes, he looked around the garden smiling broadly at no one in particular.

His home was in the Faerie Glen across the hardtop road, but he had fallen in love with this garden shortly after the man-made waterfall appeared. The elf had been a childhood companion of the lady who lived in the house with the tin roof. Even though she was all grown up now, he still enjoyed living nearby. Skuba often left his home in the Faerie Glen to spend days at a time here in his favorite garden. He enjoyed long conversations with the bees that buzzed lazily about the flowers and the frogs that hopped around the pond. He had not seen others of his kind for many years and often wondered if perhaps he was the last remaining elf on the mountain.

Skuba searched until he found a luscious morel mushroom which he sliced lengthwise and devoured one piece at a time. This was the tastiest type of mushroom on the mountain and the elf savored every bite, delighting in his breakfast which he later topped off with a handful of wild berries.

Skuba's favorite pastime was collecting things. He loved finding unusual treasures and he had just found a gleaming coin when he heard the sounds of footfalls and talking. Slipping quickly and quietly behind a tree, he peeked around to see who was making so much noise.

Pam and Bridget just happened to be walking down the path behind Skuba's garden. They moved slowly, chatting, and from time to time selecting another leaf, acorn, or clump of moss. Mother and daughter passed right by Skuba without noticing. The curious elf decided to follow them, from a safe distance of course.

Bridget was having so much fun. She thought the mountains were beautiful and she loved being with her mama and walking in the woods gathering all of the pretty things for their project. They emerged from the trees and crossed the hardtop road. As they moved into the Faerie Glen, Bridget put her hand over her mouth and gasped. Pam took her other hand and for a moment, they just stood together and gazed at the scene before them.

It felt just right to Bridget and she began to smile. Looking up at her mother, she gushed, "It's perfect, isn't it?"

Pam smiled down at her and said, "I do believe so."

The Faerie Glen had a distinct atmosphere—quiet and mystical. Bridget walked around among the old apple trees, overgrown with grapevines some of which looked quite strong. As she moved toward the center of the glen, the girl spied a large maple tree with a fat, round trunk and an opening just above the curve of the roots. Bridget got down on her knees and peeked inside to make sure that it was hollow. The interior was dark, so she put a hand inside and began to feel around cautiously. She pulled out a number of colorful bird feathers, some dried mushrooms and a few other odds and ends. Pam stooped down to help her and together they cleaned out the opening in the tree, piling its contents nearby. Before long they had the interior space emptied and Bridget used her hand to make the soil floor as smooth and level as possible.

Pam said, "I think we're going to need a flashlight to see inside a little better when we decorate the walls."

Bridget nodded her head in agreement.

The afternoon was waning, so Pam decided that it would be best to wait until the next morning to start building.   She suggested, "Let's go back to the cabin.   We can set everything that we have collected out on the table and make sure that we have everything we need.   Now that we've found our spot, we can make a sketch so that we will have something to go by when we actually begin to build. Let's hurry back now and get busy.   We have much to do before bedtime."

As Bridget stood, she placed her hand against the tree for support, then yanked it back quickly, a look of surprise on her face.

"What?" asked Pam anxiously as she grabbed her daughter's hand to examine it.   "Did you get a bug bite?"

"No, Mama," answered Bridget.   "Put your hand on the tree."

Pam complied.   The bark was rough and cool to the touch. When Pam looked puzzled, Bridget touched the tree again.   She felt a thrumming from deep within the bark, a steady, but light vibration.

"Don't you feel it, Mama?"

Pam asked, "Feel what, honey?"

Bridget looked up into her mother's face and asked earnestly, "You really don't feel it moving?"

"No, it just feels like a regular old tree trunk."   Pam tousled Bridget's hair and grinned dismissively.   "You have such a good imagination which is why this is going to be so much fun!"

Skuba watched from behind a nearby sapling.   He was

18

curious about what the two humans were doing and wondered why they were so interested in his home.   The tree that they had chosen was Skuba's own.   He took a step forward and Bridget turned to stare in his direction as if she sensed his presence.   Skuba slowly looked down so that only the top of his hat was visible.   The elf knew that it would blend with the surrounding vegetation and besides, he had always been a master at hiding in plain sight.

Pam's eyes followed her daughter's as she quietly said, "Do you hear something?   We might see a rabbit or raccoon or maybe even a deer if we are lucky."

Bridget scanned the area.   Then she shook her head.   The moment was gone.   She smiled up at her mother as she took her hand.

Then they walked out of the Faerie Glen and back across the hardtop road, talking to each other in low voices as they made their way back down the path to their cabin.   When he knew that it was safe, Skuba approached his home tree.   He scratched his head when he saw all his belongings in a pile outside.   Then he peered inside. Skuba smiled a crooked smile as he thought to himself *I wonder what they are planning*.   Then, dismissing it from his mind, he turned and headed back toward his favorite garden, arriving just in time to see the early evening fireflies light the sky.

It took several days for Pam and Bridget to complete the faerie house.   Bridget started by scooping out a pathway in front of the inverted V-shaped opening.   Along the pathway she carefully placed small seashells found on a sandy beach the previous summer. She mixed water and soil thickly to form a heavy mud. Pam spread the mud on each interior wall. Bridget smoothed clumps of soft green moss into the mud, pressing them firmly until they held. Then Pam misted the moss. The result was a living, growing "wallpaper". They sat near the tree chattering happily as they interlaced dried grasses together to form a soft, thick carpet for the soil floor of the interior.

Bridget looked up at her mother with a question in her eyes. "Mama, do you think they will come?"

"Who, dear?" answered Pam, a bit distractedly as she worked.

"The faeries", whispered Bridget. "Will they like the house and will they come? Do you think when we finish that we could watch and see if they appear or do you think they would know that we are looking for them and maybe hide from us?"

Pam looked down at Bridget's inquisitive face. She answered carefully. "This is going to be such a beautiful faerie house, honey. When we finish we will take some pictures of it. If you want to spend a day or two here waiting to see if a faerie might come along, then that's fine. We can make a picnic out of it and see what happens."

Bridget smiled happily.

Then her mother advised, "But try not to be too disappointed if we don't see anything out of the ordinary. It isn't likely, you know."

Pam didn't want to tell Bridget that there were no such things as faeries and elves, although she herself did not believe that they really existed. She didn't want to spoil the fun for her daughter and planned to cross that bridge when they came to it.

Bridget carefully placed the woven grasses onto the soil floor of the interior. It was beginning to look so nice and homey. She smiled again as she thought about the faeries. She just knew that this beautiful house would attract at least *one*.

Each day when Pam and Bridget left the Faerie Glen, Skuba came to see the changes. Today he was rolling the coin that he had abandoned several days ago in order to follow the humans. When the elf peeked into his tree home, he was drawn in by the beauty of the hand-woven grasses and the soft green walls. Once inside, Skuba walked all around admiring the thoughtful improvements made by the humans. Then he leaned his coin, a shiny nickel, against a wall and took a moment to admire this extra bit of decoration. The elf stood with his hands on his hips and turned slowly, looking at every detail. Then he touched the moss wallpaper with his finger and pushed it lightly. When it sprang back, he laughed. The grass rug felt plush under Skuba's feet. He was pleased with everything so far and he wondered what the two humans would do next.

Chapter 4

The following morning, Pam and Bridget arrived early to continue building their faerie house. They cut a number of tall sticks of similar sizes and arranged them outside the opening, leaning them together in tee-pee fashion. Pam tied the tips which formed a sort of porch in front of the tree opening. Bridget spread thick mud across the top side of the sticks. To that she attached the colorful bird feathers they had originally found inside the tree which resulted in quite an enchanting roof. Bridget and Pam looked at it critically and then smiled at each other with satisfaction.

Bridget used leaves of different shapes and sizes to form a puzzle on the floor of the newly-fashioned covered porch. Then she created a symmetrical pine cone garden off to one side of the opening along the seashell path. On the other side of that, Bridget poured a little golden sand and inverted a large, rounded out seashell with a smooth underside and a fluted back. She pushed one side of the shell firmly into the sand creating a seashell roof over the sand pile. She propped the other side of the shell up with stick supports. Dried grasses were twirled around the posts and trailed along the ground around the bottom of the supports.

Bridget sang as she worked, her soft voice carrying to Skuba who was watching everything from his hiding place. His ears twitched as he listened to the sweet melody.

Bridget used a flashlight to check the interior of the little house. She stopped singing as she reached inside the opening and felt the nickel propped against the wall. She removed it carefully and looked down in wonder. Sunlight glinted off of the silvery surface. "Mama, look!" she called excitedly. "Where did this come from?"

Pam examined the shiny nickel. "I don't know, honey. Where did you find it?"

Bridget explained, "I found it inside propped up against the wall."

Pam said, "Maybe one of us dropped it while we were working." She knew even as she said the words that this explanation didn't make any sense. Neither of them had taken any money out of their purses during the time that they were working on the faerie house. Pam quickly added, "I'm sure there is a reasonable explanation. Some animals like shiny things. Maybe a bird or squirrel found it somewhere and left it here or maybe some other people were walking nearby and dropped it when they stopped to have a look at our faerie house."

Bridget shook her head. "It was standing on end and leaning against the wall. I don't think that it could've been an animal, but maybe it was some other people." Bridget felt doubtful, but she didn't wish to worry her mother, so she remained quiet on the subject. The young girl found herself looking around frequently as they worked, but nothing seemed to be out of the ordinary. Just in case it had been a faerie visit, she left the shiny nickel just as she found it, inside the house and propped against the wall.

Skuba watched as Pam and Bridget worked. He loved everything that they built and all of the additions both inside and out. When they left for the day, he moved in closer to examine his beautiful new home. The first thing he noticed was that the bird feathers he had collected now adorned the roof. As Skuba looked at the extended porch, the shell garden and sand pile, the mountain elf's heart swelled with happiness and appreciation. It wasn't clear to him why the humans had taken an interest in his home or why they had bestowed all of these wonderful gifts on him, but he felt moved to give a gift in return. Skuba had heard the young girl talk about wanting to see faeries. He thought to himself, *I could make it happen*. As the sun edged past the horizon, Skuba smiled and disappeared into the darkening woods to set his plan in motion.

Sometime later, when Skuba returned to the Faerie Glen, he had several things with him which he placed neatly on the grass. The mountain elf admitted to being a bit of a neatnik, but preferred to think of himself as organized.

Pam and Bridget had left some grass clumps and several sticks that they had been using to build the faerie house strewn about. There were only a few items and while most wouldn't have even noticed, Skuba liked everything in its place. He helpfully piled the

24

materials near the house in neat little stacks, brushed his hands together in satisfaction, smiled and disappeared back into the woods.

When Skuba returned later, he had something rather heavy in his arms. He had to peek around the side of it in order to see where he was going. A golden moon bathed the Faerie Glen in a soft light rendered mystical by the fog that was just beginning to creep into the area. A tiny *crunch, crunch* sound could be heard as Skuba walked along the seashell path and entered the house with his heavy load.

Soon the elf emerged and gathered the items he had left on the grass before ducking back inside. First he filled the tiny clay pot with rich soil and carefully transplanted the small flower. The single bud had just started to open and already the magical fragrance of the rare bloom filled the house and floated from the entrance to spread throughout the glen. Skuba closed his eyes and inhaled deeply. He sighed as he picked up a piece of charcoal and a smooth strip of tree bark. Skuba sat crisscross-style on the floor and began to do something that most elves do not do.

As the soft moonlight reached inside and illuminated the interior, Skuba printed on the bark slowly and laboriously. He had learned this skill from the little girl who had been his constant friend and companion years ago. Many an afternoon he had watched as she practiced printing her letters. He listened as she sounded out words and he was her best audience as she read sentences and then stories. He had watched, listened, and learned.

When he was finished, Skuba leaned the bark against the wall, took one last fond look at the rare plant, then exited the house and loped all the way back to his favorite garden.

The moment Pam and Bridget stepped into the Faerie Glen the next morning, the magical fragrance captured their attention and drew them toward the faerie house. Bridget's hand flew to cover her mouth and she caught her breath sharply when she noticed the neat piles. She took her mother's arm and quickly pulled her over to the door of the little house.

Also having noticed that things were not as they left them, Pam patted her daughter's hand protectively and said, "Let me check it out."

Bridget nodded and rested against the tree. The thrumming in the trunk was more distinct today.

Pam bent down and looked inside. The indescribable fragrance was much stronger here. In the dim light of the interior, something appeared to be softly glowing. Light spilled onto a dark object resting against the wall. Pam removed this item first. It was a large flat piece of tree bark. Without studying it further, she placed it on the grass behind her.

"Bridget, move back a little, ok, honey?" Pam instructed without turning around. Her eyes were on the lighted object within and she was trying to decide whether or not it was safe to touch. After hesitating for a moment, curiosity quickly won the day. Pam was reaching for the glowing pot when she heard Bridget squeal.

Pam jerked her hand back and turned to see what was wrong with her daughter. She relaxed a little when she realized that

Bridget's squeal had not been one of distress, but an expression of excitement.   Bridget was holding the tree bark that Pam had pulled from inside the tree.

"I don't really understand some of these words, but it's like a little note!   And it was written by a mountain elf!   It says so right here.   Look, it's signed 'Skuba, a mountain elf'!"

Pam's hands shook a little bit as she gently pried the piece of bark from Bridget's tense hands.   Pam didn't know what to think about this.   She didn't want to dash Bridget's hopes, but she suspected that it was all a joke of some kind probably played by the same person who left the nickel in the house yesterday.   She looked at the print on the bark and read aloud.

"'The bloom is a draiochta.   The flower is known as Bogha Baisti or Magical Rainbow.   Place the bloom in the center of the glen.   See that it remains undisturbed throughout the day and when it opens, look, but do not touch lest a petal or a leaf fall.   At sundown the magic of the Bogha Baisti will be revealed.'"

Just as Bridget said, the note ended with the name Skuba and right beneath the name she read the words "mountain elf".   Pam was not sure what to say or do.   She was most concerned about all of this, but when she looked down at Bridget's excited face, her daughter's delight and obvious belief in the faeries convinced her to tread lightly.

"Okay, honey, let's bring the flower out into the glen so that we can take a look at it."   Pam gamely added, "Don't forget, we are not to touch it.   I will pick it up by the pot."

27

Pam didn't believe that the plant was magical any more than she thought that the note was written by an elf. She expected to find a battery operated light somewhere inside the pot. This just *had* to be an elaborate joke. Pam wondered who was trying to trick them and why? She carefully brought the plant out into the light of day. It was still a bud, but there was an opening through which a couple of petals could be seen, delicate and rich purple in color. Pam could not deny that the plant seemed to glow with a light of its own, but she could not detect a battery. It was simply beautiful and they both stared at it quietly for a while.

Until she knew more, Pam decided to humor Bridget and follow the directions given in the note. She was certain that in time they would discover the truth.

Pam carefully sat the pot with the Bogha Baisti in the middle of the Faerie Glen as instructed. Then she and Bridget finished the last details on the faerie house. They added moss to the outside of the porch and sprinkled dried flower petals over the roof and around the house, then stood back to admire their handiwork.

Bridget ran to check on the glowing plant that was basking in the sun.

Pam had brought along a picnic basket and a nice lightweight cotton quilt to spread on the grass. Since she had known that they would finish making the faerie house today, she thought a celebration in the lovely glen would be fun.

Bridget took one side of the quilt and Pam the other as they shook the blanket and watched it balloon in the air for a second, then settle evenly on the ground. As Pam grabbed sandwiches from the basket, Bridget asked, "Mama, what do you think will happen? I mean, what kind of magic do you think is in the flower?"

"I really don't know," Pam answered honestly. "Maybe the light will appear to be brighter at sundown and the glow of the plant is its own magic."

That sounded nice to Bridget, but she believed it would be more, so much more. The child walked over to take an even closer look at the plant. Then she cried out, "Mama, come look! Come look! It's opening and just look at the petals! Oh, look at the light!"

Meanwhile, in another part of the woods across the road from the Faerie Glen, a mountain stream bubbled and gurgled its way past a very old one room church. Snapping turtles laid their eggs in the stream and rested briefly on mossy rocks before taking the long journey back to their homes. The church had been abandoned long ago. Even though it still boasted red velvet curtains on the windows and rows of smooth wooden pews, it was now only used to store hay. On this peaceful afternoon the church suddenly began to buckle and roll, looking for all the world as if it were going to break asunder. The air was charged with energy. But then, as suddenly as it began, the strange motion ended, and all was still except for the muffled barking of a small dog coming from somewhere inside the church and a raspy voice asking, "Aline, Wildflower, Rosie....is everyone alright?

Chapter 5

Pam dropped what she was doing and hurried to Bridget's side. Together they stared at the plant in amazement. It was significantly larger and the flower had begun to open. Its sweet fragrance was growing stronger and the soft glow of the light had intensified. The petals practically cried to be touched. They were daintier than the finest porcelain and the varied hues were so vibrant. There was deep purple around the base, a slender streak of yellow nestled next to the purple, followed by lime green, magenta, and cyan. The effect of the slight bleeding of colors only added to the plant's exotic beauty. The center of the flower was pure light pouring out and growing brighter. Remembering Skuba's instructions, Pam and Bridget resisted the urge to touch the plant.

With some gentle encouragement, Pam turned Bridget away from the plant and over to the blanket and lunch. But even as they ate their sandwiches and chips, the magical plant held their attention.

After lunch, mother and daughter reclined on the blanket and Bridget snuggled in close. Strangely, they both felt extraordinarily sleepy. Pam gently stroked her daughter's hair as they drifted off to sleep.

Skuba walked along the stream near the old church. The mountain elf was munching on a rather large, tasty morel mushroom and thinking about the little girl who was this very minute visiting his Faerie Glen. He enjoyed listening to her sing and watching her work on his home. He smiled as he remembered the look on her face when she read what he had written. Skuba knew she believed in both him and the other Magicals and he loved her for that. He couldn't wait until dusk. Skuba wanted to see how the girl would react to what she would see and hear.

Suddenly the elf stopped in his tracks. He sensed magic and not just the magic coming from the glen at this moment. Skuba's ears twitched as he looked around trying to pinpoint its origin. Following his instincts, he began to trot toward the church. As he drew closer, he heard both a small dog barking and a Magical speaking.

Newton rasped, "Well, who could have predicted this turn of events?" The crow gazed around the smallish room. The smell of sweet hay filled the air. Cookie barked excitedly and JJ was busily trying to balance on the little dog's back.

Everyone had arrived safely, but Buddy noticed that he and the faeries were tiny in comparison to Newton, Cookie and JJ! Apparently in this world, faeries and elves were small on the scale of things. Newton, Cookie and JJ were the normal pup and bird size.

Cookie sniffed loudly. He smelled his precious Wildflower.

Then when he spotted her, out darted his tongue. Because Wildflower was now so much smaller than Cookie, that tongue looked ominous! She managed to fly out of the way just in time to avoid a drenching. "Oh, dear" she lamented. "How am I ever going to keep up with Cookie now?"

From the floor near the door, Tango looked up at Okikki, "Where are we, Mama? It smells funny in here and I don't see any tigers."

Okikki shrugged. "I don't know where we are just yet." She reassured him, "But we will do our best to find out. Anyone here have a clue?"

Newton responded, "From the windows and the pews, it looks like we've landed in a church. But with all of this hay, I'm guessing the space is being used for storage. First thing we need to do is to find a way out of here."

The others looked at him appreciatively. It was nice to have someone along who understood this world.

Tango whispered into Okikki's ear, "Where are the trees?"

Newton flew around the small room checking doors and windows, but all were closed and locked. The worst news was that the door handle appeared to be broken from the inside. Newton looked at the others sadly. "I don't know how we are going to get out of this room. Maybe if Cookie barks loudly enough someone might hear him and open the door."

Then, as if he understood, Cookie ran to the front of the church and alternated between sniffing at the crack under the door and barking excitedly. But Wildflower knew what that meant—someone must be on the other side.

Skuba studied the church door. He had heard every word and knew that there were Magicals stuck inside. His ears twitched as he tried to think how he could help. He was not tall enough to reach the handle, but he knew who could, that is, if she would.

It was a little risky, but he knew these Magicals were in trouble and he felt that it was time to believe in Bridget as much as she believed in him. He turned and looked toward the glen. He thought that the Bogha Baisti should be far enough along by now for what he had in mind. He looked back at the door once and yelled through the thick wood, "Hold on! I'm going to get some help!" Then, without wasting another moment, Skuba loped toward the Faerie Glen.

When Skuba arrived, he quickly scanned the area. The trees were already beginning to stir. He saw Bridget and Pam fast asleep on the blanket. Then he looked beyond them toward the Bogha Baisti. It was much larger and light radiated out of it, shooting lavender beams into the surrounding woods as well as into the sky above. He nodded his approval and hoped it was far enough along for what he wanted to do. As a polite gesture, since the trees were waking up, he approached the faerie house maple. The elf bowed with a flourish of his hat. The tree responded with a creaking sound followed by a soft sighing of leaves.

Skuba turned toward the blanket and walked up to Bridget.

He brought all of his powers of concentration to bear. "Child, wake up! Bridget, wake up!"

His voice carried only to Bridget's ears. She opened her eyes and found herself looking at something that she had always dreamed of seeing—a real honest-to-goodness elf. She knew it right away. She had seen pictures of elves in story books and this one had all of the important features. He was small and very cute with pointed ears and shoes that curled up at the toes.

"Hello," Bridget whispered.

"Hello, child," Skuba replied.

Bridget hoped that she wasn't dreaming as she asked, "Who are you?"

"Skuba," was the one word reply.

When the elf spoke, Bridget saw a flash of something in his eyes. In their depths she could see the image of another child.

The elf gently impressed on Bridget that they could see and speak to each other so easily because of all that he had learned from this special child and because of the magical draiochta plant, the Bogha Baisti.

Bridget sat up. She could not take her eyes off of the small elf.

Skuba said, "I need your help. Follow me, please."

Bridget pinched herself to make sure that she was not dreaming. "Ouch!"

Skuba looked perplexed.

Bridget grinned. "I'm just making sure I'm not still asleep."

Skuba thought it an odd routine, but he was still learning about humans.

Bridget said, "I need to ask my mother before I go anywhere."

Skuba warned, "She will not be able to see me, at least not yet."

Bridget asked, "Why not?   I can see you just fine."

Skuba tried to explain.   "You see me now because you already believed.   Your mother does not yet believe that I could really exist."   Then he promised, "But she will see me when the Bogha Baisti is ready."

Bridget said, "Even if she can't see you yet, I still have to ask her."   She tapped her mother's arm.   "Mama, Mama, Skuba (the elf who left the note) is here and he needs our help!"

Pam surfaced from a fog of sleep to see Bridget's face very close to her own.   As soon as Pam's eyes opened, Bridget spoke, "There you are!   Skuba is here and he needs our help.   He wants us to follow him!"

Pam sat up and looked around.   "Bridget, honey, no one is here.   You must have been dreaming."   Then she felt Bridget's forehead just to make sure that she was not feverish.

"Mama, I'm fine.   He said you wouldn't be able to see him, but he's here, right here."   Bridget pointed to the spot where Skuba stood waiting.   There was such an urgent look on her face, as if pleading for Pam to understand and believe her.   "He said you would see him later.   May we *please* go with him and help him?"

Pam looked at Bridget's face.   Then suddenly her eye was

drawn past her daughter to the flower that sat in the middle of the Faerie Glen. She gasped.

When Bridget saw the surprised expression on her mother's face, she also turned to look. "Oh, wow, look at that!"

The flower was now quite large, about five to six feet across. The beauty of the petals alone was awe inspiring, but there were no words for the majestic lilac beams of light shooting into the sky and into the surrounding trees, changing the colors of clouds, branches and leaves. When they were able to pull their eyes away from the Bogha Baisti, they could see that the garden had also changed. The trees had moved and now formed a circle around Pam and Bridget's blanket as well as the draiochta plant.

Skuba skipped over to the flower and greeted it with a respectful bow and a few Elven words.

Bridget loved the fluid sound of his voice. Was it her imagination or did the flower shake its petals a tiny bit in response? She also noticed that the flowerpot was broken into pieces. The flower had pushed free of its container and sent roots deep into the earth.

Skuba walked over to Bridget. "Child, we must hurry so that we will be back in time."

Bridget nodded and relayed the information to her mother.

Pam looked around her. Although she did not see an elf, she could see the magic taking place in the garden. She looked into Bridget's hopeful eyes. Pam may not have believed in elves and such, but she strongly believed in her beautiful daughter. She took

Bridget's hand, smiled into her eager eyes and simply said, "Lead the way."

Bridget was surprised at how quickly the elf moved. But as they crossed the hardtop road, it became more difficult for her to see Skuba. At first it seemed he was just blending with the background extremely well. Then he began to look transparent and she strained to see him. Finally he disappeared altogether. Bridget stopped in her tracks.

"Skuba, where did you go? I can't see you anymore."

The elf had been afraid that this might happen as they moved away from the magic in the glen. He spoke to Bridget, "Follow my voice as best you can and I will bend the grass as I move along. Look sharp!"

When that no longer worked, Skuba found it necessary to double back and tug on the hem of Bridget's jeans. She felt his touch even though she could no longer see him. The elf led the child and the child led her mother. It was in this manner that they approached the old church. Very soon, the trio heard the barking of a dog.

When they drew nearer, Pam and Bridget looked with delight at the picturesque scene of a one room church nestled in the clearing with a bubbling brook rolling past.

Along with the barking, they heard what sounded like the squawk of a bird. Skuba could hear what they could not—the voices of the Magicals.

Chapter 6

Buddy comforted his friend Okikki.   She was afraid that they were stuck between worlds in this little room full of dried grasses. Her baby Tango bounced around like the bundle of energy that he was, climbing up and down hay bales.   Newton flew around still trying to find a way out of the building.   Aline, Rosie, and Wildflower were not sure what they could do to help, so they waited quietly for Newton's instructions.

All that barking was starting to make Cookie's voice sound a little hoarse.

JJ talked to the papillon a mile a minute.   "What's that?" he asked.   "I hear voices outside.   Has someone come to rescue us?" Then the little bird grouched, "Cookie, could ya be quiet just a minute so I can hear?   What am I thinking?   Of course you can't be quiet."

On the other side of the door, Skuba spoke to Bridget.   "They are all trapped inside.   Could you please open the door?"

She grabbed the door handle and pulled, but it would not budge.   Looking up at her mother anxiously, Bridget explained, "Someone is stuck inside.   Skuba wants us to let them out."

Pam shook her head as she thought out loud, "How in the

world did anyone get stuck in there?"   She didn't say so, but she also wondered how Bridget knew to come here in the first place.

Pam tried the door handle, but it was stubborn.   After checking, she decided that it was not locked, just old and difficult to open.   "Bridget, if you help me I think we can do it."

Mother and daughter grabbed the door handle and pulled down and out at the same time.   With a groan of protest, the door finally creaked opened.   Out flew Cookie and JJ like a shot.   The green parrot was barely able to maintain his hold on Cookie's fur as the dog ran straight to Bridget and jumped up and down.   Cookie, sporting his best doggie grin, greeted the girl with tongue lolling.   In the midst of this activity, JJ finally came unseated and fell to the ground with a thud.

"Aw, man," complained the offended bird.

Bridget was well-occupied with the excited Cookie, but Pam noticed the small green bird and leaned down to carefully pick him up.   For once JJ was very quiet.   As he gazed at Pam, vague memories stirred in the back of his mind.   He remembered kind hands just like hers, warm tasty meals, beautiful toys...   He blinked up at Pam and his little heart filled with love.

Okikki and Tango ran out of the building next.   As the squirrels stopped short and sat up tall to get a better view of the new elf and the two humans, Bridget exclaimed, "Oh, look!   A beautiful red squirrel and a baby squirrel too!"

As the three faeries flew out into the late afternoon, Bridget thought she saw a flutter of wings just for a moment, but then it was gone.   Buddy and Newton exited next.

Bridget exclaimed, "That is the biggest, fattest crow I have ever seen!   It is a crow, isn't it, Mama?"

Pam nodded, speechless.

When Skuba caught sight of Buddy, his face lit up.   Here, at last, was another elf.

Skuba greeted Buddy in Elven.   "Welcome to the Blue Ridge Mountains, my brother.   I haven't seen another elf in a very long time.   I was beginning to think that I was the only one left in the whole world."

Buddy responded, "There are many of us where I come from."

Skuba smiled, "That's good news to me, but tell me, how did you get stuck in the man-made building?"

Buddy answered, "I'm not exactly sure.   Victoria sent us through the portal and that is where we landed."

Skuba asked, "Have you come here for a particular reason?"

"My friend Newton is here on a research mission for our world, and the rest of us seek a tiger," Buddy replied.

Skuba's ears wiggled.   "A tiger?   I don't know of any tigers here in the mountains.   May I ask why you are seeking a tiger?"

Buddy responded, "It's for a birthday elixir."   Then he explained all about his elixirs.

Skuba listened with interest.   The mountain elf looked at Bridget and then turned back to Buddy with a smile.   He leaned closer and quietly asked Buddy a question.   Buddy turned and looked at Bridget too.   Then he smiled conspiratorially and nodded.

Skuba clapped him on the back. The mountain elf had wanted to give a special gift to Bridget and Buddy's special talent gave him an idea that he was sure would be one of the highlights of the evening.

Wildflower watched as Cookie jumped all over the little girl. She smiled and shook her head. "That little scamp," she exclaimed as she looked at the dog fondly.

Aline fluttered around the two humans and said, "They don't see us, do they?"

Rosie answered her. "They seem to be able to see Cookie and JJ and the squirrels and Newton too. But you're right. I don't think they see those of us who are from Pixieland."

JJ was sitting on Pam's shoulder, looking into her ear. Before long he was grooming her and making little twitter noises of delight. Cookie had finished greeting Bridget and now focused on barking at JJ. He had just noticed that his very own feathers were on that tall person and he wanted them back.

Pam was amazed. What a strange group of creatures and none of them seemed to be a bit afraid of humans. Okikki sat within easy touching distance. She had one eye on Pam and Bridget and her other eye on Tango who had finally found the trees and was busy scampering up and down one at this very moment. Newton perched on a branch nearby and watched all of the proceedings with interest. But Skuba felt a sense of urgency. His voice reached Bridget once again. She stopped petting Cookie and listened carefully.

"Mama, Skuba says we must hurry back to the glen."

At the same time, Skuba turned and invited the newcomers to join them.   Glancing at Buddy, he said, "Bogha Baisti is in the glen and is nearly ready."

Buddy rounded up the crew.

"Mama, Skuba says the little dog wants you to put the bird on his back."

Pam complied and Cookie quieted immediately.

"Aw, man," JJ complained under his breath.   "Can't a fella take a break now and again?"   He cast one more enamored glance in Pam's direction and then walked foot over foot until he reached Cookie's shoulders where he wrapped his toes around two hunks of hair and held on tight.

"That is about the funniest thing I have ever seen," laughed Pam as she looked at JJ sitting on Cookie's back.

All of the Magicals turned toward the Faerie Glen.   They felt the pull of the Bogha Baisti.

Bridget led her mother by the hand.   Pam was only slightly surprised when all of the animals fell in behind them and followed. She was not sure that she would ever be much surprised by anything again, but then she did not know what was in store for them during the evening ahead.

Buddy sniffed and wiggled his ears.   His eyes closed as he breathed in deeply.   "Bogha Baisti," he sighed.

Skuba smiled and nodded in mutual appreciation.

As the unlikely group approached the glen, Skuba became

increasingly more visible to Bridget. But that was not all. Out of the corner of her eye, Bridget could also see another elf! Filled with excitement, she stopped and turned to see a faerie flying along beside the crow. Next to that faerie was another faerie and yet a third! Bridget's face was suffused with wonder and joy.

"Mama, they *did* come! The faeries came after all!"

Mesmerized, Bridget took a couple of steps toward the faeries and pulled Pam with her. Pam was shocked. She hadn't expected to see such creatures as faeries and elves, but there they were! They seemed to be somewhat transparent and there was a soft glow around each of them. Pam noticed the rapid beating of the faeries' wings and then took a closer look at the elf who was beside her daughter.

Skuba spoke. "We should press on. There will be time for proper introductions and visiting after we arrive."

Pam heard him when he spoke this time. As they drew ever closer to the glen, the unusual fragrance of the Bogha Baisti became stronger. Thanks to the plant's great power, Pam could now clearly see the Magicals. The flower had matured enough to allow Pam's eyes to open to many things hidden in the world around her. When they reached the edge of the Faerie Glen, Bridget and Pam stopped abruptly and stared. Nothing could have prepared them for the spectacular sight ahead.

Chapter 7

The Bogha Baisti was visible from where they stood at the edge of the glen.   It had grown to about ten feet wide.   The flower rested lightly on the grass, the stem very thick and curved.   Each bowed petal was gigantic in size, but still quite delicate and each held its own bright color.   The beams of light from the center of the Bogha Baisti were larger and stronger than before and reached high into the sky and deep into the surrounding woods, spilling lilac onto the trees.   Soft light shot out from each petal and filled the garden with the various colors reflected from the flower.   This gave the appearance of many separate rainbows arching out and away from the Bogha Baisti.   The draiochta plant was achingly beautiful and compelling to both sight and smell.   Pam and Bridget wanted to go closer.   They longed to touch the petals, imagining their soft, silky texture.

At that moment, they noticed that the trees were swaying gently as if they had been awakened (which indeed they had) by the light from the plant which bathed them in its lovely tint.   Limbs moved and stretched in a rhythm that spoke of an ancient ballet. The sun dropped below the trees and the first faint sounds of twilight started up in the glen, a rich counterpoint to the rustling of the leaves among the dancing trees.

Skuba brought the group into the heart of the glen well inside the circle of trees, but still several yards away from the flower, the magnificent centerpiece of the Faerie Glen.   In their absence, logs had been arranged in a semi-circle.   Skuba invited everyone to sit. They might have considered chatting among themselves, but they were all focused on the moving trees.

Skuba and Buddy stepped over to the Faerie House Maple, followed closely by Aline, Wildflower, and Rosie while Pam sat holding Bridget's hand.   Mother and daughter watched excitedly to see what would happen.   They were both awed by this exceptional magic.   What at first glance appeared to be a lovely lady stepped right out of the tree, stately and tall and majestic.   A closer look revealed that her hair was a mass of leaves and her face, while almost human in its appearance, had a much stronger visage.   The tree lady's arms and legs were long and she moved with incredible grace and beauty.

Tango chose that moment to ask, "Mama, may I climb that moving tree, huh?"

Okikki whispered in his ear.   "That is not a tree for climbing. You may climb another tree later."

Okikki wrapped her paws around Tango and looked around the glen.   She could not see even one tree that looked suitable for climbing.   They were all moving about and from her point of view, they looked, well, a bit frisky.

Bridget squeezed her mother's hand and whispered, "Mama,

45

what is THAT?"

Pam softly breathed the answer. "I think she must be a dryad."

All at once the tree lady turned her eyes toward Pam and Bridget. In one fluid motion she was suddenly standing directly in front of them. They were both startled because neither had seen her approach.

The dryad spoke in a low, rich voice and while it was clear that she was addressing Pam and Bridget, they had no idea what she was saying.

Luckily, Skuba stepped forward to interpret. "She whose name cannot be pronounced in your language says, 'Many have come to this Faerie Glen. Most pass through it without further thought. A few take things, such as apples from the trees, mushrooms when they can be found, saplings, stones or other gifts from the woods. We give of ourselves freely and do not ask much in return. To be allowed to exist and continue as we have for many, many years is our one hope. But you did something different. Skuba watched as you came day after day. You took the small gifts of the woodlands—moss sticks, leaves, feathers—and made with them a larger gift, not a gift for yourselves, but a gift that will remain here in our woods. A gift for Skuba. A gift for the faeries. A gift for the tree.

Skuba wishes to return your kindness. He has honored you by inviting you to see what few of your kind ever see. Perhaps some have seen faeries and elves and maybe even glimpses of other

Magicals, but for you Skuba has planted the precious Irish seed of Bogha Baisti. It is a most rare flower that when in bloom allows humans to see and interact with Magicals. Because of what you have given, you will now receive. Welcome to our Faerie Glen, Bridget and Pam.'" Skuba addressed the rest of the group now seated around the mother and daughter. "We would also like to welcome the other newcomers. I hope that all of you enjoy this exceptional night."

When the pale moon rose, owls screeched in the nearby trees and coyotes howled in the distance. Bridget snuggled a little closer to her mother, and JJ clamped his little toes more tightly around Cookie's fur. The dryad slid closer to her tree.

What Bridget saw next caused her to squint and point. "Mama, are those fireflies?"

For a moment, Pam did indeed think that the Faerie Glen was filling with fireflies. But instead of the soft intermittent glow one would expect to see, their lights appeared to look more like sporadic, jagged flames. Then something spiraled down toward them. As it drew closer, two tiny creatures holding a basket between them became visible. When they landed on the log nearby, Pam and Bridget could see that they were teeny tiny dragons, perfectly formed and only slightly larger than bumblebees. One was golden in color and the other was a deep crimson. The golden one turned his head toward Pam and Bridget and spoke with a tinny sounding voice. His eyes spun rapidly and a tiny flame escaped his nostrils lighting his face. Bridget thought she had never seen anything so unusual in her

47

life.

Skuba nodded at the small dragon, then delicately reached into the basket and removed two rings. He turned toward Pam and Bridget. "Volcano says that his people, the Nomads, wish you to have these gifts. There is a ring for each of you made with precious golden dragon scales. It is hoped that you will enjoy the beauty of the rings. Each ring contains the power to grant one wish. Wear them well and when the time comes, wish wisely."

When Skuba stopped speaking, both dragons bowed their heads, extended their transparent webbed wings and with a snap of their tails rose into the air. They hovered just overhead and watched while Skuba assisted Pam and Bridget in placing the rings on their index fingers. Mother and daughter took a moment to gaze admiringly at the beautiful craftsmanship of the bands.

Then Pam said, "Please tell Volcano that we thank him and his people for such special rings."

After receiving Skuba's words the two Nomads joined the others of their kind who were busily lighting up the night sky.

JJ stared at the dragons and expressed the sentiment that was no doubt shared by several of his friends. In his own blunt manner he simply said, "Well, I never!"

Then dryads stepped out of the moving trees that surrounded the group. The rainbow lights from the draiochta plant splashed them with bright colors as they slowly entered the glen.

Night draped its velvety cloak over the mountain. However, the Bogha Baisti provided its own light. The bright petals—every vibrant color—glowed in the dark. The individual rainbows shone more softly, but each one was visible as they arched away from the bloom. Lilac light continued to pour out of the center of the flower, reaching up and out in magical celebration. As the dryads swayed gently to and fro, a number of faeries entered the glen.

"Ohhhhh!" exclaimed Bridget as the dainty faeries gathered around the Draiochta plant.

They formed a line across the top of the plant's rainbows, each faerie different from her sister, but all very beautiful. They glowed both by their own design and by the light streaming from the Bogha Baisti. A faerie with long blond hair smiled and gestured invitingly. In response, Aline, Rosie, and Wildflower flew over to the group and joined them on the rainbows. An air of excitement was building in the glen. When each faerie was in position, the flower and its rainbows of light slowly began to revolve. Pam and Bridget leaned forward.

There was a faint sound of hoof beats heading their way, the thump-thump growing steadily louder. Pam and Bridget strained to see what would happen next. Before long their curiosity was satisfied as a magnificent centaur burst into the glen at a full gallop. His chestnut hair was full and unkempt; his craggy face sported a goatee. When passing by Pam and Bridget, he eyed them curiously. Then a dryad called to him.

As they conversed, Skuba took the opportunity to explain to Pam, Bridget and the Pixielanders, "That is Bristol. He has come to provide music for the dance of the faeries."

A large tree began to creak and groan, sounding as if it would break apart. The trunk bent instead and its branches swept low. Reaching out to Bristol, the tree gave him a lovely wooden stringed instrument which looked much like a violin. Another nearby tree swiftly passed him a bow. Bristol moved closer to the Bogha Baisti and stood on one side of the plant. The lilac light poured over him, changing his color and appearance. He lifted the bow and rested it on the strings.

From the very beginning, the music caught everyone in its spell. It started low and then spiraled upward, gaining both volume and momentum. As Bristol played, the music curled about the glen, wrapping itself around the trees and weaving among the Nomads blinking in the warm night air. Then it gently cradled Pam, Bridget, and the remaining Pixielanders seated on the logs. From there it skipped over to the faeries and took them by the hands. Moving to the music, they performed the faerie dance that had been passed down through generations from a time too distant to remember. Their wings vibrated with the beat while their arms and legs moved in graceful accord. The music ran the gamut of emotion, moving from unbearable pathos to unspeakable glee and left both Pam and Bridget with tears in their eyes.

Chapter 8

It was not clear how much time had passed, but everyone felt a little sad when the faerie dance ended. The faeries flew down from the rainbows and gathered under the trees. There was much chatter among them and their joyous laughter filled the glen.

Bristol returned the instrument and then rounded the glen until he reached Pam and Bridget, addressing them as he stroked his goatee. Skuba asked a question of the centaur because he could not believe what he had just heard. Bristol nodded his confirmation.

Surprise registered on Skuba's face as he made the translation. "I don't know when such a gift has been offered, but Bristol wishes to allow the human child to ride on his back."

Bridget's eyes widened in surprise as she turned to Pam. "May I, Mother?"

Pam nervously locked eyes with her daughter. "Aren't you afraid?"

"Well, a little, "Bridget admitted, "but he seems nice and I think he will keep me safe."

Skuba agreed. "Yes, she will be perfectly safe."

Pam granted permission, but watched anxiously as Bristol lowered himself so that Bridget could climb onto his back.

Skuba gave some instructions. "Sit up high toward his shoulders and hold on to the hair on the back of his head, but be careful not to pull. Squeeze with your legs and don't worry. He will know if you become afraid or if you wish to stop."

As Bristol slowly rose to his full height, Bridget swallowed hard and grasped his hair tightly. When she looked down, it seemed such a long way to the ground, but Bridget concentrated on sitting up straight just as Skuba had instructed. Bristol waited patiently until she was settled then began by walking slowly. At first Bridget was tense, but as Bristol continued to walk she relaxed. When he moved a little faster, Bridget held on more tightly until she realized that his gait was not going to be a bone jarring trot. By the time the centaur broke into an easy canter, Bridget's fear had diminished so that she could simply enjoy the ride. The canter was her favorite gait so far and as she whirled past her mother, she smiled.

Pam relaxed a little when she saw the blissful expression on her brave daughter's face.

Bridget felt the ripple of muscle as the centaur cantered. She loved how it seemed as if the trees streamed past them as they raced swiftly around the circle. When Bristol knew that Bridget was entirely comfortable on his back, he became playful, dancing in and out of the trees surrounding the glen in a weave pattern. Bridget could see the faces of the dryads and the faeries watching as she rode past. She was having the time of her life, but all too soon the ride was over and Bristol had dropped to his knees so that she could slide off. Impulsively, she leaned forward and hugged him.

"Thank you, dear Bristol."

Although he did not speak their language, the centaur understood the hug and the emotion behind her words. After Bridget slid off of his back, he looked into her eyes and smiled before trotting away.

The blond-haired faerie came forward. Her shiny tresses were silky soft and fell just below her waist. They glistened with a smattering of faerie dust and moved gently whenever she turned her head. The faerie's delicate wings were the same blond color as her hair. She was dressed in earth green and wore a pair of rather smart green boots as well. The faerie blended well with her surroundings and moved with an easy grace. When she spoke, her voice sounded like the tinkling of little bells.

Skuba once again interpreted for Pam and Bridget. "Her name is Morella. She has lived here in the mountains for a very long time. She is skilled in the use of herbs, roots, berries, and other forest treasures which support the health of mind and body. Also, she tends the highly prized morel mushrooms found in this part of the mountain and she has taken their name as her own. This night, Morella represents all of the faeries here and has prepared their gift to you."

Skuba nodded to Morella who then placed two vials of an amber liquid into Pam's hands. Her wings beat rapidly as she hovered just inches away from them. This was the closest Pam and Bridget had been to any of the faeries. Bridget fought an impulse to reach out and touch Morella. She loved how the tiny faerie glowed softly and the tinkling sound of her voice. How she wished Morella would land on her hand, if only for a moment.

Morella spoke again and when she finished Skuba explained. "Keep this gift safe until the time is right. It is a magical cleansing soup and is to be consumed when healing is needed. There is one for each of you."

Pam thanked Morella for such a generous gift.

In all of the excitement, no one noticed that Buddy had left the Faerie Glen—that is, no one except for Newton. From his vantage point overhead, he had seen the young elf speak to Skuba for a moment and then slip into the trees. But now his attention was drawn back to the scene around Pam and Bridget. The faerie house tree's dryad had drawn near them again. The tree lady towered over the pair of humans looking wild and dangerous, yet nurturing and kind all at the same time. There was tenderness in her expression as she gazed down at a bundle that was cradled in her arms.

As she spoke, Skuba explained, "The gift of the dryad is precious indeed. Please accept two of her children. Treat them gently and watch over them with love. Plant them where you will, but within calling distance of each other. Care for the baby saplings until they grow strong enough to care for themselves. The young dryads will grow as the trees grow and if the trees thrive, the sisters will not depart."

When Skuba finished, the dryad presented the two small maple saplings to Bridget and Pam. The little trees were swaying back and forth much like their adult counterparts. Bridget reached for a baby and as she held it up to get a better look, she heard a giggle. For a moment Bridget could see a dimpled baby face with dancing eyes peeking out from within the tree. The baby giggled once again and disappeared from view. Then Bridget could only see the gently moving tree. She looked up at Pam and said, "Mama, there is a baby in my tree!"

Pam patted her hand, "Yes, I know and there is one in mine too." Pam had to admit to herself that she felt like a child again, lost in the wonder of this remarkable experience. She smiled radiantly at both the dryad and Skuba, but she directed her words to Skuba. "Please thank the lady for so precious a gift. Tell her we will follow her instructions and we promise to take excellent care of these young trees."

The dryad nodded. She could see from the human faces that this gift was treasured and that her children would be well loved.

Chapter 9

Two cats entered the Faerie Glen followed closely by Buddy, who was smiling from ear to ear. He spoke with Skuba for a moment while the two cats wandered over to Pam and Bridget looking for a little attention.   Bridget stroked their soft fur.

"And what are your names?" she asked, not really expecting an answer.

Much to her surprise, a mellow voice responded, "I am Coty and this is Sasha."

Bridget laughed, "You can talk!"

"Sure we can!" informed Coty a bit smugly.

Sasha chimed in, "We helped Buddy and Skuba!"

Bridget asked, "How did you help Buddy and Skuba?"

Sasha started to explain, "Well, you see, we..."

Coty shoved her a little, "Shhh, Sasha, that's not for us to tell."

Sasha grinned, "Oh, oops, sorry."

Bridget really wanted to know how they had helped the elves, but she could see that they were not going to tell, so she changed the subject.   "What kind of cats are you?"

"Ahh, that's easy," exclaimed Coty.   "Our people tell us that we are very special kitties.   We are rescues!"

Sasha, who was swishing her tail proudly, said, "Yes, and they say that we are very lucky too."

Bridget hugged them both, but they wiggled away just as soon as it was politely possible.

When Skuba finished his conversation with Buddy, he walked over to where Pam was sitting watching Bridget and the two cats. He motioned for her to lean down so that he could speak into her ear.

Cookie sat watching Bridget and the cats. He was not a talking dog, but he liked children and he especially loved attention. So he walked over to Bridget and sat as close to her as he could plaster himself, nuzzling her with his muzzle.

She giggled and said, "What do you want, fella? Huh?"

Cookie whimpered and nudged Bridget's hand until she began to pet him too. Then he rewarded her with a wagging tail and his best doggie grin.

JJ grouched, "Cookie, do ya have to sit so close to her? You're gonna knock me off again if ya don't watch it."

Of course Cookie was not paying any attention and JJ had to do some fancy footwork to stay on the little dog who was leaning against Bridget.

Pam interrupted, "Bridget, you are not going to believe this!"

"What, Mama?"

"Buddy has a gift for us too!" Coty cleared his throat and shot Pam a meaningful look, so she corrected herself. "Excuse me, Buddy, Coty, Sasha and Skuba have conspired together to make this gift for us."

Bridget was so excited that she could hardly wait. "What, Mama? Tell me please!"

Buddy and Skuba were both smiling.

Pam beamed at Bridget. "I'll give you a hint. What is your favorite game? You know, the one that you love the most when you are playing make believe?"

Bridget didn't even hesitate. "I love to pretend that I am a kitty!"

"Right," said Pam and then she added, "Buddy has made a special elixir. He says that if you drink it, you will turn into a real, live kitty! Sasha and Coty were nice enough to donate some kitty hair to help with the elixir. Buddy says it will only last for a short time and then you will turn back into yourself."

Bridget was stunned. "Wow! That is so awesome! How did he know that I wanted to be a kitty? When can I drink it?"

Pam paused. The Faerie Glen was awash with color and magic. The Bogha Baisti and its rainbows were no longer moving, but each color was as vibrant as ever. While Pam and Bridget were discussing Buddy's gift, the garden had begun to fill with wonderful and mysterious cooking aromas. The dryads had summoned large wooden tables seemingly out of nowhere and they were laden with all manner of delicacies just waiting to be enjoyed. It was no surprise that the delicious morel mushrooms were featured in many dishes. There were also several warm breads, a nutty pudding, a variety of soups, a rich mixed berry cobbler and other tasty treats too numerous to mention.

Pam knew that Bridget was eager to drink the gift potion, but the cooking smells reminded her that they had not eaten in hours. She had also noticed that the Magicals had started to gather around the tables. "I think we should have something to eat first. Our hosts have kindly prepared a meal."

Bridget didn't really want to wait, but since they had gone to all that trouble and her tummy was rumbling she reluctantly agreed. "Ok, Mama, I guess I can wait until after we eat. I am pretty hungry!"

Tango had been eyeing the vines hanging out of the trees for some time. He tugged on Okikki.

"Mama, may I climb the trees and play on those vines, pul-eeease?"

Okikki smiled down at him. "Right after you eat. That is, if it's ok with the dryads." She cast a wary eye at the swaying trees, then patted Tango lovingly. Okikki tried to distract her son by sniffing the air in an exaggerated manner. "Is that nutty pudding I smell?"

It worked beautifully. Tango's ears perked straight up. "Oh, boy! Nutty pudding! Yum! I want a BIG bowl!"

Okikki put her arm around the young squirrel and maneuvered him toward the feast.

Pam filled plates for both herself and Bridget. After the first bite, their eyes opened wide and Bridget voiced what both were thinking. "Oh, wow! This is the most delicious food I have ever eaten!"

Pam looked around at the unusual scene.   She felt as if it was all an elaborate dream.   It just didn't seem possible that she could really be casually having a meal with all of these magical creatures. Pam observed her daughter's animated face.   All along, Bridget had believed that faeries were real and all along Bridget had been right.

Mother and daughter sat on the grass finishing off their meal with a healthy portion of mixed berry cobbler.   The crust was light and flaky, very buttery and the juicy fruit, sweet and tart at the same time.   It was a perfect conclusion to a perfect meal.

As soon as she had swallowed the last bite, Bridget asked, "May I have the gift now?"

Pam produced the glass container.   The liquid was a lovely shade of purple; it looked like grape juice.   Bridget reached for the glass and pulled on the cork that fit snugly in the mouth of the bottle. When Buddy noticed that the girl was about to drink the elixir he stepped closer to watch.   Skuba and the two cats also joined them. Bridget was very excited, but she felt a little nervous at the same time.   She really didn't know what to expect.   After boldly downing the liquid, she licked her lips.   Surprisingly, the elixir tasted just like cherries.

Bridget noticed that her tongue felt rough to her skin, like sandpaper.   Out of the corner of her eye she could see fur on her face.   The sights and smells in the garden had become greatly intensified.

Skuba clapped his hands together and exclaimed, "That was the smoothest transition I've ever seen!"

Bridget had to agree that it had happened quickly and she was relieved that it was completely painless.   Looking down, she spotted her four furry white feet.   She held up a paw to examine it more closely.   She retracted her claws and then released them again. *Wicked*, she thought.   Bridget gazed down the length of her new body and admired the sleek beauty.   Her medium length fur was a deep shade of red/brown with the exception of four white "socks" and the white tip of her long tail.

"Mama, what color are my eyes?" she asked curiously.

Pam put her hands behind Bridget's ears and tilted her feline face up.   "They are very green!"   Playfully she said, "Now you really are mama's little kitty!"

Sasha meowed impatiently.   "Come on, Bridget.   Let's play."

Bridget gave her mother a questioning look and Pam nodded. After asking permission of the dryads in the garden, Sasha, Coty and Bridget climbed up the trunks of different trees and called to one another.   Each cat tried to be the one who climbed the highest. Bridget noticed Tango swinging on the vines that hung from the trees. It looked like so much fun.   She wondered if she could do that too. She was way up high in her tree of choice and just below she could see a vine swaying...very tempting.

"Hey, Coty," she called out, "do you ever swing on the vines?"

Coty replied.   "No, cats aren't really made to swing on vines. You aren't thinking of trying that, are you, Bridget?"

"You are up too high," Sasha joined in.   "You could fall."

Bridget was ordinarily a cautious child, never one to take any sort of risk.   As a matter of fact, she was not even a tree climber even though she did love to swing on low-hanging vines.   However, in her feline form she felt much stronger and more agile.   Bridget's brand new cat claws had made it so easy for her to climb that tree. The new confidence went straight to her head making her feel like she could do anything.   Bridget's cat eyes danced back and forth in the same rhythm as the wagging vine below.

Coty watched as Bridget prepared herself to launch.   "NO, BRIDGET, STOP!" he cried, but it was already too late.

Chapter 10

With feline precision, Bridget estimated the distance and sailed through the air toward the fat vine.   When it slapped against her, she wrapped her front legs around it and sunk her claws deep. Her back legs flailed in mid-air, but could not gain purchase.   She swung a time or two, then lost her grip, meowing her distress loudly as she slid down the vine with ears pinned back against her head. Everything seemed to move in slow motion.   Coty and Sasha called for help.   Bridget looked down to see her mother's pale, frightened face.   Skuba was jumping up and down, barking out orders to someone.

Bridget managed to cling to the vine, but could not stop slowly slipping down its length.   She didn't want to think about what would happen when she came to the end of that rope.   Then suddenly from the far side of the glen something moved rapidly toward her. By the light of the moon and the Bogha Bahisti it looked like a plush flying carpet.

Skuba called out, "Bridget, when they get right beneath you, let go of the vine.   Then drop onto their backs.   Crouch down.   Do not move and don't forget to sheathe your claws.   Do you understand?"

Bridget nodded down at Skuba. It was all she could manage. When the magic carpet was directly beneath her, she gulped audibly and released her grip. But she never really fell. Her hind legs were supported by the "carpet" almost before she had even let go with her front feet. Following Skuba's instructions, Bridget crouched down, sheathed her claws and then looked to see just exactly who or what had come to her rescue.

Bridget could hardly believe her eyes. Instead of a magic carpet, there were thousands of tiny Nomads, the micro-dragons that she had thought were fireflies when she had first seen them flying overhead and spitting tiny flames. The dragons rippled up and down as they flew in tight formation and they seemed to be somehow connected to each other which created the carpet effect.

Pam and the Pixielanders were clustered together below and everyone's eyes were glued to the spectacle in the air as the micro-dragons, with Bridget on their backs, rounded the glen in wide circles.

JJ piped up with an all too familiar, "Well, I never..."

Each time the dragons circled they flew a bit lower and in this manner they gradually dropped low enough to glide in for a gentle landing.

As soon as her feet hit the ground, Bridget thanked them profusely. She was in mid-sentence when Pam scooped her up and hugged her. There were tears of relief in both of their eyes. It had been a close call.

Pam and Bridget thanked Skuba and the Nomads for the

incredible rescue. Then Pam wasted no time telling Bridget to be sure to keep all four paws on the ground from now on.

The kitty contritely replied, "Yes, Mama."

Fully recovered, she bounded away chasing Coty and Sasha, pausing only briefly to allow Tango a kitty-back ride. Tango hung onto Bridget and shouted, "Giddyup!"

Cookie suddenly jumped up and took off after the cats, barking merrily.

JJ almost fell off and yelled, "Cookie, could ya give a fella some notice before takin' off like that? Man, oh, man..."

Cookie never missed a beat and soon he and a reluctant JJ were frolicking around with Tango and the three cats.

Bridget enjoyed being a cat. She had always loved cats, but now felt that she really understood the felines in a special way that wouldn't have been possible if she hadn't been transformed into one of them. Later when she changed back, she wanted to explain it to her mother, but couldn't find the right words.

The Faerie Glen was bursting with magic. It was a night that Pam and Bridget would never forget. Pam felt as if she could almost remember something from long ago. The sights and sounds in the garden seemed strange and yet so familiar all at once.

The "magic carpet" Nomads dipped and swirled overhead, spewing flames here and there which were immediately painted lavender by the light from the unspeakably compelling Bogha Baisti plant. The faeries flittered around the glen tossing sparkling faerie dust on everyone and everything.

As Bridget watched the gentle shower of magic dust, she began to feel quite drowsy.   She leaned back against Pam who had also started to feel very sleepy.   Skuba stepped forward with a knowing smile and touched Bridget's hand.   She turned toward him and returned his smile.

She heard him say, "I will not forget you, child."

There was a moment of sadness.   It felt like goodbye.   Just before sleep claimed her, Bridget listened to the sound of rushing wind through the trees and looked up one final time to see the large black crow.   The child wondered why he had remained on that perch and so strangely quiet all evening long.   He tilted his head and looked down at her with brilliant blue eyes.   Bridget could barely hold her own eyes open, but she asked herself, *Do crows really ever have blue eyes?*   She thought that she must have spoken out loud when a rasping voice chuckled and said, "Rarely."

As Pam and Bridget slept, the Bogha Baisti faded.   The Magicals left the glen as quickly as they had arrived with the exception of Skuba, Morella and the group from Pixieland.   By the time the sun peeked over the top of the mountain range to greet the new day, Newton, Buddy and their friends were also preparing to leave.

Buddy explained to Skuba and Morella what the other Pixielanders had planned.   Morella was so intrigued that she decided to accompany them on their journey in search of a tiger.   Aline was already beside herself with excitement.   She just knew that this was going to be the best birthday ever and was thrilled at the possibility of seeing a real live tiger!

When Pam and Bridget woke up, the garden was back to normal. There was no sign of the draiochta plant and all of the trees were in their original locations. It was a lovely morning and they both felt refreshed from their deep sleep. Pam opened the lunch basket from yesterday and placed the baby trees inside. They took one last look at the faerie house.

Pam remarked, "It's beautiful, Bridget. You did such a wonderful job!"

Bridget fingered one of the feathers on the roof of the little porch.

She asked, "Mama, will we ever see the faeries again?"

Pam looked around and shook her head. "That I do not know, honey."

Bridget looked up at her mother. "Do you think we will ever see Skuba again?"

Pam answered honestly, "I wish I knew."

Bridget scanned the Faerie Glen, but didn't see any sign of the mountain elf.

Grabbing her mother by the hand, she asked, "Well, can we come back again next year?" When Pam didn't answer immediately, Bridget continued, "The faerie house may need repair and we could bring a gift for Skuba. I mean, maybe we would see him again or even if we didn't see him, we *know* he's here and we could still leave his gift. Oh, please, Mama?"

"Of course we can return next year.   We will just plan to do that very thing."

Then after one more look around the peaceful Faerie Glen, mother and daughter turned and walked away.

Skuba watched them from a distance, his ears twitching. When he was sure they were gone, the mountain elf skipped over to where the Bogha Baisti had been the night before.   Leaning down, he found and pocketed the precious seeds.   Smiling from ear to ear, Skuba left the glen and loped down the road, back to the garden with the waterfall, the house with the tin roof, the two cats, Cody and Sasha, and their keeper, his best friend in the entire world.

As Pam and Bridget were driving home, Bridget sat in the back seat so that she could nap.   She already missed Skuba and wondered how she was ever going to tell her best friend Brooke about what had happened this summer.   She was sure that Brooke wouldn't believe her if she mentioned all of her new magical friends.   Bridget reached over to move the picnic blanket to one side and noticed something attached to one corner of it.   She drew in her breath sharply when she saw that there were two tiny eggs lying on the blanket!   Bridget glanced to see if her mother had noticed, but Pam was totally focused on the road ahead.   A whisper of excitement filled Bridget's heart as she wondered what could possibly be inside those eggs.   Could they be magical?   She carefully covered them with a corner of the blanket.   Later she would ask herself why she didn't tell her mother right away.   But for now she gazed out the window of the car and watched the trees fly past with one trembling hand cupped over the two unexpected passengers.

Part Two:
Never Catch a Tiger by the Tail

Chapter 1

On the day following the blooming of the rare Bogha Baisti plant and the magical gathering in the Faerie Glen, the group of Pixielanders closed down their small camp and made preparations to begin the search for the tiger. Aline had been fluttering around since early morning, bringing nectar to her friends and chattering endlessly about how wonderful it was going to be to get to see a tiger in person. While she zoomed around the camp barely containing her excitement, Newton opened his beak and raised his voice to get everyone's attention.

"I have an announcement to make. As some of you know, I am here on important Pixieland business. Victoria herself has requested that I return here to my home world in order to find one Dr. Armantine Obrial. For reasons that will be made clear at a later time, I must seek his advice." Newton pulled himself up to his full crow height and swaggered about in a somewhat pompous manner as he continued. "While I'm away on business, I will leave you in the capable hands of Buddy and Morella. They will be in charge of tracking the tiger. And please do be careful. I think most of you already know that tigers are very dangerous." Newton looked at each one of them in turn. He paused when he reached Tango who was fidgeting. Okikki put a paw on her son's shoulder to hold him still.

The impatient youngster whispered loudly, "But, Mama, he's taking forever!"

Okikki clapped her other paw over Tango's mouth and flashed a tiny embarrassed smile in Newton's direction.

Newton cleared his throat and continued. "I know that Aline will be pleased to hear that the tiger is not too far away. Morella knows where to find him and I have asked her to tell us all about it." Newton smiled at Aline, then gestured to Morella.

"I am sure that those of you who know anything about tigers are wondering how one could be living in these mountains," said Morella. "Well, let me tell you the story. Some years ago there was a zoo nestled in the nearby foothills. It was family-owned and even though it was small, the zoo was very popular. The kind family treated the animals well and they watched everything carefully to make sure that none of the guests did anything to tease or harm the animals that lived there. Eventually the family decided to move away from the area. Although they tried to make sure that the zoo passed to good hands, the man who purchased the zoo from them didn't care nearly as much about the animals as he did about making money.

The new owner added some extra animals to bring in more people, but that resulted in overcrowding. Some of the smaller creatures were even living in plastic containers. As people noticed the conditions, they became angry and stopped coming to the zoo. Town officials received many complaints, so they sent a group of people to investigate.   After seeing the living conditions, the owner was told that the zoo would be shut down if he didn't make certain improvements.   He paid no attention to their orders.   Instead, he focused on ways to bring people back to the zoo.   He decided that the best way to do that was to buy a Siberian tiger.   The man kept her in a metal cage near the center of the zoo.   Her name was Rasheteike.   The zoo owner put signs everywhere advertising her as his main attraction.   And people *did* come to see the beautiful tiger. The man hired to tend the animals was no better than the owner and was often careless as he went about his duties.   One night after a few weeks of feeding the tiger (much less than he should have in order to save money), the man failed to latch the cage properly.

Rasheteike was tired of feeling hungry and living in such small quarters.   She waited until it was late and all was still, then she pushed open the cage door and escaped."

Everyone listened intently as Morella continued.

"Rasheteike moved quickly and by dawn she had made her way well into the mountains.   Her escape created a lot of turmoil among the humans.   The zoo was closed shortly after that and fortunately the animals went to larger zoos with more natural habitats.   They have Rasheteike to thank for that.   If she hadn't escaped, who knows how long it would have taken the good humans to be able to help the animals.   Anyway, trucks rolled through the mountains for days and men searched the woods hunting for

Rasheteike. But she was not found, at least not for a while. Rasheteike was smart and stayed away from humans, blending nicely with her surroundings. She hunted and lived off of the land, only taking what she needed. She often moved about in stream beds which minimized her footprints. But there was something about Rasheteike that even the zoo owner did not know."

"What?" Tango asked eager to hear Rasheteike's secret.

Morella was not long in answering. "Rasheteike was going to have a baby! When her time came, she gave birth to a healthy baby boy and named him Rashka. Rasheteike tried to teach her baby every caution, but from the beginning it was clear that he had a mind of his own. The cub thrived and grew into a very large tiger. He was far more fierce and dangerous than Rasheteike. He was also much more careless. Then one day, something happened that changed everything."

Tango piped up, "What happened?"

The young squirrel was completely caught up in the tale, as were the other Pixielanders. Other than pictures in Buddy's book, none of them had seen a tiger, nor did they have any real idea about what a tiger was like.

Chapter 2

Morella knew that this was going to be a dangerous adventure. She was as brave as anyone, but she had her concerns. It was one thing to see a tiger in the woods and another thing altogether to approach said tiger and attempt to take a few hairs from the top of its head. Such a violation of the beast's personal space could result in unfortunate consequences.

Morella smiled at Tango, took a deep breath and continued her story. "After a while, the trucks of humans didn't come as often, but they still searched for Rasheteike. She was careful, but her son was not and he left footprints to be found by trackers. The men didn't know about the cub and they believed that the footprints belonged to Rasheteike.

Rashka had never seen a human in his life. However, his mother had been around them all of hers. She didn't really fear the men, but she didn't wish to return to the cage at the small zoo. It was also important to Rasheteike that her son remain free. He had always been free and she feared that he wouldn't do well in captivity.

One day Rashka was tracking game near the road when he heard the rumbling sound of a truck. His mother happened to be nearby and when she realized that the truck was moving toward them, she tried to coax her son away from the road and out of sight. But Rashka would not listen. He growled, 'How bad can it be? Have I not taken down the wild boar and the bear? Am I not the strongest beast in the mountains? I will face these humans and we will see who is the strongest!' Then he let out a roar that would have cast a shadow of fear in many a brave heart.

Rasheteike swiftly ran toward the sound of the vehicle until she was running level with the truck and in plain view of the people inside. The man in the passenger's seat pointed at her. Then the driver turned the truck around and followed as she led them away from her son. She fell quickly when a tranquilizer dart hit her side. The people seemed pleased with her recapture. A woman spoke into a metal thing in their truck to let others know that Rasheteike had been found and that she would now be safely transported to her new home. After they loaded Rasheteike into the truck I heard the woman say, 'Sleep on beautiful tiger and when you waken, you will be home at last. There is a nice, natural habitat waiting for you and excellent care and plenty of good food. There are other tigers too. You are going to be so happy.'"

Morella paused for a moment. Everyone leaned forward just a little as she resumed, "I was glad to hear that Rasheteike would never want for anything again. I would love to have seen her reaction when she entered her new home for the first time." Morella sighed. "However, I was still worried for her reckless son."

Then JJ spoke up, "What did happen to her son?"

JJ's eyes welled with emotion as he listened to the story of

Rasheteike and her love for her cub.   He didn't want the others to notice, but as he looked around at the group, he could see from their expressions that everyone was feeling pretty much the same thing.

Morella had the group's full attention as she answered the little green bird.   "That's the most interesting part of the story. Rashka was furious.   The truck was gone before he arrived on the scene, but he knew his mother had been taken.   He was angry and roared so loudly that he awakened Akron!"

Everyone except for JJ took in a sharp breath simultaneously.

Buddy breathed, "No!"

Wildflower shook her head.   Rosie and Aline exchanged worried glances.

Confused and feeling left out, JJ stared at Morella and asked, "Who is Akron?"

Morella wondered why the little bird had not heard of Akron.

Buddy noticed the incredulous look on her face and explained, "We found JJ in the woods or I should say that Cookie found him in the woods.   We think he may have had some sort of accident because he doesn't remember his past."

Morella nodded sympathetically.   "I see.   Well, then, I will tell you.   Akron is one of the four Nature Guardians and she is very powerful.   Akron is hard to describe.   Most often she looks very much like a dryad, like a dryad princess.   And she can change her size in the blink of an eye!   I have seen her quite small and I have seen her very tall.   Even though her appearance changes as she wills, Akron is much more than a shifter.   She does many things to help ensure the proper balance of nature. If there is a dry season and trees are dying from lack of water, she wakens. As you know, dryads do not leave their home trees on a whim. But they must go if their tree dies and the trunk begins to harden." Morella shook her head. "Sadly, they resist change and don't always leave the dying tree soon enough. Akron works hard to prevent that from happening by leading the dryads out of the fading trees and homing them in new growth before it's too late. I have seen her in action. She moves swiftly through the trees in a parched land calling to the dryads to depart from their dying homes. I have watched them follow her for many miles until the land is lush and healthy trees are plentiful.

When she sleeps, she takes on the appearance of a large boulder. Although no human has ever seen her awake, many have walked right past her as she slept. Mostly, she does not interfere with the woodland creatures, but she may if she chooses…and Rashka was a foolish tiger. He hadn't learned to respect others. His mother had tried to teach him, but he turned a deaf ear. He thought her too soft and he felt that he knew best. Rashka believed that he was the strongest animal in the mountains. He had let it go to his head and had become quite proud.

On that day, when he awakened Akron, she called out, 'Who is bellowing so loudly and disturbing my sleep? Is there a forest fire? I don't smell fire. Is there another kind of catastrophe? I think not.' Let me tell you, I was nervous when I saw her heading toward Rashka."

JJ asked, "Was Akron angry with the cub for disturbing her sleep?"

Morella answered, "I don't think so, at least not at first. I think she was mostly annoyed and curious."

Buddy grew more and more concerned. "I have a question, Morella. Is Akron still awake?" Buddy was not entirely successful in keeping the quiver out of his voice.

"Yes, she is still awake," Morella answered.

Buddy raised a hand apologetically. "I don't mean to interrupt the story, but about how long has she been awake this time?"

Morella hesitated as she considered the answer. "About two years."

Buddy responded, "I see...please do continue."

Tango blurted, "Yeah, I want to know what happens next."

Aline glanced over at Buddy. She wondered why he looked so worried and could tell that something was really troubling him. She decided to speak with him about the matter at the first opportunity.

Everyone listened intently as Morella resumed the story. "I can only imagine what Akron must have thought about Rashka. He is one of the most beautiful animals on the mountain, but I'm sure that Akron knew he didn't really belong here. Besides that, he was making too much unnecessary noise and if he didn't soon learn some important survival lessons, he would eventually attract unwanted attention from humans. As I told you, Akron is all about the balance of nature and this young tiger was knocking a pretty good dent in things with his reckless behavior.   Something had to be done before every hunter on the mountain descended upon the area.

I could tell Akron wasn't happy about what she witnessed. The tiger cub had stopped bellowing and was bullying a family of rabbits.   They hid in their burrow and quaked as he growled into the opening of their home.   Rashka was not hungry.   I am sorry to say, he was just being thoughtless and more than a little bit mean. Akron interrupted his game.   'Tiger, why have you awakened me?' Rashka sized her up quickly and didn't seem to feel threatened.   'It's not my fault you're awake.   Why should I care?   And if you don't get out of here, whoever you are, you'll regret it.'   Then Rashka revealed every one of his large pointy teeth."

Chapter 3

Morella's eyes widened.   "Can you *believe* he challenged the Nature Guardian?"

"Unbelievable!" exclaimed Buddy.

Morella continued, "Sparks flew from her hair as Akron shook her head and met Rashka's eyes with her dark, smoky stare.   Akron's voice went flat with the question 'Will you now, young cub?'   Just for a minute, Rashka looked hesitant.   It was probably the first time in his entire life that he ever entertained a moment's doubt about anything.   But he had a great deal of pride and he wasn't backing down.   Raska growled loudly and Akron said, 'Why so loud, cub? Do you call for help?   I hope for your sake that you do, because if you plan to attack me, you will most certainly need it!'"

All eyes were on Morella as she told the story.

"I could tell that Rashka was in trouble.   He was so full of himself that he didn't stop to think or question.   Rashka never even asked who she was.   It was a shame that he had turned out to be such an insensitive, disrespectful creature."

Morella paused.   Aline and Rosie shook their heads in dismay.   As the story progressed, Buddy looked more and more uncomfortable.   Wildflower had noticed and moved closer to him.

A light breeze was blowing and it lifted Morella's blond hair, swirling it around her head like a soft cloud as she spoke. "As Rashka leapt through the air, I could see his big clawed feet. It looked as if he would have given Akron a good raking if he had landed as he planned. But with a simple wave of her hand, Akron suspended him in mid-air. The look on his face was really quite frightening. And then Akron changed forms. I saw it with my own eyes! The sparks in her hair turned into flames that seemed to engulf her and I could feel the heat from my spot in the tree. Then it was like Akron disappeared because through the fire came the largest tiger I have ever seen! She was much larger than Rashka and quite well-muscled. Her coat was sleek and white with black stripes. While I was watching, Akron looked straight at me with her penetrating cat eyes. I froze instantly, but then she smiled and winked at me. I should've known she would sense that I was there. (The cub was still hanging in mid-air by the way.) Anyhow, with a wave of her paw, time was restored and I could have sworn I heard her say to him rather sarcastically, 'Come to Akron'. As Rashka collided into her, a veil dropped all around them and I could neither see nor hear anything except the ordinary woodland sounds. Whatever Akron had in mind, it was going to be a private matter."

Tango was puzzled. He asked, "Well, did she hurt the tiger? When did you see them again?"

Morella's smile held a hint of mystery as she continued, "I stayed in the area. Even though Rashka was naughty, I cared about him and wanted to know what had happened. I felt afraid for the tiger cub, but kept remembering the wink and smile that Akron gave me before she hid the two of them from view.   It was like a gift, you know?   It was comforting, and I believe she was letting me know that I didn't have to be afraid for him.   For several days all seemed perfectly normal, and I could tell that many of the animals who had been bullied by Rashka for the past year were much happier as they went about their daily lives.   I don't think anyone missed him except for me."   Morella sighed.   "I don't even know *why* I missed him. Maybe it was for the sake of his beautiful mother and her sacrifice for him.   Maybe it was because I remembered when he was just a tiny thing, rolling around and growling like a kitten."   As she recalled this stage of his life, Morella's face softened.   Then she smiled and said, "You should have seen him when he was little.   He was just the cutest thing.   I don't know what went wrong, but I always believed that underneath it all he had a good heart.   Somehow he just lost his way."

A few days later I was picking some wild onions along the road and as I rounded a bend, there they were walking along up ahead. As I observed them, it became clear that Akron was teaching him respect for others as well as some much needed survival skills.   She was pointing out old footprints Rashka had left everywhere and teaching him how to hide his signature so that he would not be so easily detected.

Rashka looked perfectly fine.   There was only one mark on him—a jagged cut over one eye.   It didn't seem to trouble him though and appeared to be healing well.   Akron stayed with him constantly for several days which, as you know, is quite unusual for a Nature Guardian. Apart from that one cut, the only real change was his attitude. Gone was the reckless tiger, replaced by one who was obviously much more thoughtful. He seemed a willing pupil and Akron a patient teacher. I have often wondered how she managed to get through to him during the days spent behind that veil. I believe that Akron was thoroughly enjoying Rashka's company and indeed he was much nicer to be around. He's an adult now, but still Akron comes to him often."

JJ asked, "How does she help him now that he's grown?"

Morella replied, "I have seen her hide him if humans approach. She knows that if they found out that he was living on the mountain, they would take him away. This is the only home he has known and he's happy here."

Buddy spoke up. "I think we should find another tiger."

Everyone stared at Buddy.

Aline blurted out, "What? Another tiger? Why, Buddy? After hearing Morella's story, I want to meet Rashka."

Everyone nodded in agreement.

Wildflower rested a hand on Buddy's shoulder and asked, "Buddy, what is troubling you?"

"Don't you see?" Buddy responded. "It's difficult enough to get close to a tiger—any tiger—to get some hair from its head. Approaching a tiger who is befriended and protected by a Guardian is going to be practically impossible. When Morella told us that Akron had been awake for two years, I just felt in my heart that she had taken a special interest in Rashka. It's a wonderful thing for the young tiger, but not such a great thing for us. I know that most of you don't know much about tigers, but even the nicest ones are wild and dangerous animals. We will have to be very clever and very careful. If we choose Rashka, then we should get permission from Akron in advance." Buddy shook his head. "I think it will be too difficult. We really should find another tiger." Buddy turned to Morella. "Do you know where the next closest tiger is?"

Morella answered, "As far as I know, tigers in this part of the world (other than Rashka) only live in zoos or wildlife parks. And there aren't any around here now that the old zoo is closed. You would have to travel many miles to find such a place." At this point, Morella glanced at Cookie and JJ. "I know that some of your group must walk, so travel will be slow. It could take weeks, maybe even months, to find another tiger."

As Buddy thought about this, his ears wiggled. It was so quiet that you could have heard a pin drop as everyone waited for Buddy's response. Buddy didn't know how long it would take Newton to conduct his business with the specialist, but he was reasonably sure that the group needed to get the tiger hair in a matter of days, not weeks or months. He glanced at Aline. Her sweet face looked both eager and hopeful.

Buddy had serious misgivings about pursuing the mountain tiger, Rashka. However, he could not bear to disappoint Aline and the others. He wished that Newton had not already flown away. It would have been nice to get an opinion from him. After all, Newton knew more about this world than any of them except for Morella.

Buddy asked, "What do you think, Morella? As you know, we need to be able to approach Rashka and remove a few hairs from the top of his head. Do we have a chance for success?"

Morella looked thoughtful then replied, "I don't know. I believe it can be done, but it will be risky and someone could easily get hurt. Rashka is alert and dangerous. That is enough reason alone to give us pause. Then to further complicate things, there is Akron. You are right. We'd better ask her first."

Buddy looked at the group. "Should we stay and look for Rashka or should we look for another tiger? I propose that we put it to a vote. Everyone has heard what Morella said. Each one of you should have a say in this."

Aline quickly raised her hand. "I would like to stay in the mountains and see if we can get the hair from Rashka."

Rosie supported Aline by adding her affirmative vote to the count. Then Wildflower raised her hand as well.

JJ hesitated. "Well, you know the whole bird and cat thing...but if my friends are going, you can count me in too. Not sure how much help I will be, but if Wildflower said yes then Cookie will go. Someone has to keep him in line and it might as well be me." JJ sighed heavily as if watching after the little dog dumped the weight of the whole world squarely on his shoulders.

"Well, then," Buddy shrugged, "I guess that settles it. Majority rules. We will stay in the mountains and try to find Rashka. We're going to need a plan." Buddy gazed at the group of Pixieland friends. "Does anyone have any ideas?"

Chapter 4

There was stillness all around as everyone was thinking. Finally Wildflower broke the silence.   "Is it possible for us to speak with Akron?"

Aline brightened at this thought and added, "Yes, that's a good idea, Wildflower.   Maybe we could just tell her what we want and that we mean no harm to Rashka.   She might help us."

Morella looked doubtful.   "I'm not sure.   She is known to be unpredictable and..."

Aline interrupted, "But, Morella, she smiled and winked at you."

Buddy chimed in, "Aline makes a good point.   Akron has acknowledged you in a most direct way, Morella."

Rosie asked in her gentle voice, "Do you think Akron noticed you because she felt a common bond?"

Morella turned to Rosie.   "You mean..."

Then Rosie and Morella both spoke at the exact same time, "a love for Rashka."

Morella continued in a thoughtful tone, "I never thought of it that way before, but it would make sense."

Buddy chimed in again, "Then it might also make sense to

think that she would consider speaking directly with you, Morella."

Aline pleaded with her, "Oh, please, would you try?"

Morella smiled, "Of course, I will try.   But you all must come along with me."

Everyone smiled and nodded and began to chatter excitedly. That is, everyone except for Okikki and Buddy.   Each still had their doubts and as the group became more excited, the pair exchanged worried glances.

Morella admitted, "I do know the area where Rashka can usually be found.   I have watched him often.   He is very beautiful, as I have said, and there is an aura of power and majesty about him. There is no animal on the mountain quite like him."   As the group was pondering this last statement, Morella suggested, "I really don't know how to go about seeking an audience with a Guardian.   I agree that we need to talk to Akron first, but even if I did know where to find her, I have no idea how to approach her.   We might see her as we travel, but it would be a stroke of luck that we cannot count on. However, as we get closer to Rashka, maybe Akron will come to us."

Okikki emphatically stated, "I certainly hope that she isn't feeling angry when she sees us!"

Tango cupped a paw and spoke into Okikki's ear, "Is Akron mean?"

Tango's whisper was a bit loud and Buddy overheard.   He smiled at the young squirrel and answered, "Not mean, Tango, but maybe a little, well, intimidating.   It's just that we must always show great respect for Akron."

Tango nodded at Buddy's words. He understood what it meant to be respectful.

Buddy smiled and lightened the mood by asking, "Who's hungry?"

Tango yelled, "ME!"

Everyone else chimed in as well. Wildflower and Aline built a campfire while Buddy gathered some ingredients for a wild veggie stew. Rosie brought back water from a clear mountain stream. Morella provided seasonings. Everyone chattered and talked as they worked together. When the stew was ready, the friends agreed that it smelled wonderful and tasted even better. Wildflower strained the broth from some of the soft vegetables so that they would be easier for JJ to eat.

Cookie gobbled his meal with his usual "shovel mouth" technique. It was a very special talent that he had for scarfing down a large portion of food in a very small amount of time. When the little dog finished, he ran around begging for seconds from everyone else.

JJ chastised him, "Cookie, that's NOT polite! Ya ate yours, now let everyone else eat in peace. Sheesh!" Cookie only gave JJ a passing glance as he ran to the next person in line and continued to beg. JJ shook his head, "I'm never gonna teach that stubborn canine anything. I can feel it in my bones."

Wildflower almost choked on her soup as she struggled to hide her laughter from the proud little bird.

After everyone finished eating, Morella led the group out of the clearing, calling over her shoulder, "Follow me. I will travel slowly enough so that Cookie and JJ can keep up with us."

The friends followed her down a foot path and into the trees. As they entered the woods, Tango's voice could be heard saying, "Mama, are we there yet?"

Everyone laughed and Okkiki rolled her eyes.

Aline was so excited. It was difficult to believe that the time had finally arrived and she was on her way to find her tiger. She didn't know which she looked forward to more—seeing a real live tiger for the very first time or drinking Buddy's elixir and actually becoming a tiger for a day.

Rosie noticed the anticipation on Aline's face and smiled in response. Rosie was a Caller and skilled in communicating with animals. She had a feeling that her special talent would be helpful when they finally found Rashka.

Okikki motioned to Tango and they quickly climbed a tree, moving effortlessly along the branches. Even in this world, the comfort of the squirrel skyway helped settle her nerves. Okikki knew Buddy quite well and she could tell that he was not confident. Knowing that Buddy was worried amplified her own fears.

Chapter 5

It was mid-afternoon, Rashka's lazy time of day. He had found a lovely, soft, grassy spot of sunshine and was stretched out with his eyes closed. The usual woodland sounds were like a distant hum as the large cat drifted into a light sleep. One of his ears moved when he heard Akron softly approach. The young tiger's mouth turned up slightly, but his eyes never opened. The Nature Guardian came and went frequently and Rashka had grown accustomed to her presence. Indeed she had become his best friend. He respected her greater strength and power. Akron had taught him much in these last months and with her help he had become both stronger and wiser. When she did not speak, Rashka drifted off again.

Akron settled herself on a fallen log. Today she appeared tall and slender. Her green hair was filled with leaves that were studded with ladybugs. At the moment, her features were similar to the strong, almost human, look of the dryads. White silk cloth spun by the most talented spiders adorned her. There was a circlet of gold in her hair which featured a single uncut emerald. Her fingers and toes dripped leaves and rustled when she moved. Once settled, she did not speak or move again, but her smoky eyes never left

Rashka as he slept.

As the cat dozed, he dreamed. Once again he heard the roaring of a truck coming down the road. Rashka watched from a great distance as the people took his mother and placed her in the truck. Then he panicked as the vehicle turned around and rumbled back down the road. He tried to reach them, but they were much too swift. In his dream, Rashka bellowed in frustration and vowed that he would make them pay, the same vow that he had made on the day that his mother had been captured. This one thing he harbored in his heart and kept to himself. Rashka listened for the sound of that truck. He would know it from all of the others that passed by and when it came near again, he would have his revenge.

Sometime later Rashka woke up and turned to see the curious eyes of Akron watching him. He rose and stretched his powerful limbs. Akron had taught him silence for his own protection, so he contented himself with small cat noises and low sounds that rumbled deep within him as he greeted her. Akron rose from her sitting place and rested a lanky, leaf-strewn hand on the tiger's back. The two of them moved together through the woods toward the stream where Rashka would take a long cool drink.

Amyra was a wildlife specialist and a forest ranger. She was proud to have been a member of the group responsible for the recapture of the beautiful tiger, Rasheteike. Afterward she had visited the wildlife preserve where the Siberian had been relocated and was pleased to see that the beautiful tiger appeared to be happy.

On this particular day, Amyra was in the truck that had been used in that recapture.   She was glad to be driving it for the very last time, for the truck had proven unreliable and repairs were becoming more frequent and costly.   As she wheeled onto the car lot, she anticipated the brand new truck purchased by the county.   Amyra pulled around to the back of the building where Lou, the dealership owner, was waiting.   He waved as she parked and exited the truck.

Amyra patted the hood and said, "Goodbye, old friend!"

They engaged in small talk as Lou escorted her to the new truck.   By the time she pulled out of the lot, the older vehicle was already being driven into a service bay.   At the same time, Lou picked up the phone to call his cousin, Jeb.

After their conversation, Jeb hung up the phone.   He was smiling, but on his rather unpleasant face it looked more like a sneer. Jeb went to the fridge and searched behind cartons of leftover takeout to find a drink.   He popped the cap, leaned his head back and swigged almost half of it down in the first gulp.   Then Jeb went to the torn screen door and yelled into the yard.

"Yo, Billy.   That was Lou on the horn.   That ol' truck he was tellin' us about is bein' fixed up right now.   Gonna be ready tomorrow."

Billy was underneath the ancient Ford pickup tinkering with the transmission, but it was pretty much a lost cause.   From beneath the metal heap his muffled voice could be heard.   "That's sure a relief.   I'm not gettin' anywhere with ol' Bessie here."

Jeb was in good humor after receiving the news from Cousin Lou. "Well, then climb on out from under there and let's hit the town tonight. We oughta celebrate. Lou is gettin' us that truck for a song!"

"Hadn't we oughta save our money to pay for the thing?" questioned Billy.

Jeb laughed aloud. "Nawwww. Remember? I told you about that fancy shop in the mountains. We're gonna give that place a little visit, you know? There's never anybody there this time of year and the girl that runs it goes to the back to eat around noon most days. We're gonna hit that cash register while she's gone and see what we can find. We'll be out'a there before she knows what hit 'er!"

Both men laughed loudly.

"They so high priced there oughta be some bills in there. Maybe if we luck up it'll be enough to pay for the new truck," hooted Billy.

Far away in a mountain glen, Rashka turned an ear toward the road. He was always listening...

Chapter 6

Night had fallen in the mountains. Everyone in the group was asleep except for Buddy. He was reclining on a sturdy branch in an oak tree. Clasping his hands behind his head, he gazed up at the myriad stars above. He could hear Cookie who was at the base of the tree curled up in a little ball snoring lightly. Occasionally there was a flutter of wings as JJ adjusted his position on Cookie's back. It was a still night without a cloud in the sky. The pale, white moon shone brightly, like a priceless gem set against a dark and velvety background.

Buddy played connect the dots with the stars, forming various shapes in his mind's eye. Sleep wouldn't come. He just couldn't shake the feeling that something bad was about to happen. The elf had a strong premonition that seemed to be growing by the hour. He loved each and every member of the group and could not bear to think that anything might go wrong during this adventure. He hoped his instincts were incorrect as he continued to search the sky until his eyes finally closed in sleep.

About three hours before dawn, Cookie raised his head. His ears perked as he stared into the trees. Then he stood and trotted into the woods. JJ would have fallen off except that his feet were tightly clenched into the little dog's fur, as was his habit. By the time the small bird was fully awake and aware, they were moving well away from the group.

"Cookie, where ya goin', bud? It's still dark. What's up?"

Of course, Cookie did not answer. JJ heard the howl of coyotes in the distance. He fluffed out his feathers and tightened his grip on Cookie's shoulders. "Cookie, let's go back. It's not safe out here. Where are we going anyway?"

Cookie paid no attention. JJ spent his time alternately attempting to memorize their trail so that he could find the way back if necessary and fuming about little dogs who thought they were big wolves. As they continued on, JJ felt increasingly worried about getting lost or worse.

As the sun peeked over the horizon, Buddy's eyes opened. The others were also beginning to stir.

Soon Wildflower asked, "Where are Cookie and JJ? Has anyone seen them?"

No one had, so Buddy helped Wildflower search the area.

Wildflower called, "Cooookieeee, JJ, where are you?"

Okikki climbed high into the trees and looked as far as her eyes could see. Rosie, Aline, and Morella concentrated their search in the area where Cookie was last seen, the base of the large oak tree. Morella followed what was to the others a mostly unreadable trail that disappeared into the trees. Before long she was back.

"Ok, everyone, I have good news and bad news. The good

news is that I have Cookie's trail and we can follow him.   The bad news is that he has a good head start."

Wildflower's heart sunk as she heard this news.   Buddy gave Morella a thankful look as he quickly organized the group.

"Let's get started.   If you're hungry, grab some berries or mushrooms along the way.   We will keep moving until we find them."   Buddy continued, "We should all stay behind Morella so that no one accidentally smudges the trail that she is following."

Wildflower asked, "Should someone stay here in case they return?"

Buddy shook his head.   "Remember that they don't know the lay of the land here.   If they return, they will have to follow their own trail back and then they will run right into us."

Everyone thought that Buddy's words made sense.   Morella moved on ahead tracking Cookie while the others followed.   Okikki and Tango scampered through the trees above and stayed level with Morella, looking around for a possible sighting of the little dog and his feathered friend.

About thirty minutes away from the camp area, Cookie finally found what had drawn him.   Leftovers from a picnic shared by some hikers were in a metal can designated for trash.   Cookie stretched up as tall as he could and pushed against the can.   He was trying to dump it over so that he could reach the contents—a partially eaten sandwich and some stale potato chips.

JJ asked "What are you doing, Cookie?   It's late and nippy out and I'm sleepy.   Let's go back to camp.   What do you want with that old can anyway?   It's too heavy to be moved."

Cookie barked at the can, then snuffled around on the ground where he found some crumbs.   The papillon gobbled them up in short order.

JJ snorted.   "I bet you were planning to raid that can.   Well, it's going to be disgusting, but I can help you…I guess.   It's probably going to make you sick and then I will no doubt get the blame."

JJ continued to fuss to himself as he flew to the top of the can and stared inside.   Cookie whimpered as his feathers moved away. JJ smiled at him.

"See, my wings are getting better.   I can fly a little now!"

Cookie tilted his head to one side and barked.   JJ disappeared into the can.   His voice echoed back to Cookie.

"It's nearly empty in here.   Just this old food…"

Cookie listened with interest to the sounds of JJ scuffling around inside.   When the little bird finally emerged from the metal can, his beak was full of leftover ham sandwich.   He would never want to admit it, but it tasted pretty good.   He decided that it might not make Cookie sick after all.   He fluttered down to the ground and put the piece of sandwich on the grass.   Cookie grabbed it almost before JJ had a chance to release it from his beak.

"Whoa, Cookie, wait just a minute!   Give a fella a chance to put the food down before ya go grabbin' it up.   Someone would think ya haven't eaten for a couple o' days!"

JJ shook his head and made raspy bird noises to himself as he

100

disappeared into the can for a second time. "This could take a while." His voice echoed out to Cookie. "My beak can't hold nearly as much as you can gobble up in one bite."

Cookie tilted his head and whimpered softly as he eagerly anticipated the next morsel of food. After some time of flying back and forth, JJ finally offered the last bit of sandwich. It was clear that Cookie would have loved more, but JJ was glad to have finished fishing bits of bread and meat from the garbage bin. He was tired and more than ready to go back to camp.

"Ok, Cookie, ya ate everything in sight. Now let's go back. We'll hardly have an hour to rest before everyone wakes up."

Cookie waited quietly while JJ flapped onto his back and positioned himself. As soon as the little bird was settled, Cookie took off at a trot. Instead of moving toward the camp, he headed in the opposite direction.

"Aw, man..." JJ complained. "Where are ya goin' now?"

Cookie moved quickly through the woods. JJ would have enjoyed the ride if it weren't dark and if they were not in an unfamiliar world.

"No tellin' what's in these woods. This is wrong. We need to go back, Cookie!"

JJ sighed in exasperation as it became clear that Cookie was not paying any attention to him whatsoever. It was then that they heard the howl of coyotes again. But this time they sounded much closer. JJ was frightened. However, Cookie seemed oblivious to any danger. He was making some noise of his own snuffling along the ground.   It was obvious that he had uncovered an interesting scent.   As Cookie followed his nose, JJ could only hope that the little dog was NOT tracking the coyotes.

Cookie moved along, snuffling like a bloodhound.   JJ sat quietly clutching the little dog's fur.   He didn't want to attract the attention of the predatory coyotes, so he kept his beak closed and hoped that the sun would be rising before long.   To JJ's relief, when the coyotes tuned up again, they sounded much further away.   Just as he began to relax, he heard a noise in the brush ahead of them. Cookie stopped short and started barking.

JJ spoke in a harsh whisper, "Just what kind of trouble you gettin' us into now, Cookie?   Shhhhhh!"

Cookie was alert and focused as he stood staring at that brush and barking as loudly as possible.   He knew exactly what was in the shrubs.   Cookie had a great memory for scent and he knew he had chased this creature before.   Cookie ran straight toward the brush.

Chapter 7

JJ yelled, "Wait a minute, would ya!"

Of course, Cookie did not do any waiting whatsoever, so JJ flattened himself down as low as possible and hoped the brush would not rake him off as Cookie squeezed through. The little bird heard scuffling sounds and glimpsed a flash of bright blue and a bit of white. Then he heard a loud yelp as something or someone tried to scramble away. When Cookie finally pushed all the way through the underbrush into a clearing, JJ was still on his back holding onto the canine's fur as tightly as possible.

"Who and what in the world are you?" asked JJ as he stared in amazement at the creature standing just a few feet away from them. Cookie bounded forward and the character backed away from them. "Cookie, would ya stop it!? You're scarin' him!"

JJ fluttered onto the top of Cookie's head and stuck his face down in front of Cookie's eyes. The little bird looked upside down to Cookie and his rather large beak was dangerously close to Cookie's tender nose. Then JJ said loudly and distinctly, "Stop chasin' him and stop barkin'! NO BARK!" He glared into Cookie's eyes with a no nonsense expression and snapped his beak to punctuate his words.

Cookie looked cross-eyed at JJ. The little bird had finally gotten his attention. He calmed down just a little bit, but was still quivering with excitement as JJ took charge of the situation. JJ returned his attention to the creature. He had never seen anything like it. The animal had a large head which sat on what seemed like an impossibly thin neck. Its torso was ample in size and the creature was hugging itself with arms which were short and thick in contrast to long, thin legs. JJ stared for a moment at those two feet which were long and wide. The creature had bright eyes, a well-whiskered black nose and big, round flexible ears that twitched this way and that. He was dressed rather smartly, nautical-style in a white and blue sailor outfit.

JJ repeated his question. "Who and what are you?"

"I am a mouse of course!" answered the creature in a shaky voice. "My name is Ernie."

The mouse pulled his long, tapered tail into his hands and stroked it nervously as he glanced briefly at JJ. He quickly returned his attention to Cookie, ready to bolt if the dog started to chase him again.

JJ responded in a doubtful tone, "You aren't like any mouse I have ever seen."

Cookie knew Ernie was a mouse. The little dog remembered him from Pixieland. Cookie loved to chase mice and he had chased this one some time ago just before finding JJ in the woods. Ernie had disappeared before Cookie could catch up to him. It made no difference to Cookie that Ernie was large. Cookie did not know size.

He thought of himself as big and bad, able to handle anything that came his way. He growled low in his throat. JJ popped him with a wing.

"Stop it, Cookie! You're acting just plain rude!" JJ rolled his eyes and shook his head. "I'm sorry, Ernie. I am trying to teach him some manners, but he is as stubborn as they come. You sure you're a mouse?" Then before Ernie could answer JJ said, "You must be from this world 'cause I've never seen anything like you back home."

Ernie was calming down some. It seemed that JJ had a pretty good handle on the canine. Still, Ernie was not going to take his eyes off of Cookie, at least not for long.

He peered at JJ hopefully and asked, "Are you the doctor?"

JJ looked confused.

Ernie continued, "They said the doctor would be large with black feathers. You are small and your feathers are green, but as far as I can see you are the only bird in your group."

JJ looked at Ernie as if he were speaking a foreign language. He had no idea what the mouse was talking about. "What group?" Then realization dawned on JJ. "Have you been following us?"

The mouse had enough good manners to look mildly embarrassed as he admitted, "Just for a couple of days. I should have been here sooner, but I arrived at your portal a little late. All of you had already stepped inside, so I hopped in, but was separated from you at destination."

JJ stared at the blue mouse in amazement. "So, you are from

Pixieland and you followed us here?"

The mouse nodded, then questioned again, "Are you the doctor?"

JJ could not remember his past, but he was pretty certain that he had never been a doctor.   Then he recalled what the mouse had said earlier.   "You said large bird with black feathers?   That describes Newton perfectly, but what do you want with him?"

JJ did nothing to mask the suspicion in his voice.   The small parrot was automatically cautious about this mouse who had been secretly following him and his friends.

Ernie looked interested as he asked, "Where is Newton now?"

JJ responded, "He flew away on some important business, but I don't see how he could be a doctor."   JJ lifted his own wings as he hinted, "Wings, ya know?   Instead of hands?   If you are looking for a doctor, you'd be better off to look elsewhere."   JJ changed the subject.   "You said you're from Pixieland.   So, why haven't I seen you or anyone else like you before?"

"That's easy," Ernie replied.   "I'm a sailing mouse, I am. Mostly I live on my boat.   Her name is the Reliant."   Ernie couldn't keep the pride out of his voice.   He looked as if he wished that he were still on the Reliant as he explained, "My people live on the other side of the ocean and as far as I know, I'm the only one to have ever set foot on your shores."   He paused wistfully and then speaking aloud reminded himself, "I need to keep my mind on the task at hand."

JJ looked at him sharply.   "Speakin' of, what exactly IS the task at hand? Followin' folk around without tellin' um and then askin' for a doctor. Are ya ill?" JJ peered at the mouse. "Ya don't look ill."

Ernie's face reflected his surprise. "Oh, no, I'm perfectly fine. It's not just ANY doctor that I'm looking for, you see." He watched JJ's face carefully for some sign of understanding. Then after looking around as if he thought someone might overhear, he dropped what he thought was a bombshell. "The dynasts sent me."

It was clear to JJ that Ernie expected him to react to that bit of information, but JJ had no idea what the mouse was talking about. The green bird was impatient and more than ready to get to the bottom of things. Every answer from this mouse just seemed to create more questions.

JJ responded in a clipped tone. "Who *or what* are the dynasts?"

Ernie was aghast. He couldn't believe what his large round ears were hearing. It was astonishing that this bird didn't know about the dynasts. He reacted by whistling through his teeth in surprise.

During most of this conversation, Cookie was as calm as he could be when he wanted to do something very badly and felt restrained. He didn't understand what was being said, but he knew his feathers were getting upset. In his doggie mind, the mouse that he so badly wished to chase was to blame.

JJ was so focused on Ernie that he overlooked the fact that Cookie was trembling with excitement again. When Ernie whistled, all bets were off as Cookie started barking and then bounded toward Ernie, dumping JJ off of his back in the process.

The blue mouse ran as if his life depended on it. JJ yelled at Cookie, but no one could hear anything except Cookie's loud barking. Then as quickly as it all started, it ended. Before Cookie could catch up to the running mouse, Ernie disappeared. It was as if he had never been there at all. Cookie cast around for a few minutes, then gave up. JJ was right where he had been dumped when the puzzled papillon returned. When Cookie snuffled JJ with his wet nose, the green bird tapped his foot and glared at the little dog.

JJ said, "Nevermind tryin to tickle me when ya know ya been a bad dog." JJ quickly stepped aside, narrowly escaping a drenching from Cookie's (not so contrite) tongue. He climbed onto the papillon's back and just shook his head in frustration. "Now look what ya done! Ya chased Ernie away. We didn't even find out what he wanted. I'm never gonna teach ya nothin' and that's a fact!"

Cookie whimpered, but he did not look very sorry as he continued on down the path in the opposite direction from the camp.

Chapter 8

Morella had no trouble following Cookie's trail.   Within a few minutes, the group arrived at the metal trash can.   It was clear that Cookie and JJ had been there.   Wildflower tried not to think about what the two of them were doing around that can.   She was well aware that Cookie would be looking for anything edible, no matter how stale.   She just hoped that whatever he had found would not make him sick.

Wildflower understood why Cookie would want to explore this strange world.   It was certainly very different from Pixieland.   She knew that the little dog would love all of the different sights sounds and smells.   It was a comfort to know that JJ was with him and that Cookie wasn't wandering around all alone.

She turned to Aline.   "I am so sorry that Cookie and JJ have caused a delay in getting to the tiger.   I know how excited you were to be on your way to find Rashka."

Aline rested a hand on Wildflower's shoulder.   "It's fine! We will get there soon enough and right now it's more important to find those two."

Wildflower smiled gratefully.   "Thanks, Aline."

Morella chimed in, "Truthfully, we are sort of heading toward

Rashka's territory and we aren't too far from the path we were going to take."

As the group continued on, Morella grew a bit anxious when she realized that Cookie seemed to be leading them a little too close to the main road. She decided not to mention it just yet. After all, the small dog was unpredictable and he might turn back into the woods and avoid the road altogether.

It was not like Jeb and Billy to be up so early in the morning, but they had decided to go into town and take a look around, maybe case the small business that they were planning to rob later in the day. They had tinkered with their old truck and finally had it running fairly smoothly.

Jeb glanced at Billy and said, "Listen up, Billy. I figure we can hang around in town til lunch time. Lou said the truck we're gettin' would be ready by then. When the girl who works at that there fancy tourist store goes to the back, we grab the dough from her cash register and run. She won't know a thing til after lunch. By that time we'll have picked up our new truck, dumped this one and be on our way."

Jeb smiled as he thought about the money that had probably been sitting there in that cash register all week long just waiting for him and Billy to snag it.

Billy asked, "We gonna pay Lou with that stolen money?"

Jeb looked doubtful as he said, "Well, now, I don't rightly know about that. I thought about it and Lou says he'll wait a little if we don't have all the dough at one time, so why give him all our money?"

Billy could tell that Jeb had no intention of paying Lou if there was any way that he could wiggle out of it. That struck Billy as funny, so he snickered and then laughed boisterously. Soon both men were laughing.

Billy wiped tears of mirth from his eyes as he pointed at a small building ahead. "Yo, Jeb, pull in here at this burger joint. They make a mean sausage biscuit. Let's git a bag full of um."

As Jeb pulled up to the drive thru window, he patted his stomach and said, "I could shore do with some breakfast right about now."

Jeb grimaced as he grudgingly dug the money out of his pocket to pay the employee at the window. Then he slapped Billy on the back.

"Liven up there, Billy. This here's gonna be a good day for us."

Billy stared through the window at the young man as he counted sausage biscuits then put them in a sack.

When they had finished eating, Billy wadded the sack into a ball and threw their leftovers onto the back seat where it landed on top of coke cans, bottles and other debris.

Jeb bragged, "Yep, Billy, this is gonna be a good day alright. We'll be sittin' pretty before you know it."

Billy nodded. "If this goes good, I say let's do it again somewhere else. Maybe that burger joint. Whaddaya think?"

Jeb laughed out loud.   "Now yore talkin!"   Then he took one hand off of the steering wheel and slapped Billy on the back once again.

"Here," directed Billy, "let's take this ol' road.   It's steep in places, but it'll be shorter."

Jeb thought that was a good idea and obediently yanked the steering wheel, just barely making the turn in time.   It took a moment to right the old truck, but Jeb was a good driver and soon had the vehicle chugging steadily along the mostly deserted mountain road.

As Morella continued to follow Cookie's trail, her fears about his path were confirmed.   She decided that she shouldn't delay telling the others, so she stopped and turned around to face the group.

"I think you should know that if Cookie continues the way he is going, he will soon be very near the road."

Tango could see that Morella was not pleased about this and asked what several of them were wondering.   "What is 'the road'?"

Morella smiled at Tango as she answered, "That's a very good question, Tango.   You see, in our world there is a large population of humans.   They are clever and have many inventions.   They drive in large metal machines and build passageways which connect their cities and towns.   Then to reach each other, they drive their metals along these roads.   It's quick, like flying, but they move along the ground."

Tango asked, "May we go close enough to see the metals? They sound like fun!"

Morella answered, "Some roads are full of metals, but this one is traveled infrequently. We might not see a metal for a long while. Even so, I should warn you that the metals are dangerous and animals around here don't fare well if they get in the way, especially at night."

Tango was disappointed, but after what Morella had said, he felt a little afraid of the metals and was content to follow her lead.

Morella told everyone, "I just wanted you to know, if you hear a loud roaring sound, it could be a metal, but it's not alive and is not really issuing a challenge. Just remember that the humans control them and the metals are strong and powerful inventions. Stay clear of them, please."

Chapter 9

Cookie ran up a small hill and through a row of trees which opened onto the shoulder of the road. Neither Cookie nor JJ was disturbed by the ribbon of asphalt. There was a smattering of gravel lining the side of the road and some soft grass that covered a broader area between the gravel and the trees. Cookie sniffed around in the grass and gravel, then moved onto the road to inspect an oil spill. He was making his usual pig-like snuffle noises as he investigated the strong scent.

JJ yawned. The little bird was getting sleepy and decided that since it was so quiet here and Cookie was occupied, he might just as well catch a couple of winks. Then maybe he could convince Cookie to head back to camp...right after this nap. He clutched Cookie's fur tightly, fluffed out his feathers and closed his eyes.

Cookie heard the engine first. He lifted his head and perked up his ears. As the truck came over the hill, the early morning sun bounced off of the metal grill causing Cookie to squint. JJ woke up to see something very large and noisy rapidly moving toward them.

At the same time that Cookie and JJ were looking at the truck, its occupants were also looking at them.

Jeb said, "Would ya look at that!"

Billy grabbed his specs and peered through the dirty windshield. "Well, what in tarnation! Slow down there, Jeb. I got me an idear." Billy gestured to the side of the road. "Pull over an' let me out a minute."

Jeb drove onto the shoulder, his eyes never leaving the little dog and bird. Billy reached into the back seat and grabbed the wadded up sack of leftovers. "We gonna grab those two. I'm purty sure that dog is somethin fancy an' if we can git that bird too, we got somethin that someun will pay a purty penny fer."

Jeb rubbed his stubbly chin as he thought. "You don' think someun will recognize those two. It ain't everday ya see a sight like that—a bird on a dog's back? It looks like a circus act." Jeb looked around as if he expected to see a circus wagon somewhere in the vicinity.

Billy just laughed as he exited the truck. Then he leaned into the open window and said "Jeb, you worry too much."

Billy walked heavily across the gravel toward Cookie and JJ. Cookie ran a few steps away from the man, then turned and started barking. JJ whispered loudly in the papillon's ear. "Run, Cookie!"

As the man approached, Cookie stood his ground until the last minute. Then he retreated a few paces and turned to bark once again. Billy was not afraid of the little dog. *After all, how much damage could such a bit of a dog do?* he asked as he advanced toward them. JJ glared suspiciously at the man. Then Billy slowly reached into the bag and produced the food. The smell of sausage and bread filled the air and Cookie's nostrils. Cookie stopped barking and sniffed noisily. Then he wagged his tail.

Uh oh, now we are in trouble, thought JJ who was fighting the urge to fly away. This was a powerful instinct, but even stronger was his devotion to Cookie and his unwillingness to leave his canine friend alone in the face of possible danger.

Billy had a tight little smile on his face as he clumsily crouched down to coax Cookie. "Here, fella, don't you want a bite of this nice biscuit?"

Cookie didn't hesitate. He came forward eagerly to accept. Billy grabbed him as soon as he was within reach, knocking JJ off in the process. Billy stood up with Cookie in his arms and chuckled as he rewarded the little dog with several more bites of food.

JJ was truly frightened. He flew around the two of them twittering and fussing. Even though JJ was a talking bird, everything he said sounded like chirps and twitters to Jeb and Billy.

After Cookie gobbled the food, he began to feel trapped. He didn't like being held so he growled.

"None o' that!" Billy said sharply as he turned and walked back to the truck, eyeing JJ who was buzzing around his head like an annoying bee. "Too bad I don't got a net or somethin' to catch that bird," he complained.

Jeb barked, "Would ya get yo' self in the truck 'fore that mutt's owner shows up?"

Billy opened the door with one hand while holding on to Cookie. As JJ flew around the vehicle, Billy slammed the door and

Jeb cranked up the engine. Just before they rolled away, JJ flew straight into the open passenger window and landed on Cookie's back. Billy laughed out loud.

"Well, would ya look at that...yessiree, someun is gonna pay a purty penny for this act."

Morella stopped at the edge of the woods and Okikki called down from the trees. "I think that must be the road just ahead." Then she added, "I don't see any metals."

Morella said, "Thanks, Okikki. That is indeed the road. I think it would be best for all of us to stop right here. If everyone agrees, Buddy and I will go take a look. It might be safer if we don't all go."

Wildflower was very worried and her voice shook as she asked, "Do you think they crossed the road?"

Morella looked at her sympathetically as she answered, "They may have, but I want to be certain before we all go across."

The rest of the group waited patiently as Buddy and Morella set out through the last line of trees and toward the long snake-like road. The pair moved silently across the thick grass that lined the gravelly shoulder. The morel faerie's eyes were glued to the ground as she followed Cookie's trail.

Buddy was a fair tracker himself, but he had to admit that Morella was much quicker and more skilled. He was thankful to have her help right now. He didn't know anything about roads or metals and was glad that there were none in Pixieland. As the two of them crossed the gravel and stepped out onto the blacktop, Buddy noticed that it smelled funny. It was a strong odor and Buddy sniffed a time or two. "Morella, what is that smell?"

Morella glanced up briefly as she answered, "It's the smell of the road—a mixture of the ingredients that humans use in their construction. Also, the metals that travel here sometimes leak and leave an oily residue that mixes with the road odor. I know, it's most unpleasant when you are right on top of it as we are now."

Buddy happened to notice something lying on the road just ahead. "Morella, look!"

The two of them hurried to the spot. It was a small green feather. Their eyes met and Buddy's face blanched.

Morella read the concern in his eyes and placed a hand on his arm. "I see no indication that they were injured here. Give me a minute to read all of the signs." Morella moved with cat-like steps as she examined both the road and its shoulder.

Buddy waited patiently as Morella worked. It felt like a knot was forming in the pit of his stomach, that nervous twinge that always seemed to take hold of him when he knew that something was terribly wrong.

Morella bent down on one knee to examine the gravel. Finally she swept her long blond hair up and away from her face with a delicate hand as she looked at Buddy. Her eyes were sad and her wings drooped.

The nervous knot in Buddy's stomach suddenly felt like a lump in his throat, but Buddy reminded himself that he had never been one to shy away from the facts. He squared his shoulders in preparation.

Morella spoke slowly, "It seems that Cookie and JJ were here. From the metal tracks and human footprints in the gravel as well as the crumbs on the road, my guess is that at least one human in a metal saw Cookie and JJ and stopped. The human may have lured Cookie with this bread. Since there is no further sign of Cookie or JJ, I feel certain that the human took them into the metal and away. I cannot say for sure about JJ since he can fly and might not leave any tracks, but I don't think that he would abandon Cookie, and I feel sure that he would have found us by now if he were still here."

So many questions crowded through Buddy's mind all at once. Why would a human want to take the little dog and where did they go? Would the small dog be treated kindly? Would the group ever see Cookie again? Where was JJ? Was he with Cookie or roaming around somewhere lost and looking for them? Buddy didn't know what to say.

Morella spoke. "Buddy, I think we should camp nearby for a few days. There is a chance that JJ is still in the area. We should give him every opportunity to find us."

Buddy knew that she was right, but at this moment he could not trust himself to speak and they were both quiet as they made their way back to the group.

When Buddy relayed the disturbing news, Okikki took Wildflower's hand in her paw mothering her as best she could. Later while the others set up camp, Wildflower flew around the area and on both sides of the road, looking for more clues.   Everyone kept an eye out for a little green bird, but when night fell they were no closer to finding Cookie and JJ.

Chapter 10

Later that evening the friends were settling down to get some much needed rest. Aline curled up comfortably near the top of a tall pine. The branch beneath her swayed gently. She watched Wildflower as the restless faerie bobbed in and out of the trees searching and hoping to catch sight of those she loved and missed. Aline felt sad, but her eyes grew heavy and before long they closed in sleep. On the ground below her, Buddy was tending a fire. He had built it just in case JJ was still in the woods. He hoped the light from the flames would serve as a beacon and show the bird where to find them.

Sometime in the middle of the night, Aline woke suddenly. She thought she heard a cat spitting and hissing. When she looked down she could see that Buddy was dozing by the fire. In the heat of the flames a large log had suddenly shifted positions. Aline thought that maybe the crackling log was what caused the spitting noise that had wakened her. Everyone was asleep, even Wildflower. As Aline's eyes began to close again, she heard something a second time. It sounded further away and was not so much a spitting sound as a low thrumming noise. She sat up and looked around. No one else had stirred. Aline scanned the area, but couldn't see anything. The faerie wondered if she should wake the others, but she decided to let them sleep and investigate on her own. As Aline flew out of the camp an almost full moon shone down on her and danced along her beating wings.

The sound was further away than Aline had at first suspected, but as she drew closer the thrumming noise filled the air and seemed to be coming from every direction. The faerie landed high in a gnarled oak and took a look around. Her surroundings were suffused with a soft misty light cast from the bright moon above. She carefully searched the area and then suddenly she spotted something lying stretched out on a long flat rock. Aline shook with excitement. She could hardly believe what she was seeing. He was much larger than she had imagined, but she knew exactly what he was from the picture in Buddy's book. How many times had she stared at that picture and dreamed of the moment when she would see a tiger for the very first time. His fur looked like spun gold, rich and tawny. He was well marked with crisp, black stripes that formed in contrast to his honey hide. Golden eyes reflected the moon and shot lasers of light into the night. The tiger's ears were rounded with tufts of fur inside.

Aline breathed, "Rashka...exquisite!"

So transfixed was she that it did not occur to her that her words had been spoken aloud until he lifted his large head and looked her way. The cat's face filled with an alert focus that is a characteristic of the great predators.

Aline held her breath and dared not even blink as she watched the muscles ripple along the tiger's shoulders.   His tail flicked back and forth much like that of a domestic cat, but this was no tame beast.   Rashka moved quickly and stealthily toward her tree.   He stretched full length up the trunk with two powerful back legs acting as a brace.   Two giant front paws complete with sharp claws sunk deep into the rough wood almost reaching the lowest of the branches.   Those golden eyes searched for her among the foliage. But before he discovered her hiding place, a voice distracted him. After one more penetrating stare, the great cat pushed away from the tree and ambled back toward the rock slab.   As the tiger chuffed a greeting to the newcomer, Aline quietly sat down on the branch, breathing an inward sigh of relief.   When she had recovered, the faerie leaned forward a little to see who or what was with Rashka.   A low voice floated up to her waiting ears.   When the owner finally moved into view, there was no doubt in Aline's mind that she was looking right at Akron the Nature Guardian.

Akron wore a shimmery soft gown, the pattern resembling the wings of a monarch butterfly.   Aline had never seen such a beautiful garment.   From the Guardian's waist to the ground there was an enormous amount of fabric which billowed and flowed like moving water.   Her face was soft, yet strong and flawless.   Dozens of monarch butterflies covered much of the Guardian's head and shoulders like a living cowl, their wings moving up and down slowly. Akron's hair resembled long sweetgrass and when she turned her head it appeared that delicate wisps broke free and drifted down. Aline thought that there should be piles of the tendrils at the

Guardian's feet, but it must have been an illusion because she didn't see anything on the ground below.

Never had she seen such obvious power and beauty. At first Aline wondered why the Guardian didn't fit the description in Morella's story and then she remembered that Morella had said that Akron changes her appearance at will.

Raska's long tail seemed to have a life of its own as it flicked back and forth. It was so close that Aline felt strongly tempted to fly down and touch it. An idea popped into her head. She remembered that Buddy said the hair should come from the head of the tiger, but she wondered if by chance hair from that twitching tail might work just as well. As she gazed at the powerful tiger, Aline thought better of her idea, deciding that it would never under any circumstances be a good plan to grab a tiger's tail.

Aline's eyes shifted back to the Nature Guardian. Akron's skin was luminous as if it shared an unspoken secret with the nearly full moon above. Her smoky eyes revealed her fondness for Rashka. The two of them charged their surroundings with an enormous energy that practically stole Aline's breath away.

Aline felt a little lightheaded as she watched Akron and the tiger speaking to one another. She couldn't tell what they were saying, but the sound of their voices had an almost hypnotic effect. Aline began to feel sleepy, but she was determined to stay awake. The tiger seemed almost tame as he gazed fondly at the Nature Guardian and relaxed so quietly at her feet. Aline wondered what it would be like to sit beside him and stroke his silky looking fur.

Sometime in the middle of the night Akron departed and afterward the glade seemed less alive. Although Aline would not have believed it possible to do so, eventually she fell asleep.

Chapter 11

That morning when the group began to stir and it became clear that Aline was missing, there was panic in the camp. Buddy thought it was bad enough that both Cookie and JJ were missing. It was beginning to look like their group was disappearing one at a time.

"My voice carries well. I will climb this tall tree and call to her," volunteered Okikki. Without another word, the red squirrel scampered up into the waiting branches. She stood ram-rod straight and snapped her tail rapidly as she cried, "Aline, where are you?"

Luckily, Aline was within squirrel shouting distance and heard Okikki through the fog of her sleep. The groggy faerie sat up abruptly, stretched and looked around. Rashka was no longer there. Okikki called again and this time Aline responded.

When she had left camp last night, Aline had every intention of returning as soon as she solved the mystery of the strange sound. It was difficult to believe that she could have fallen asleep. The remorseful faerie flew toward Okikki's shrill voice as fast as her wings would allow. She hadn't meant to worry her friends. She called to Okikki as she flew and very soon the squirrel could hear her response. The two continued to call back and forth until Aline arrived safely in the camp.   Everyone surrounded her and they were all speaking at the same time.

"Wait a minute, wait a minute," ordered Buddy.   "One at a time, please.   We all want to know where Aline went and what she was doing.   Now that we know she's safe, let's give her a chance to talk."

Buddy's words calmed and focused everyone.   When all were quiet, Aline smiled a bit shyly, but her eyes sparkled with excitement. There was an air of anticipation in the camp as her friends waited to hear her story.

Tango's eyes never left Aline's face as she told everyone about last night's adventure.   She lingered over the descriptions of both Rashka and Akron.

Rosie breathed, "Oh, how I wish I had seen them too!"

Everyone talked among themselves going over every detail of Akron and Rashka's appearance.   Only Aline stood quietly.   She was remembering that tiger's tail flicking back and forth so near her hiding place that she could almost have reached down and touched it. The question that she had asked herself last night popped back into her mind so she tugged at Buddy's sleeve to get his attention.

"Buddy, would hair from the tail of the tiger be as good as hair from the head of a tiger for the elixir?"

Buddy ran a long fingered hand through his dark hair.   "It's an exact recipe, you see.   I think that if I don't follow the instructions there would be no way to predict the outcome.   Why do you ask? Do you have some hair from the tiger's tail?"   The elf raised one eyebrow and looked at Aline as if expecting her to produce the hair in question.

She responded, "No, I just wondered. The tiger's tail was so close to me that I was tempted to fly down and touch it. I thought maybe that hair would work and it would surely be easier to get. But I chickened out!"

Buddy smiled at Aline. "It might sound like a good idea, but I am sorry to say that it would probably not produce the desired result and it certainly would not have been safe for you to try to take the hair on your own."

Aline sighed, "I understand. " Then she confessed, "I know that I really did find Rashka last night and I watched both him and Akron for a long time. But this morning when I woke up they were gone and I wondered if it had all just been some elaborate dream."

Wildflower's wings drooped as she sadly turned away from the group. She had to admit that Aline's brush with Akron and Raska was exciting, but she simply could not stop thinking about Cookie and JJ. She had so hoped that Aline had spotted some sign of them in the woods last night.

Billy held Cookie in his lap. When Cookie realized that he was not free to move about, the little dog began to whine. JJ fluttered down and perched on Cookie's front leg. From this vantage point he made a clumsy attempt to comfort his canine friend.

"Now look at the trouble you've landed us in, Cookie. No telling what these bozos have in mind for us."

In spite of JJ's words, he snuggled against Cookie. The bird was really frightened, so he wanted to stay as close to his doggie friend as he possibly could.

Jeb shook his finger and glared at Billy. "Shut that mutt up."

Billy looked at Cookie with a puzzled expression. "Don't look like he cottons ta bein held, but I ain't got nowhere to put him, so quit yer bellyachin', Jeb. We are flat gonna make some bucks off these two."

Jeb looked somewhat appeased as he thought about the money. "Well, then give him some more food. Just shut him up. We need to talk."

Billy felt around in the back seat with one hand and found the rest of the sausage biscuits. He brought the sack up front. It worked like magic. Cookie stuck his entire head into the sack and began to gobble bits of crumbs as quickly as possible. JJ rolled his eyes and sighed.

Jeb said, "Give the bird somethin' too. It's about noisy, ain't it?"

Billy offered some bread crumbs. JJ clamped his beak shut and glared at the man. When all was quiet except for the wheezing of the truck's engine, Jeb said. "Well, finally! Now, let's go over tha plan again. Here's what we'll do. We gonna park right in front of that store so we can see the girl thru the window. When she goes to the back, that's when we make our move, see? I'll go in first an' then you come right behind me. You stand lookout while I reach over the counter and open the cashbox. When I grab the cash, we both run fer the car.   She may run out an' see our truck afore we get clean away, but here's the funny part.   We gonna go right over to Lou's place and pick up the new truck.   Then we ride on home just as easy as ya please."   Jeb smiled with satisfaction.

Billy asked, "What we gonna do with these here critters while we rob tha place?"

"Just leave 'um in the truck for now.   We can get 'um a cage an' make whoever buys 'um pay for that too.   After we pick up the truck at Lou's we can stop by the Allmart and find sumthin'."

Billy thought that sounded like a good idea.   Soon they pulled up in front of the gift shop.   They sat in the truck and watched until the girl behind the counter finally looked at her watch and then went to the back for lunch.   Jeb and Billy clambered out of the truck, slamming the doors quickly.   Billy's window was open just a little, but there wasn't enough room for a papillon to escape.   JJ could have squeezed through and he considered it for a moment, but he wasn't willing to abandon Cookie.

Chapter 12

The young clerk did not hear the doorbell as the two men entered. She had just stepped out the back door to get her sack lunch from the car. She had forgotten to bring it in that morning and that one little detail gave Jeb and Billy the time they needed to empty the cash register. By the time she popped back into the store, the pair had already come and gone. She gazed curiously through the shop window as the two rough looking men opened the doors and disappeared inside an old truck. The girl could see a little dog on the passenger seat. It looked as if it was trying to jump out, but the man grabbed it before he sat down. She found it a little humorous that these burly men would own such a dainty toy dog. After watching them pull away, she took one more look around to make sure that the shop was empty, then stepped into the back room to eat her lunch.

Billy stayed in the car with Cookie and JJ while Jeb went into the Allmart to find some sort of cage for the animals. Jeb searched until he found the aisle where the crates were located. He stood there staring at them until a friendly clerk noticed his confusion and offered to help. After finding out that Jeb's pet was a dog, the clerk asked for the dog's size.

"It's no bigger 'n a loaf a white bread and hardly weighs anythin' either," explained Jeb.

"What breed of dog is it?" asked the clerk.

Jeb rubbed his chin with a grimy hand. "Well, now, ya got me there. Can't say as I know jest what he is, but that don't make no nevermind. Jest hook me up with a cage an' i'll be on my way," Jeb snapped.

The salesperson was surprised that this man didn't know much about his own dog, but he answered politely, "I would suggest this smaller crate."

Jeb snatched it from the employee, turned his back and stalked abruptly toward the checkout line. When Jeb returned to the truck, Billy reached for JJ to put him into the crate. However, JJ bit down hard on the man's finger as soon as it invaded his space. Billy wrung his hand, then swore and threatened JJ, but the big man was only bluffing. He thought that the bird was too valuable to injure. Instead he stuck Cookie in the crate first and laughed as the feisty JJ followed of his own accord. "Look a there, Jeb. That bird sticks to that dog like glue. Yessiree, we gonna make a purty penny off a these two."

Ignoring Billy, Jeb ordered, "Count that dough again. I wanna know exactly what we got."

Meanwhile back at the shop, the clerk rang up her next customer. When the drawer popped open, she was shocked to see that it was empty.   Later when the police questioned her, she used her excellent memory to give a detailed description of Jeb and Billy as well as the truck.   Much to the surprise of the officers, she was even able to recall a partial tag number, explaining that she had only noticed the plate because it was so badly dented.

When Jeb and Billy arrived at Lou's place, Jeb wasted no time trying to wheedle out of paying for the truck.   "You know, cuz, times is tough.   I can pay for the truck, but it's gonna take some time to get up the cash.   Uh, I meant to have it, but if you can see your way clear to give us the truck, I'll get the money to ya real soon."

Lou wasn't so sure, but family was family, so he decided to take a chance on Jeb and float him for a couple of weeks.   He patted Jeb on the back and said, "Ok, ok, Jeb, I can wait a couple of weeks, but I'm gonna have to keep the title until you come up with the cash."

Lou wagged the truck title under Jeb's nose and then left the room to file it away.   As he was returning he saw Billy waving a wad of cash.   He was mildly curious, but since it seemed to be Billy's money, Lou didn't ask any questions.

When Billy noticed that Lou was watching him, he shoved the bills into his pocket and nervously cleared his throat.   After a small amount of conversation, Jeb and Billy said goodbye to Lou, loaded the crate with Cookie and JJ into their newly acquired truck and took off down the quiet road that wound through the mountains.

Meanwhile, somewhere nearby, Rashka had an ear turned

toward the road.   He was always listening...

Aline offered to take the others to the thicket where she had seen Rashka and Akron the night before.

Buddy put an arm around her shoulders.   "We all would love to have been there with you last night."

Tango said, "I want to see the tiger AND Akron."   Then he looked up at Okikki.   "Can we go now, Mama, huh, can we?"

Morella advised, "Since Rashka and Akron were gone when Aline woke up this morning, I think we should wait until we see if we can find out what has become of Cookie and JJ."

Wildflower nodded in agreement.   "I am going to check the road again."   She sighed heavily.   "I don't know what good it will do, but I have to do something."   The distraught faerie stifled a sob.

Rosie went to her and gave her a hug.   "Let's go, Wildflower. I will go with you."

Aline chimed in, "Let's all go.   More pairs of eyes will give us that many more chances to find a clue."

The Pixieland friends scoured the road surrounding the area where Buddy and Morella had found a green feather.

Wildflower felt so sad.   There was no sign of Cookie and JJ anywhere past this spot.   Originally she had hoped that they were still nearby, but now she was convinced that her two companions had indeed been captured.   She looked both ways and realized that she had no idea which direction the men in the metal had traveled after taking Cookie and JJ.   Her wings drooped and she sat down.

Suddenly she thought of something. "Morella, do you have any idea which way the metal went?"

Morella carefully studied the tracks again. "I think it went this way toward the town."

Wildflower looked hopeful. "Then maybe if we go to the town we might find them?"

Morella responded, "It would be a long shot and I might be wrong about the direction the metal took. I'm going by the tracks in the gravel and a few crumbs of bread. My idea about them being taken is just a theory."

Buddy commented, "No one has come up with anything better. I believe that your idea is very likely correct. It makes sense that whoever took Cookie and JJ might have been on the way to their town before finding the pair. They would probably continue on to wherever they were planning to go in the first place. I say let's move in the direction that Morella thinks they went. Stay close to the road, but just out of sight."

Everyone agreed that this was a good idea. Tango's eyes widened at the prospect of seeing a real human town.

Okikki cautioned, "Stay close to me, Tango, and be your best quiet self. We don't want to draw attention with any loud chattering."

Tango solemnly promised to be good. "I can be quiet, Mama. I'm not a baby anymore."

Okikki beamed at her son in spite of the circumstances, "You are growing up so fast, Tango. I am very proud of you."

Tango smiled shyly and everyone began the journey toward the little mountain town.

Chapter 13

Akron relaxed on the spongy moss bank of a mountain stream. She was entertained by Rashka who was splashing about in the water, chasing the rapidly moving fish. It was a game that he loved to play. His face was aquiver with excitement as he stared into the water, eyes darting back and forth like twin metronomes. In a sudden movement, the cat leapt forward scattering a spray of glistening water into the air as he pounced on a fish. Rashka was rewarded with a tasty snack which made the game that much more fun.

Akron enjoyed watching him play and she greatly appreciated the effortless grace and energy of the young tiger. The other three Guardians questioned her affection for the cub, but that didn't trouble her in the least. Always strong willed and unpredictable, she had taken a fancy to Rashka and that was that. Akron was also concerned that left unchecked the great cat would cause problems that could not be easily solved. The Guardian felt it best to keep an eye on the tiger and it was merely an added bonus that she happened to enjoy his company.

On this day Akron was dressed in a long, fitted powder blue robe spun from the very rare Tekka plant. The fabric was satiny soft and light as a feather. Akron's face was a work of art. A tattoo of colorful koi danced across her forehead, down her right cheek and across her chin. Silver water bubbles appeared to trail from the outer corners of her smoky eyes to her cheekbones. Her long hair resembled seaweed and there were some yellow strands mixed with various shades of green. Small beads of water adorned her hair and larger ones formed a necklace around her slender neck. When she laughed at Rashka's antics, her melodious voice filled the air inspiring nearby songbirds. As the woods filled with the music of birds, Rashka lifted his great head. Water dripped from his chin as he stared toward the road.

Akron was familiar with Rashka's ways—all of his likes, dislikes and subtle movements. In the months that she'd known him she had never seen an expression such as this one on the young tiger's face. It was a mixture of purpose, satisfaction and something else...something dangerous. She could see that trouble was afoot. As Rashka bolted through the trees, Akron began to fade from view. The last thing to disappear was the powder blue dress. Its perfect shape gave way to a soft blue mist rapidly moving in the tiger's wake.

Cookie was NOT enjoying the close confines of the crate. He barked at first and when that brought no response, he began to moan and howl. Jeb slammed a fist on the steering wheel.

"Billy, shut that mutt up once and for all. I ain't a gonna listen to it no more!"

Billy smacked the flat of his hand across the metal front of the crate in an effort to silence Cookie. If JJ had teeth, they would have rattled from the resulting jolt.

Cookie was quiet for at least two minutes before he started barking again.

Billy yelled, "SHUT UP!", then he clapped his two meaty hands over his ears in a useless effort to muffle Cookie's barking. The papillon was just reaching his stride with a regular rhythmic barking that, in very little time, resulted in a torturous effect on the two men in the front seat of the truck.

At first JJ tried to comfort Cookie with such words as, "This is entirely your fault, ya know...can't control your appetite...had to eat that man's dumb ol' food and walk right into his trap, ya silly dog." Then he realized how much Cookie's barking was annoying the smelly men so he added his own voice to the effort. JJ closed his eyes, flung his beak open and released a high-pitched stream of chittering, twittering, and squawking.

Jeb angrily slammed on the brakes, threw the truck into park and jerked open the door.

The group of Pixieland friends had not gone far when they heard a loud roaring sound. Morella told everyone that the noise meant there was a metal coming their way. But Wildflower heard something else above the whine of the metal. It was faint, but steady. "Is that Cookie?"

Buddy and Okikki looked at Wildflower. Buddy raised a hand to signal everyone to be quiet. The entire group stopped and stood still, straining to make out what Wildflower was hearing. Buddy smiled and grabbed Wildflower by the hands, dancing her around in a circle.

Wildflower laughed. "It's him! It's him!"

Tango jumped up and down. "Mama, it's Cookie. I hear him and JJ too! I didn't know JJ could squawk like that!"

Okikki touched the young squirrel's shoulder. "Shhh, Tango. That is not polite."

Tango muttered, "Sorry."

Okikki patted his shoulder affectionately. Everyone felt relieved. From what they heard, Cookie and JJ sounded just fine.

Morella advised, "They are not safe yet. They must be inside the metal that is headed our way. Metals go very fast, so we could lose them still. They might go swiftly past us and on down the road."

Everyone sobered at that thought.

Buddy asked, "Is there any way at all to stop a metal?"

Morella paused to listen again. "The metal's whine has changed. It has stopped on its own, but it is still running and could take off again at any time."

Suddenly, Buddy had that familiar feeling of dread right in the pit of his stomach. He was very worried for Cookie and JJ. However, the elf did not want to alarm his friends, so he kept his fears to himself and suggested, "Come on everyone! Let's hurry! Perhaps we can rescue Cookie and JJ while the metal is standing still."

The group moved quickly toward the familiar sounds of their captured friends.

Not too far away Rashka paused and made a slight correction to his trajectory, then he continued running, rapidly reaching peak speed, a black and gold blur slicing through the trees followed closely by the blue smoke of Akron.

Jeb yanked on the door leading to the back seat.   He pointed a chubby finger at Billy.   "I'm gonna shut them two up myself!"

Billy whined in response, "Now, Jeb, don't you go hurtin' those critters.   We can make some good money off 'um, but not if they ain't right!"

Jeb yelled, "Ain't nobody gonna pay nuthin' for those noise makers."

By this time, Jeb and Billy were both yelling in order to be heard above Cookie's piercing barks and JJ's indignant chattering. Jeb attempted to open the metal door of the crate.   JJ fussed loudly and tried to bite the man's fingers through the opening beside the latch.

Cookie stopped barking in anticipation of being freed from his small prison.   Jeb yelled at JJ and slammed a fist heavily against the stubborn door.   Both JJ and Cookie retreated to the back of the crate which turned out to be a good thing. For at that very moment Rashka catapulted through the trees and skidded across the road.

Billy had been sitting in the passenger seat calming his frazzled nerves by counting the chunk of stolen money.   He was the first one to see the tiger and he could not believe his eyes.   Billy dropped the money on the seat.   Using both hands to rub his eyes, he looked again.   In a hoarse voice he yelled, "JEB, GIT BACK IN THIS TRUCK RIGHT NOW!"

Chapter 14

Morella, Buddy, Aline and the rest of the group moved quickly toward the sounds of Cookie, JJ and the metal.   Soon the truck came into view and the smell of spent gasoline hung heavily in the air. Cookie and JJ had fallen silent.   The group could see one human standing on the road beside the truck.   He appeared to be agitated and he was vocalizing loudly.   His ire was directed at something or someone in the back seat of the metal.

Aline spotted Rashka first.   In a low voice she alerted, "Look! Over there!   It's Rashka."

The large cat was magnificent.   And frightening.

Wildflower whispered, "What is he doing?"

Morella responded in a tense voice.   "He is stalking his prey. Oh, this is not good..."

Buddy thought Rashka was one of the most beautiful animals he had ever seen.   The pictures in his book did not do the tiger justice.

Okikki said, "He is so, so big!"   She was completely mesmerized by the great cat.

Tango kept quiet, just as he said he would, but his eyes mirrored his excitement and he was eager to take a closer look.

Rosie sensed something—a great anger in the heart of the tiger. She could feel it as if it was her own emotion and the strength of it overwhelmed her. She gasped and leaned against Buddy for support.

Buddy asked, "Rosie, what is it?"

Rosie exclaimed, "It is Rashka. He wants revenge for what he believes is a great wrong that has been done."

Buddy warned, "Be careful, Rosie. He looks scary."

Wildflower tried to catch a glimpse of Cookie and JJ through the windows of the metal, but she couldn't see them.

Suddenly Cookie barked again. This time it was a warning bark. Cookie had caught the scent of the tiger.

Rashka was completely focused on the vehicle. All of his senses were honed in on this monstrosity that had taken his mother. He considered the man standing on the road to be an appendage to the metal. Unfortunately, everyone and everything inside the truck was also at risk. At the moment, Rashka's whole world was the vehicle before him as he zeroed in on his enemy. The air around him was charged with dangerous energy. The stalking cat was only dimly aware of the group of friends who were witnessing this drama unfold.

Buddy watched quietly, but he knew time was short and his mind worked feverishly, searching for a solution while Wildflower fearlessly flew past him and over to the truck.

Cookie's bark changed again as he recognized the faerie hovering outside the back window on the opposite side of the metal. Billy and Jeb were not sensitive enough to be able to detect Wildflower.

Jeb, who was still standing at the rear passenger door, thundered at Billy, "Who you yellin' at—" He cut his own sentence short when he noticed the fearful expression on his partner's face. Billy was looking at something behind him. Instead of following Billy's instructions to get back into the vehicle, he took precious seconds to turn and look.

Lou heard about the theft on his police scanner. Putting together the description of the truck, the men of interest and the partial license plate, he was reminded of the wad of money that Billy had flashed earlier. Lou did not want any trouble connected to his car lot. But he couldn't deny that the description of the truck sounded suspiciously like the one he had taken in from Jeb and Billy. He went into the service bay and took a look at the plate. It was a match. He hoped that this was the wrong truck, but he decided that it would be better to let the police take a look now and get it over with. Lou went back into his office, closed the door and phoned the police.

There was not much crime in the nearby town and local police were all over this brazen theft, arriving in a matter of minutes. After viewing the old truck and speaking with Lou, they took down the new truck information and drive-out tag number. The officers thought it might be a good idea to have a little talk with the men who were seen outside of the store right after the theft occurred.   Even if they were innocent, perhaps they had seen someone in the area and could provide helpful information.   As the police car pulled out of Lou's New and Used Cars the light on top began to spin.

Rashka could hear the rumble of the truck as it idled.   There was no mistaking it.   He remembered and knew that this was the very one that had taken his mother.   His eyes were as hard as flint and his lips tightened against glistening sharp teeth.   Silently, the determined tiger gathered himself and then leapt through the air as if from a catapult.

Jeb stared in disbelief.   Could he really be seeing a live tiger...in these mountains?   He stood frozen to the spot as Rashka landed with a thump in the bed of the vehicle and then charged forward, scraping his great claws against the long window.   The frustrated cat leaned over the side to reach into the open rear door. Roaring with rage, he flipped out of the truck and aimed for the back seat.   Jeb took this opportunity to run screaming into the woods. Billy was too scared to move.

Rashka jammed his large head against the front of the crate in which Cookie and JJ were imprisoned.   The small green bird was terrified and he squawked loudly while flapping his wings.   In a rare show of defensive behavior, Cookie bared his teeth at the tiger and growled a warning.   It was clear to JJ that his friend was making an effort to defend him.   It would have been touching if he were not so frightened.

"We're gonna get eaten!" JJ panicked.

Wildflower called to the others, "Hurry, Cookie and JJ are in trouble!"

When Rashka jumped into the back seat, his large chest and forelegs shoved the driver's side seat against the steering wheel. His back legs were outside of the truck, his rear feet on the ground. Tiny fibers of material floated around inside the truck as the angry cat destroyed the seat. JJ sneezed as the fibers reached his beak. Rashka's ears were pinned tightly against his head and he smacked the crate again. Cookie yelped.

Rashka knocked the crate over on its side and then grabbed a mouthful of the seat underneath. He shredded the fabric, growling fiercely. The cab of the truck echoed with his loud vocalizations. Billy hid in the floor of the front seat, far too afraid to attempt escape.

Buddy and the group joined Wildflower beside the truck on the opposite side from where Rashka had entered. The closed door offered some protection, but there seemed to be little that they could do to help Cookie and JJ.

Wildflower sprang into action. Her love for the little papillon compelled her to try to help even in the face of such great danger. She flew around behind the tiger. Everyone followed except for Rosie who was still struggling to sort her own emotions from the powerful feelings and impressions of the tiger.

Wildflower grabbed the tiger by the tail. The others caught on to the plan and quickly came to her aid. Unfortunately, this didn't work well.   With one flick of the cat's tail, everyone went flying in different directions, much like the childhood game of crack the whip.

Fortunately none of the group was injured.   Tango felt a little dizzy, but Okikki tucked him close to her side and chortled words of comfort in his ear.

Rashka was backing out of the cab to deal with whatever had pinched his tail when Billy made the mistake of moving slightly.   The tiger turned his attention to the front seat.

Chapter 15

Akron circled the vehicle, such a soft mist that she passed mostly undetected.   She did not understand Rashka's hostility toward the truck.   Akron was strong and powerful, but she could not read minds.   When she noticed the human inside the truck with Rashka, she knew she must intervene.   After all, if the tiger harmed a human it would bring hunters and officials to find him and she did not intend to let him go.

The Guardian was surprised that with all of her teaching the cat was still considering attacking a human.   She felt that something was strange about his behavior as well as the level of his anger.   Akron was preparing to change forms in order to deal with the situation when Rosie caught her attention.

The faerie had finally sorted through Rashka's jumbled feelings and thought she might know a way to help the tiger and save those trapped in the metal with him.   Rosie placed her hand flat on the window glass.   The faerie glowed faintly in the harsh light of day as she stared at Rashka.   Then the young Caller spoke his name. The tiger turned away from the quaking man and snarled at Rosie through the window of the truck.   Akron watched with interest as the Caller reached out with her free hand and whispered for Morella.

Morella just barely heard Rosie whisper her name over the noisy metal.   She bravely flew to Rosie's side and reached for her outstretched hand.   Morella observed Rashka through the glass and felt uneasy about such close proximity to the tiger.   She could see her own reflection as well as Rosie's in his large golden eyes. Morella was just thinking that she couldn't read his expression when Rosie interrupted her thoughts.   *Morella, quick, think of Rashka's story.   Hold it to the front of your mind and try not to drift from it, please.*   Rosie drew from Morella's thoughts and used her connection to Rashka as a bridge to replay the story of his life.

Although she told the story in a manner easily understood by the group of Pixielanders, Rashka received the story in his own language of sounds, impressions and pictures.   Such was the gift of the Caller.   For the moment, Rashka forgot all about the truck as he viewed the pictures of his life which streamed across his mind's eye. When he watched the part about his mother being taken by the metal, he snarled savagely and almost broke the fragile link with Rosie.   With a great effort of concentration, Rosie repaired the connection.   In his mind, Rashka followed the truck as it rolled down the mountain road.   He watched as the forest ranger stroked his sleeping mother and promised her a wonderful new home.   Finally he was able to see his mother happy and well, roaming free with others of their kind in her new habitat.

Rashka's wild heart swelled with emotion.   He looked at Rosie through the glass and there was a lingering tenderness in his expression as thoughts of his mother slowly faded away.   The tiger

149

finally understood that his mother was safe, had good care and plenty to eat.　He lifted his giant paw and gently pressed it to the glass just opposite of Rosie's small hand.　Mewing like a kitten, Rashka backed out of the truck completely ignoring the rest of the group as he strode to the edge of the woods.　There Akron joined him.　She had seen everything and now understood what had troubled the tiger.

Akron had changed to her Dryad form.　She could see that Rashka had also changed—on the inside.　He was still a dangerous wild animal, but now that he knew his mother was safe, a weight had been lifted and he frisked around the Guardian like a young cub. Akron laid a comforting hand on the tiger, then looked at Morella and smiled her thanks.　As Akron moved away, soft honeysuckle breezes swirled out and away from her long green hair, filling the air with the sweetest scent.　Rashka calmly paced alongside her.　He looked back at Rosie once more before the pair disappeared into the trees.

Everyone stood very still for a moment after Akron and Rashka left the area.　The mood broke when Cookie and JJ began to fuss. Wildflower and Buddy quickly entered the back seat of the truck and found the crate which had landed on its side.　Cookie pressed his small black nose against the crate door.　Aline joined them to help free the pair.　She sniffed, then sneezed as tiny particles of fiber troubled her nose.　Buddy struggled with the latch on the crate while Wildflower talked to Cookie through the small, square-shaped openings across the door.　She called to the others to tell them that both Cookie and JJ were just fine.

Aline detected something sticking out of the top of the crate door.   "Wait a sec, Buddy!"

Buddy cast a puzzled look toward Aline.   He watched as she carefully removed several honey colored hairs from the door.   She solemnly held them out to Buddy.   "Are these what I think they are?"

Buddy examined the hair.

Wildflower said, "I did see Rashka hit the door of the crate with his head."

Buddy smiled at Aline.   "I think you just found the tiger hair that we need for your elixir."

Aline's eyes sparkled with excitement as Buddy carefully stored the hair in his pack.   Then he said, "I imagine that's why this latch is so stubborn.   Rashka must have bent it when he rammed into the crate door."

Cookie was whimpering eagerly and JJ finally spoke out, "Good to see all of you.   I didn't think we were ever going see any of you again."   Just then a loud squealing noise filled the air.   JJ nervously asked, "What is that sound?   It's hurting my ears."   JJ covered his offended ears with his wings.

Of course that meant he could not hear Morella's answer, but everyone else did.   "It's a police siren."   She noticed the confused looks on several faces and added, "That means more humans are coming."

Wildflower cried, "Please hurry, Buddy!"

A fearful tear spilled out of her eye and landed on Cookie's nose.   Her small hand continued stroking his fur.   The little dog's tail could be heard thumping against the inside of the crate.

Billy, who had buried his face in his hands, looked up when he heard the siren. The big man shook violently. Who knew that he would ever be glad to hear a police siren, but it sounded like music to his ears. Getting caught by the cops was much better than being eaten by a tiger. The first thing that he noticed when he opened his eyes was the absence of the tiger. *Wow, what a relief.* Billy briefly considered running from the truck, but dismissed that idea because he knew that the tiger was out there somewhere. Then he thought he might scoot over and drive away. But as he glanced back something very unusual happened.

Billy had had a rough childhood and had been a bully all of his life. But this same bad Billy could actually SEE the faeries and the elf in the back seat of the truck! He blinked his eyes rapidly and rubbed them with his fists. Then he looked again. He never knew that anything so beautiful as these creatures existed. Stunned, Billy quietly watched as Buddy worked to free the crated animals.

Billy looked from one exquisite faerie to the next. He marveled at Morella's long blond cloud of soft hair. He gazed at Wildflower's multi-colored tresses, looked at the shimmering wings on Aline and noticed the delicate hat worn by Rosie. He saw pointy toed shoes and pointed ears on what had to be an elf! Billy watched the red squirrel and her cute baby, close enough to touch. He wondered why the squirrels glistened and sparkled so much. Billy could not have known that he was seeing the faerie dust that was meant to hide animals traveling in the company of faeries and elves. He could see that they were all working together to free the dog and the bird from the crate.

Okikki offered to help Buddy with the latch. The young elf stepped back to make room for her. Okikki worried the metal with her sharp teeth, her tail flicking up and down as she worked.

Since most humans do not see faeries and elves, the Pixieland friends hadn't been terribly concerned about Billy. Both Okikki and Tango had been covered in faerie dust as a precaution and none of the magicals thought that they would be detected. Tango was the first one to notice that Billy was watching them.

"Hey, everyone!" he cried in dismay. "That human knows we're here!"

Okikki looked up when she heard Tango's alarm. When the large man realized that they were looking at him, he smiled a small tight smile. Buddy bravely smiled in response. Billy slowly reached into the back seat. Everyone stood very still and Buddy gulped as he watched the big hand reaching toward him.

Chapter 16

Billy thought that he knew everything that was important about this world. After he dropped out of school, he learned lessons of survival on the streets. Life had been a struggle. Finally a few years ago he met Jeb and the two of them just sort of clicked. Jeb was like the older brother he never had and Jeb had taken Billy under his wing. Jeb was smart too. He knew lots of ways to get money. Billy admired him and up until this very moment he had gone along with every one of Jeb's hare-brained schemes.

Billy had been feeling very low since Jeb had run off and left him to get eaten by the tiger. But something happened inside of Billy the moment he laid eyes on the faeries and the elf in the back seat. His heart filled with wonder. There had not been much beauty or joy in his life. But here, right here in the confines of this truck, he was seeing a truly unexpected sight and he felt some measure of joy. Billy was shaken to the core.

As Billy watched the little ones bravely working together to rescue their friends in the crate, he knew that he was being given a rare gift and one that he in no way deserved. The wall of his anger and lack of concern for others crumbled and for the first time in many years, Billy felt the urge to do something for someone besides

154

himself.

Buddy stepped in front of Okikki as Billy's hand came close. The elf felt a light breeze as the hand moved past him to grab the latch and force open the crate.   Cookie and JJ lost no time in exiting their former prison.   Cookie licked Billy's hand and wagged the entire rear part of his body—after all, this was the man who had fed him a sausage biscuit.

JJ was not as forgiving.   He shook his head and rolled his eyes.   "That's right, Cookie.   Go on an' make friends with the very one who trapped us in that cage in the first place."   JJ's voice dripped sarcasm, but in the next minute he was on Cookie's back and settled into his favorite riding spot.

Billy removed his hand carefully without touching any of the Magicals.   As he glanced up to see the policemen approaching the truck, Billy spoke softly to the group in the back seat.   "Ya best be gettin' along.   Here come the cops an' ya don' want them ta see ya now."

No one understood what he said and everyone continued to watch him carefully except for Cookie who was busy greeting Wildflower.

Morella unknowingly repeated Billy's advice.   "We need to move.   The sirens have stopped.   The police might see Cookie and JJ even if we use more faerie dust.   *This* man could see all of us."

JJ needed no further prompting.   He urged Cookie to jump down out of the truck.   Cookie eagerly complied since that's exactly what he wanted to do.   The little dog ran across the road and into the trees.   Wildflower and the others followed.

As the policemen exited their vehicle, one of them scratched his head.   "Hey, Mac, did you see that dog?"

"Yup, I did.   We can call Animal Control, but I'm not going into the woods after it."

Mac's partner Carl responded, "Yeah, ok, but I'm just wondering...did you see a bird on his back?"

Mac repeated, "A bird on his back?   Man, you need to get your eyes checked.   A bird on his back indeed.   Ha!"

Mac turned his attention to the vehicle idling in the middle of the street.   As soon as they had seen it, the officers knew that it fit the description of the theft suspects' second vehicle as described by Lou.   When they were in position, Mac demanded that all occupants exit the vehicle slowly and with their hands up.

Billy made no effort to resist them and followed their orders. He immediately confessed to the theft and handed over the stolen money.   The two policemen were surprised at how easy this had been.   Carl stayed with Billy who was handcuffed in the back seat of the patrol car as Mac checked out the truck.   He gazed in surprise at the shredded fabric of the back seat, then his eyes fell on the crate. He lifted it out of the back seat and examined it.

Walking back over to the patrol car, the officer asked Billy, "What happened to that seat?"

Billy explained, "You see, Jeb was driving and he stopped the truck because the dog and the bird was making so much noise.

Then when he opened the back door to make tha animals quiet down, a tiger came an' jumped into the back seat. Then tha tiger tore up the seat."

Mac and Carl exchanged looks. Mac spoke sharply, "Surely you can do better than that. Were you thinking about hiding the money inside that seat?"

Billly shook his head. "No, Officer. I'm tellin' ya the truth, for real."

Mac had been a policeman for years and could usually tell when someone was lying. As crazy as this man's story sounded, Mac was pretty sure that Billy believed that what he was saying was true. He obviously had a screw loose somewhere.

Carl took a kinder tone. "Tell me about this Jeb. Where is he now?"

Billy's eyes widened and he wiped a hand across his forehead. "He ran into tha woods when tha tiger came. Maybe tha tiger got him. I don' know."

Mac hid a laugh as he suggested, "What say you take us to his place? I mean, just in case he made it through the woods and all." Carl snickered. As an afterthought Mac said, "Oh and one more thing. How did your dog get loose? He was in the crate, right? We saw him run into the woods." Then he could not help but grin as he added, "Aren't you afraid the tiger might get him too?"

Billy looked very uncomfortable. He squirmed a bit. He could not think of what possible reason there could be to let the dog go, but then it struck him. Mac was watching him closely as his face brightened suddenly. "I let him go 'cause we stole him an' when I heard your siren, I got scared an' let him go." Then he added, "The bird too."

"Bird too?" questioned Carl, shooting Mac a look that said "I told you so."

Billy didn't even ask what would become of the truck. After he told them Jeb's address he never said another word. He sat silently looking out the window and scanning the woods. Billy hoped for one more glimpse of the dainty little people and their animal friends. He was willing to serve time for what he had done, but told himself that when he was a free man again life was going to be different. Billy planned to stay out of trouble and do an honest day's work for an honest day's pay. He was going to help people whenever he could, just like the little people he had seen helping each other. Billy smiled as he gazed out the window of the car. The woods looked quiet and empty, but Billy knew better...

Chapter 17

From the shadows well inside the tree line, Buddy and his friends watched as Billy and the police car swiftly rolled away. Morella led the group back to their camp so that they could all rest and welcome Cookie and JJ properly. Tango fired questions at JJ. The young squirrel wanted to know all about the metal—what made it go, how it felt to ride in it and how he and Cookie ended up there in the first place. JJ was so relieved to be back with his friends that he patiently answered the questions as best he could.

Cookie greeted everyone quite happily and was none the worse for wear.

Everyone seemed relaxed except for Aline. She couldn't stop thinking about Rashka. The faerie wondered if she would ever see the beautiful tiger again.

Feeling restless, Aline spontaneously hugged Buddy and thanked him again for making this whole trip possible. What an amazing adventure it had been from start to finish and she was still looking forward to the tiger elixir!

Aline cornered Morella, "Do you think that the two of us could follow the path that Akron and Rashka took just to see where they went?"

Morella's eyes twinkled mischievously and she slowly nodded.

With safety no longer a concern, everyone found cozy spots to rest. Tango cuddled up to Okikki for a nap and soon Cookie's light snoring could be heard, music to Wildflower's ears. Aline and Morella waited until everyone else was asleep before quietly making their way toward the road.

Morella searched for and found the exact spot where Akron and Rashka had entered the woods. Aline felt excited as they followed what would have been, for most trackers, a very difficult trail indeed. Morella could tell that Rashka had learned his lessons well. It took a little bit of magic and a great deal of determination for Morella to identify the faint trail left by the tiger. Soon the faeries heard the distant sound of rushing water which indicated that a waterfall was somewhere close by.

Morella said softly, "I think I know where these tracks are going. That waterfall feeds into a mountain stream. I have seen Rashka playing there before."

Aline smiled delightedly at the prospect of seeing Rashka at play. When the sound of the waterfall became a comforting rush in their ears, the faeries could smell the blend of green earth, water and wet rock. Aline watched the spray dancing to its own tune while Morella examined the area. Aline's eyes sparkled with excitement and Morella was also looking forward to what they might see.

Then Morella spotted something further downstream. "Aline, look at this."

The Morel faerie pointed at two boulders. One was round

and smooth. Less than two feet away from it was a more chiseled looking formation. "They are sleeping."

Aline was puzzled at first until she remembered what Morella had said about the Guardian sleeping much of the time and only waking when she was needed to help restore balance. "You mean Akron is sleeping?"

Morella slowly shook her head. "No, I mean Akron and Rashka are BOTH asleep. Don't you see? The Guardian has found a way to take him with her."

Aline stared wide-eyed at the boulders. Then she asked, "May I touch them?"

Morella nodded. Aline landed on the ground and stepped over to the large rocks. She first touched Akron's smooth surface and then finally rested a hand on the rough surface of the sleeping tiger. She felt a moment of sadness. This was not the farewell that she had contemplated. Morella waited quietly.

Aline sighed and looked up at her friend. "Morella, will Rashka be alright? Do you think that he will ever return?"

Morella replied, "Rashka will be fine. He is in the care of the Guardian. And, yes, I do believe that the two of them will return sooner or later. I don't pretend to know the ways of the Guardians, but I do think that if Akron found a way to take him with her, she will find a way to bring him back when the time is right. I believe that she is protecting him from detection. If anyone should come looking, he will not be found."

Aline nodded. "Then I'm glad she has taken him. I want

him to be safe."   Aline's heart filled with emotion and she blurted, "I just love him.   He is the grandest creature I have ever seen."

Morella took Aline's hand.   The two of them sat very still for a while just listening to the rush of water and looking at the sleeping rocks.

Chapter 1

Aline and Morella spent most of the afternoon at the waterfall before returning to camp.

Wishing to lift her friend's spirits, Morella reminded Aline, "Don't forget, Buddy is going to make your tiger elixir just as soon as we get home.   It should be ready in time for your birthday."

Aline brightened, looking forward to Buddy's gift.   "I can only imagine what it will be like to be a noble tiger for a day," she sighed.

The faeries flew side by side chattering continuously until they reached the camp where the welcome sound of Cookie's light snores greeted them.   Aline and Morella soon settled down to rest with the others and before long sleep claimed the two wanderers.   The late afternoon sun slanted down on the resting party and everyone felt warm and cozy under the sleepy pines.

Just before nightfall the group of friends began to stir. Cookie woke up first then barked long enough to rouse everyone else. Wildflower yawned and smiled.   She was so glad to hear his little voice again that she could forgive the extra barking.

JJ grouched, "Aw, Cookie, can't a body wake up easy-like without having to listen to all of that noise?"

Cookie just looked at him quizzically and grinned his doggie grin.

JJ cast an affectionate glance at the little dog and said, "I guess not. Ya been barkin' at me for one reason or another ever since I laid eyes on ya. Ya need to learn some manners and that's for sure."

With that said, JJ ruffled his feathers and flew into a nearby berry bush where he helped himself to a little snack. The entire bush rustled as JJ pulled berries and popped them open. The sweet juice drizzled down his throat and then he ate the pulp of the berry, discarding only the skins. Wildflower stroked Cookie's fur and whispered into his ear until the little dog finally calmed down and was quiet.

Buddy said, "Now that we have the tiger hair, we need to head back to the Faerie Glen. Skuba promised to keep an eye out for Newton in case he gets back before we do."

As Buddy and the group made their way through the woods, things were anything but calm back in Pixieland. It was true that the trees, meadows, gardens and their inhabitants all appeared completely normal. However, in the very deepest part of the ocean, trouble was brewing.

Far from the sandy shores of Pixieland and down through the warm water, down into the coldest reaches along the ocean floor, the great kingdom of the Mer people stood shimmering in the dark. Its algae-covered walls contrasted sharply with shining golden gates and delicate spires extending up through the glistening water like outstretched arms.   The Great Kingdom was a place filled with soft mystical light and extraordinary beauty.

The Mer folk were a private people, seldom seen by those who walked on land.   They possessed a great love for building things which was evidenced by their breathtaking city.   The beautiful architecture and wealth of materials used in its making were rivaled by none.   It seemed as if all of the ocean's treasures had been poured into this one great city constructed by the loving hands of its people.

The Mer folk were presided over by their dynast who was also considered to be the mother of the entire Mer nation.   But this most recent reign had been unusual.   For the past five hundred years the Great Kingdom had been ruled by twin dynasts.   At first the citizens did not know what to expect from their two leaders since such a thing had never happened before.   Even so, the Mer folk received their new dynasts warmly and the people were not disappointed. Throughout the years Summer and Sandrea ruled wisely and well. They were in perfect accord and always agreed on every decision.

However, recently there had been much excitement among the people because a very special egg had been spotted among the other eggs in the incubation chambers.   In the beginning, the egg had been white like any other.   But it had gradually changed to pale blue, then to royal blue overnight.   The rich blue color confirmed that a dynast was within, signaling that the reign of the twins was drawing to a close and new leadership loomed on the horizon.

The dynasts recognized that a smooth transition of leadership was an important key in maintaining balance for all of Pixieland. This egg meant everything to the Mer people and Sandrea took it upon herself to check on the egg each day. In the beginning stage, the egg is quite soft and must not be touched or moved. Unfortunately, something had gone horribly wrong.

Summer gracefully swam down the beautifully tiled Halls of Valiancy, through the Greeting Room and finally into a small door that lead to the Incubation Chamber. She urgently called to her twin, "Sandrea, Ernie is waiting."

Turning from the egg to face her sister, Sandrea's concern was evident. "How does Ernie seem? I mean, do you think he has good news for us?"

Summer answered, "The Guard said that he looked nervous, so I'm not sure."

Sandrea joined her sister and they talked as they swam. Ernie was waiting several miles away in a quiet cove that had been their meeting place ever since the trouble first began.

Even though they were twins, the sisters did not look alike. Sandrea's flowing hair was the color of ripe corn. In contrast, Summer's long tresses were as black as octopus ink. Sandrea preferred to wear her thick mane loose and flowing while Summer enjoyed catching her locks up in decorative combs although a number of tendrils always escaped in a rather charming way. Their slim arms were adorned by many bracelets, treasured gifts from the Mer children of the kingdom.

The twins used their slightly webbed fingers as paddles to help propel them through their watery world.   Powerful strokes of their blue-scaled tails moved them quickly and effortlessly through the deepest parts of the ocean where there was not much light.   But they were well-equipped for these icy depths.   The mermaids relied on a type of radar that easily guided them over and around obstacles until the darker waters gave way to the upper region where sunlight sliced through, making it possible to switch to their keen eyesight.

They were greeted by several giant seahorses floating toward them.   Sandrea smiled showing her tiny, evenly matched, pearly white teeth.   The twin dynasts acknowledged the gentle giants with pleasure and the animals swam alongside for some distance.   In less worrisome times, the sisters would have lingered and played chase with the creatures, but at this particular moment they needed to keep moving.   Finally the mouth of the cove appeared and the royal twins swam into calmer water.

Ernie had been hiding in some bushes nervously twisting his nautical cap around and around in his hands.   His whiskers twitched and his ears turned this way and that as he watched for the dynasts' approach.   The blue mouse looked quite fetching in his nautical suit in spite of the gravity of the circumstances.

Summer's head popped up first.   She moved effortlessly across the remaining distance to a large rock that jutted out of the water close to shore.   Soon after she pulled herself onto the rock, her sister Sandrea broke the water's surface.

Ernie stepped out of the bushes.   The blue mouse couldn't help feeling nervous.   He had been a sea-faring mouse all of his life and had seen many beautiful and magical creatures, but he still felt breathless in the presence of the dynasts. As if that weren't enough, he did not have good news. He dipped his head and thumped his chest in respect, then waited to be addressed.

Chapter 2

"Hello Ernie. It's good to see you," Sandrea said. "Did you find the doctor in Otherworld?"

Ernie's ears folded back against the top of his head as he hesitantly replied, "I found the whole Pixieland group and followed two of the party members when they left the camp. One was a dog and one was a green bird. The dog didn't like me much, but the green bird was nice enough. I asked him about the doctor. He told me that there was not a doctor in the group."

The twins looked puzzled. Summer spoke for them. "You didn't see the black crow?"

Ernie responded, "No, there was no black crow with them. The green bird said that the crow had flown away."

The mermaids spoke to each other in low voices while Ernie stood and waited.

Sandrea reached toward Ernie and he took her hand. Her slick fingers felt cool and strong against his fur.

"Ernie, it is urgent that you locate the doctor. We will speak with Victoria and have you returned to Otherworld immediately." Lady Sandrea pressed a small metal container into Ernie's paw. "You must give him this message when you find him and please do not delay.   We are depending on you."

Ernie put the container in his pocket.   "I will do my best, but I don't know how or where to look for the doctor.   Will there be any clues?"

Sandrea advised, "Find the elf named Buddy and let him know that you are sent by the Dynasts of the Kingdom of the Sea.   Tell him you must speak with Newton the Crow."

Ernie wondered how a crow could be a doctor and he asked himself what kind of doctor he could be with wings instead of hands. It was a curious thing, but Ernie was too polite to ask.   Instead he said, "I am ready to go immediately, Lady Sandrea and Lady Summer."

The relieved twins smiled, then spoke in unison.   "Victoria will contact you right away.   And Ernie, thank you."

Sandrea and Summer slipped into the water and were soon well on their way home.   As they swam along the shallow bottom of the cove Summer picked some soft grass.

"I will just tuck this around the egg.   You know they say a warmer egg hardens all the more slowly and we could use some extra time."

Sandrea flashed a wry smile.   "And you know that is just a tall tale."

Summer responded, "Well, maybe not.   There could be some truth to it."

Sandrea's expression grew more serious.   "Sister, how long do you think it will take for Ernie to find the doctor?"

Summer shook her head. "I don't know, but I hope it will be

soon."

When Sandrea and Summer arrived home they went directly to check on the egg. Summer gently placed the soft grass around the bright blue shell.

"Oh, dear," she cried. "Come and see. It looks worse!"

Together they examined the surface of the egg. A long scratch extended almost halfway down one side.

Sandrea said, "I think it may indeed be a little worse, but only just a little. There is still time, but we do need some help soon."

Summer sniffed. "Do you really think she can be saved?"

Sandrea patted Summer's hand. "We must believe that the doctor can help."

The queen egg had a long journey ahead in order to reach its destination. Several mermaids had already been selected to accompany the egg on the first part of its journey. The kingdom's greatest treasure would be fitted snugly into a specially designed cart with much padding for protection. Then with its entourage it would be sent miles away to a secret place where it would be watched over carefully until the day of hatching. When the young queen was old enough, she would begin the long journey home. It was both an ancient tradition and a rite of passage for their new leader. When each new ruler swam through the gates of the Great Kingdom for the very first time she would be announced by the Guard and then greeted by her people. The feasting and celebrations held in her honor would go on for days finally ending with a lovely coronation. The new dynast would then take her rightful place as the leader and mother of the kingdom.

Summer's thoughts drifted to the day when she and her sister had come home for the first time. She would always remember her first glimpse of the beautiful spires. All of her life before that moment culminated with her arrival at those golden gates. There was a shocked silence among the Mer people within the city when they realized that there were two dynasts. The twins had entered the gate only to hear loud murmurs and stares of disbelief. Summer smiled to herself as she remembered the thunderous cheers that went up after the Guard cried, "Welcome to the twins, Summer and Sandrea, the new Queens of the Great Kingdom!"

Summer's thoughts were interrupted by Sandrea who had just re-entered the room after preparing a snack.

"I hope this is not too salty," she said as she sat large shells filled with seaweed salad on the nearby table. She glanced at her sister and when she noticed Summer's far-away look and pensive smile, Sandrea ventured, "A sea shell for your thoughts."

Summer took a bite of the salad and absentmindedly replied, "It's not too salty at all. It's very good. Thank you."

Sandrea pondered, "I wonder if Timna knows that the egg is finally here."

Summer answered right away. "Oh, I believe she does. She has a sixth sense about these things. You know she has nurtured and cared for each new queen for thousands of years. I think she is probably already preparing for the egg's arrival." Summer's face softened as she remembered Timna. Unlike human babies,

174

mermaids can remember all of their experiences from birth and many of the sounds heard while inside the shell. Summer allowed her thoughts to continue drifting back in time.

Timna's face was the first thing Summer had seen after she hatched from the egg. She remembered well the great caretaker's eyes, so kind and full of wisdom. Even Timna had been surprised that the egg held two babes, both of them so small, but round and dimpled with the lovely blue, shiny scales on their tails that visually distinguished dynasts from the rest of the Mer family. Timna had sighed as she looked from one adorable baby to the other.

She shook her head and remarked, "Well, I will do what I have done for lo these many years, but I will now do it times two."

Timna taught the twins everything they needed to know from where to gather food to how to be the best possible leaders. She helped them discover their individual gifts and explained how they would be called on to use these talents and abilities to benefit their world and their people.

Summer's thoughts returned to the present and she looked at the royal egg hopefully. So much rested on this one little egg.

Chapter 3

Meanwhile, in another part of Pixieland, Moziac walked right up behind Ernie before the mouse even knew that she was there. "BOO!"

Ernie jumped and spun around to face the mischievous cat. "How do you do that?"

Moziac pretended to be baffled. "Do what?" she asked innocently.

"Sneak up on me. You always sneak up on me!" Ernie pouted.

Moziac maintained her innocent look for a little while longer, then relented and smiled her clever cat smile. "Just having a little fun with you." She raised her paw and with a poof of her special brand of magic, the mischievous cat transformed into a more serious Victoria. The Portal Guardian asked, "Ernie, do you have plenty of ghost fish oil? You know it's your main protection against the many dangers that lurk in Otherworld."

Ernie checked his stash. "Yes, there is plenty. I used it a couple of times. Once in Otherworld when that dog chased me and before that I tested it here when there was a bear following me. It worked like a charm. They couldn't even see me and I was less than a stone's throw away from them both times!"

Victoria nodded, satisfied.   "Well, then, if you are ready, I will send you back to Otherworld right now."

Pixieland became a shimmery, wavy place and Ernie squinted against the shifting landscape as Victoria sent him through the hastily opened portal to Otherworld.   Ernie thought that Victoria looked magnificent with her white hair whipping around her face and her arms outstretched.   Seeing her like this, Ernie had to admit that people aren't always who they seem to be.   Just as this thought crossed his mind, the blue mouse landed with a thump in the small building near the Faerie Glen.   This was the same old church house where Buddy and his friends landed when they had first come to Otherworld.   The light streaming in through the building was pink where it spilled across the floor.   Ernie stared at it with some curiosity, but he soon realized that it was only a reflection of color from the red drapes that adorned the windows.   He sniffed fresh air coming from somewhere.   Ernie followed his whiskered nose which led him to the front of the building where he found an open door.

The blue mouse remembered the directions that Victoria had given him.   He found the landmarks right where she said they would be and it was not long until he entered the Faerie Glen.   The first thing he noticed was the beautiful faerie house at the base of one of the trees.   After admiring it, he called into the entrance. "Helloooo, is anyone here?"

Hearing no answer, Ernie timidly peeked into the opening. There were various treasures stacked about and a bed of feather down and soft grasses against the back wall. Although things were neat and tidy, it was obvious that whoever lived here liked to collect from the surrounding woods.

The mouse had hoped that Buddy and his friends would be meeting Newton here. Since it appeared that no one was home, he decided to find his way to the camp site where he had seen the group last. Maybe they were still in the vicinity. If not, Ernie hoped that he would be able to track them.

Realizing that he had a long hike ahead of him Ernie decided to have a quick snack before getting started. The blue mouse pulled a small hunk of cheese and a piece of bread from his pocket and, sitting up on his haunches, he rapidly stuffed his face using his two tiny paws. Hearing a twig snap, Ernie whirled around to see an elf standing right behind him looking at him with a curious expression. In a muffled voice (for his mouth was still full), he queried, "Buddy?"

The elf raised an eyebrow. From his point of view, Ernie looked pretty funny with his bulging eyes and his cheeks full of food. Still, the elf managed to understand the question and he shook his head. "No, I'm not Buddy. I'm Skuba."

Ernie gulped as he swallowed and asked, "Are you from Pixieland?"

Skuba shook his head again and proudly stated, "I am a mountain elf and these mountains are my home." He spun around and gestured expansively toward the mountain range.

Ernie could not deny the beauty of the mountains and he certainly understood why the elf standing before him sounded so very pleased to live here, but Ernie's mind was on his mission, so he asked, "Do you by chance know Buddy?"

The elf smiled, "Yes, I have had the pleasure."

"Can you take me to him or tell me where he is right now?" Ernie asked. "I must find him. It's a rather urgent matter."

Skuba eyed the mouse just a wee bit warily. "Are you a friend of Buddy's?"

Ernie's ears flattened against his head as he nervously replied, "Well, no, not really, but I have been sent to locate the doctor and I was told that his good friend Buddy could probably tell me right where to find him."

Skuba mused, "Hmmm, a doctor... I did not see a doctor, but I will help you find Buddy and then you can sort it all out. Did this doctor have a name?"

Ernie nodded. "Yes, of course, his name is Newton."

Several expressions chased across Skuba's face, not the least of them surprise as he pondered this information. He looked thoughtful as he asked. "Do you mean Newton the Crow?"

Ernie nodded. "He's the one I am sent to find."

Skuba rubbed his chin as he thought about this. He gazed at the mouse wonderingly. "I don't want to say that you are mistaken and I do know that people and things are not always what they appear to be. But he has wings, you know? A bird is a doctor? I wouldn't mind getting to the bottom of this myself. Come with me!"

Skuba led Ernie out of the Faerie Glen and down the path that

Morella, Buddy, and his friends had taken. They were easy to track because the little dog that was with them left such obvious signs. As they were traveling along, Skuba asked Ernie about his life back home. Ernie told one tall tale after another. He gestured broadly and twisted his little face into so many different shapes as he spoke that it kept Skuba laughing and wanting to hear more. The mountain elf was fascinated with the whole idea of the ocean. He never tired of Ernie's stories which was a good thing because when Ernie was not nervous or afraid he could be a very big talker indeed.

Ernie told stories of life on his boat in the great ocean whose waves gently washed the sandy shores of Pixieland. Skuba listened closely. He had never seen the ocean even though he could have shown Ernie the biggest waterfall in these mountains or led him to the banks of bubbling brooks and clear blue streams. He could even have taken him down by the river. But he had never seen so much water all in one place like the ocean that Ernie described.

Ernie asked, "Would you like to hear it?"

Skuba looked puzzled. "Hear what?"

Ernie flashed a lopsided grin. "Hear the ocean, of course."

Skuba seemed confused. He knew that there was no ocean nearby. "Right here? How?"

Ernie produced a small conch and the elf reached for the shell. It had bumps and ridges and a chalky look. But when the mountain elf turned it over, he could see that the opening on the underside was surrounded by a deep salmon-colored, glazed lining. It was both cool and smooth to the touch. Skuba's eyes widened as he examined this beautiful treasure, like nothing he had ever seen.

"Now, hold it up so that the opening of the shell is right against your ear," instructed Ernie.

Skuba did as he was told and with Ernie's help (the blue mouse could not keep his little paws from adjusting the shell for maximum effect), Skuba could hear the rushing sound. He looked at Ernie with wide eyes and smiled. Ernie flashed his lopsided smile in return and the two became instant friends.

Later in the afternoon both Skuba and Ernie began to feel hungry. Skuba searched around the base of an old apple tree and found two tasty morel mushrooms. He proudly handed one to Ernie. "I bet you don't have these in Pixieland!"

Ernie took a nibble. He closed his eyes, enjoying the bite of 'shroom, but they popped open again as he said, "I have an idea. Let me show you something neat."

Skuba curiously followed as Ernie collected two sticks. The blue mouse trained his eye down each one muttering under his breath and then he pulled something out of his pocket. It was a tiny knife which he used to sharpen the tips of each slender stick. He told Skuba, "Now break the mushroom apart and put some pieces onto each stick while I get the fire going."

Ernie collected a few twigs along with some dried grass and positioned them carefully. Then he coaxed a tiny flame by rubbing two sticks together and before long a small fire was burning. Ernie held one of the mushroom-laden twigs over the flames and Skuba followed suit. The heating of the morels released an intoxicating aroma and the two travelers made short work of their mushrooms on a stick. As they sat around the small fire with full tummies, Skuba asked, "So, why are you looking for Newton?"

Ernie's ears flattened against his head as he considered Skuba's question. Not sure how to answer, he responded, "I guess the best I can do is tell you that the mermaids need the doctor, so it's important that I find him as soon as possible." With this reminder of the task at hand, Ernie stood.

Skuba looked concerned. He carefully extinguished the fire and the two of them spread things around to cover their tracks. The elf said, "No more stops for us then. If someone is ill, we should hurry." As they trotted down the path, Skuba added, "I sure hope you are right about that crow...I just don't see how he could be a doctor."

Ernie didn't like to admit it, but he was a little nervous about the whole thing himself. What if the Ladies Sandrea and Summer were mistaken? They could be wasting time looking for a crow who wasn't really a doctor. Then what would they do? The mouse wondered if there would still be time to get the help that they needed.

Chapter 4

Newton the Crow stretched his wings and flew over the familiar house. He spotted the rose garden he had spent so many hours tending. He remembered it well. The blooms weren't as large as they used to be, but all in all it looked pretty nice. There was the bus—his pride and joy—still in the driveway.

After retiring from practicing medicine, Newton had lived alone without much contact with his two sisters who lived overseas with their husbands and children. He had no other family and because he had completely devoted himself to his work, he really had no close friends. There were things that he missed here, but he loved Pixieland. His old life had been centered around his practice and his patients, but now he had been given a chance to do something different (although he was not completely sure what) that would positively impact an entire world. He only knew that Victoria was leading him along, one step at a time. Newton recognized that his role was considered important and he felt honored that the Book of Crows had chosen him.

He had been perfectly happy living in Pixieland and being Newton the Crow. But he had wanted to come here to test his feelings, to find out how it would be to see his old house again.

Victoria, or the Sentinel of the Main Portal, as she was otherwise known, had told him that he had been called to Pixieland for a purpose. It was not by accident that he had stumbled into that strange room in Norman's junk shop on that rainy Saturday. It was not by accident that The Book of Crows had been placed in his hands by that elderly librarian. And it was no accident that he had found the ornate ring in the back of the book, the very ring that had ultimately taken him to Pixieland.

Much had been shrouded in mystery. But things were beginning to happen and some things at least were clear. Victoria had sent him back to his own world for one important reason. Newton must find a way to meet with the very famous Dr. Hammond Obrial. He hoped that his own medical background would provide enough credentials to be granted a meeting. Dr. Obrial was a world renowned agricultural specialist and had headed the team responsible for making some dramatic strides in the cultivation of plants and the care of farm animals. Newton hoped that Dr. Obrial would be able to provide the solution to the problem now facing all of Pixieland.

Newton spotted a great place to land on the grass close to the bus. Feeling sentimental, he walked up and down, imagining what it would be like to sit behind the wheel again. He did love that rumbly old bus. Its blue color reminded him of the sky-blue popsicle that was his favorite when he was a child. Before leaving the area, Newton circled the house a final time. Then he made his way over the tree tops, telling himself that flying was better than driving any day.

The black crow flew right over Norman's Junk Shop and without pausing continued on his course. A small cafe that sat on the outskirts of town offered internet service and Newton thought this might be a good place to begin his search. Behind the restaurant were a couple of trash cans enclosed by a weathered fence that would provide the privacy he needed. He knew this transformation was going to require some extra magic, so he reached down and opened the golden ring that encircled his bird leg. The crow took a pinch of the soft powder that rested inside the ring and then closed the dome. After looking around to be sure no one was in the area, he blew the powder into the air and stepped beneath its gentle fall.

It was a quiet afternoon at Pop's. There were several patrons scattered throughout the restaurant, but business was slow. The lunch crowd had departed by two o'clock and the dinner crowd was not expected until around six. Seated near the entry, some students from the local college were peering into laptops while grabbing a bite to eat. One table in the far corner held several young ladies who were sipping cola and chattering among themselves, comparing nail polish colors and purses. The buzz of small talk provided rather typical background noise as the door opened with a jangle of the bell overhead. Dr. Newton Bennett stood in the doorway. He took in the room with a glance before heading toward the red sign which identified the men's room.

The doctor turned down a poorly lit hallway and entered the privacy of the bathroom. He looked at himself carefully in the mirror. It had been awhile since he had seen the face of a man looking back. Dr. Bennett was not an imposing figure. He stood approximately five feet nine with a medium build. His eyes were blue and his hair had been light brown in younger years. Since retirement the doctor had enjoyed good health for which he was thankful. Newton had a very nice smile, piercing but kind blue eyes, and a full head of salty grey hair. He thought that he looked much the same as he had years before in his favorite blue button down shirt, crisp khaki pants and white lab coat. As he inspected himself, he found that one tiny black feather adorned the collar of his shirt. Newton carefully removed it before returning to the dining area.

He sat down in a chair which scraped across the floor as he scooted closer to the computer that was available for customer use. When the waitress arrived, he ordered a large glass of orange juice. By the time she returned, Newton was completely focused on one of Dr. Obrial's most recent papers. This one was all about a purely organic plant food developed to raise larger and plumper ears of corn. He scanned the article before finally typing "Dr. Obrial egg research" into the search engine. When the news item he was looking for popped up, he read all about the egg as seen through the research of Dr. Hammond Obrial and his team.

Newton found that there were some interesting general facts in the article. He read that eggs are covered with pores, many pores. The next section of the article indicated that Doctor Obrial's team had developed a formula for repairing the surface of a damaged viable egg. At the time the article was written, this formula was being tested on some prize chicken eggs. The article did not clearly state what, if any, success had been achieved with the paint-on repair serum. But the text ended on a hopeful note as the researcher indicated that a goodly number of chicks from eggs with minor surface damage could be saved. Newton read everything he could find on the site and cross-referenced the information. This took the better part of the afternoon, but he wanted to educate himself on the subject as much as possible before meeting with the renowned doctor.

Newton sat back and rested his eyes. It was too late to contact Dr. Obrial's office this day, so he would have to wait until tomorrow. He copied some information from the site onto the back of a napkin, left the money for the juice lying on the table, then stood up and strode out of the restaurant.

Newton paced back and forth in the downtown motel room. He missed Buddy, Rosie, Wildflower and all of his friends. It seemed like it had been such a long time since he had seen them last. Here in this mundane hotel room it would have been easy to think that they were only a dream if not for the ring on his finger. He looked at it again as if to reassure himself that he was indeed Newton the Crow—Newton the Shape Shifter.

It was the most unusual ring he had ever seen. The gold band felt warm against his skin and ever since he had shifted, he could feel it pulsing with its own singular energy. The workmanship of the nest on top of the band was quite detailed. Each golden twig and leaf had obviously been shaped by a very skilled hand. The surrounding gemstones glittered and the large pearl egg in the center of the nest glowed with a soft, luminous sheen. Newton would have been surprised if there were another ring like it in the world. It was clearly unique as well as powerful.

Studying the ring calmed Newton and he sat on the side of the bed. It had been a long flight. He was tired and the ring felt heavy on his finger. He stretched out across the mattress and before long began to feel drowsy. As he drifted off to sleep, a mysterious shadow slipped under the door and crept closer until it stood at the foot of the bed. If Newton had been awake he would have sensed the ominous tone that filled the room.

Chapter 5

Light seeping through the tiny slits in the window blinds awakened Newton early the next morning. He ordered room service, then showered and dressed while waiting for breakfast to arrive. The Shape Shifter enjoyed the meal as it had been some time since he had eaten a thick, buttery, syrup-drenched waffle. The sweet treat disappeared quickly. After breakfast, he glanced at the napkin from Pop's Place and dialed the number. Newton spoke with the office secretary who promised to call him back regarding his request for an audience.

Within fifteen minutes the phone jangled. Following a brief conversation, Newton smiled as he placed the instrument back in the cradle. Arranging a meeting with the good doctor had been easier than he thought. As Newton walked down the long corridor toward the elevator, he did not notice the strange shadow that moved stealthily along the wall some distance behind him.

After hailing a cab outside of the hotel, Newton sat back and gazed out the window while the driver wound through early morning traffic. After several twists and turns, the cab pulled up in front of a long, low building situated on the outskirts of town. The grounds were neatly manicured and the building itself was painted in understated tones. The blinds on the windows were closed. As Newton walked in the front door, he was met with a cheery environment which was a surprising contrast from the drab exterior. The reception area was decorated in a soft yellow color with blue accents. The plush leather seating was inviting and the glass side tables boasted stacks of scientific journals. After leaving his name at the front desk, Newton sank into the comfortable sofa.

A door behind the receptionist flew open and a very large dog lumbered into the room. There was a person on the other end of his leash who was clearly not in control of the animal. Newton watched as the slight young man clutched the lead and yelled, "Whoa, Mason! Wait a minute!" But Mason had other ideas. He spotted Newton right away and barreled over to greet him. It appeared to be love at first sight. The large dog did his best to climb right into Newton's lap. The animal's head was broad and well-wrinkled and he gazed at Newton with intelligent eyes. Mason's large front feet were firmly planted on Newton's legs and his giant mouth hung open as his tail slapped back and forth, thumping into the side of the poor handler.

"No, Mason! Get down," the horrified man cried as he tried to pull the dog off of Newton.

Newton grimaced as the weight of the beast pressed heavily on his legs, but he loved animals of all kinds and that included large dogs who viewed themselves as lap dogs.

Mason's handler apologized profusely as he continued to try to get the dog under control. "I am so sorry. It's not like him to take to anyone right off the bat like that."

Newton replied, "That's quite alright.   I am fond of dogs and this one is certainly a beauty.   Is he yours?"

"No, the doctor brought him here a few weeks ago."   The man grunted as he finally succeeded in pulling Mason's thick front legs off of Newton.   The animal sat down right on top of Newton's toes and stubbornly refused to budge.   Newton wiggled his feet out from beneath the dog while there was still some circulation left in them.

Extending his free hand, the poor fellow shot Newton a wry smile.   "I'm Jake.   One of my jobs is seeing to it that he gets walked several times a day."   Then he shook his head.   "The doctor couldn't leave him home alone."

Newton was about to ask why not when the receptionist spoke in a soft voice, "Dr. Bennett, Dr. Obrial will see you now."

Newton stepped around the dog after giving him a final pat on the head.   Dr. Obrial greeted him at the door to his office.   It struck Newton immediately that the specialist was an exceedingly tall man. Newton shook his hand and said, "Newton Bennett," while squelching the impulse to ask Dr. Obrial if he had ever played basketball.

With a loud snort, Mason barreled into the room dragging the reluctant Jake behind him.   The famous doctor rolled his eyes at the dog.   Jake apologized once again, but this time he was speaking to Dr. Obrial.

In a resigned voice, the doctor said, "It's alright, Jake.   Just unhook the lead and leave him with us."   Dr. Obrial offered Newton a seat.   As soon as he sat, Mason lumbered over and plopped down right beside the Shape Shifter's chair.   Jake unhooked the lead and, looking quite relieved, left the room.

When the door closed behind him, Dr. Obrial looked politely at Newton and asked, "How can I help you?"

Newton pulled out the article on the egg repair serum and in jargon that is reserved for doctors and those well-versed in medical terms, the two men discussed Dr. Obrial's findings.   Newton listened attentively to all that Dr. Obrial told him about the structure of the egg, what is needed to result in a healthy chicken, and how his repair serum works on damaged eggs.   The famous doctor produced a chart to demonstrate the current rate of success.   It was clear from his animated demeanor that this project was Dr. Obrial's passion and that he enjoyed educating people on the subject.   Newton was impressed.   He thought to himself, *Now for the tricky part.   How am I going to get a bit of that repair serum to take with me?*

All of a sudden, Newton noticed a cool draft seeping into the room.   Mason apparently sensed something too because he jumped to his feet with hackles raised.   A low growl rumbled in the dog's chest as he watched the door.   Dr. Obrial and Newton both looked in the direction of the dog's attention.   The temperature in the room dropped noticeably and the room went unnaturally still.   Small hairs on the back of Newton's neck stood on end.

Newton instinctively reached for the dog's collar although he doubted that he could hold Mason if the dog decided to bolt.   Dr. Obrial picked up the phone and in a low voice called for security.

Mason pulled away from Newton and moved closer to the door. Without further warning, he lunged forward locking his great jaws around what appeared to be nothing but air.

There was no doubt that a peculiar presence was in the room with them. Even though (try as they might) they could not see anything, what they *heard* sounded like a dog fight. Mason was making his share of the noise, but a good bit of growling, snarling, and yelping was made by the invisible opponent. Mason continued biting and snapping until he finally seemed to have a good grip on whatever it was. At that moment a shadow began to materialize on the wall of the room. Dr. Obrial gasped in alarm.

Before the shadow fully formed, the door opened and two security guards entered. Mason lost his grip and the shadow seemed to dissolve. The dog cast around for a bit, but then he began to look more relaxed as if he sensed that his combatant was no longer there. Newton called Mason over and examined him thoroughly while Dr. Obrial spoke with the security guards.

Dr. Obrial accompanied them to check on the receptionist, then re-entered the room visibly shaken. "Is it just me or did you see that too?"

Newton assured, "No, it's not just you. I did see something, but I also *felt* something strange. It got really cold in here. Have you had any other incidents like this?"

Dr. Obrial shook his head. "No. The strangest thing that has happened to me lately is the arrival of this dog." The doctor gestured toward Mason.

Newton looked up at Doctor Obrial and quizzed, "Arrival?"

Dr. Obrial explained, "Yes, a few weeks ago he was found roaming around out back. One of my team brought him here. We could see that he was a well-cared for dog and figured his owners would be looking for him. I ran ads that said 'Pure bred dog found' and listed the area. I received a few calls, but nobody could accurately describe him. I put the word out on a couple of web sites, through vet's offices and shelters. At first I had trouble believing that he could have possibly been abandoned until I left him at home alone. When I returned, my favorite shoes had been mostly eaten and the neighbors had called the police because of all the noise the dog was making. They reported that he barked all day long. When I brought him to work with me, he seemed just fine, nice and quiet, although maybe a little stubborn."

Newton turned his attention to Mason. The dog was lying as close to him as possible, his sides moving in and out as he panted. He seemed tired but content.

Dr. Obrial continued," I want to see him get a good home, but I feel it's important to be sure I have left no stone unturned in finding his owner."

Newton agreed. He could see that the dog was beautiful—well-built, muscular, and massive. Mason's head was big for his body and his upper lips hung thickly down over his powerful undershot jaw. His coat was short and soft to the touch, the color was particularly nice—a rich shade of red with gold undertones. His legs were thick and he had giant cat-like feet. The dog's tail was long, reaching to his hocks and his red-gold eyes twinkled brightly. Yes, Mason was very beautiful and very strong.

Newton said.   "It's not every day you see such a nice Dogue de Bordeaux.   I wish you good luck in finding his owner."

Dr. Obrial nodded.   He still felt uneasy after what had just happened.   He was a man of science and the fight Mason just had with the invisible creature was not adding up in his mind. Nevertheless, he was pleased to have Newton there and so interested in his research.   Dr. Obrial had done some checking just before Newton's arrival and he had heard good things about Dr. Bennett. He thoroughly enjoyed talking about his most recent project and he was comfortable sharing his findings with Dr. Bennett.

He clapped a hand around Newton's shoulders in an effort to put them both at ease.   "Let's go out to the lab.   I will show you the egg repair serum in action."

Chapter 6

Newton was fascinated with the egg repair formula. Dr. Obrial explained that it fills small cracks and tiny tears in the egg surface, bonding but with flexibility. Apparently the repair serum works by keeping dirt and bacteria out while sealing and strengthening the egg. Newton wondered if it would work on the softer mermaid egg and remain effective over time as the egg hardened. There was only one way to find out. Newton fervently hoped this would be the answer that the Mer people needed. He came right to the point. "Dr. Obrial, your research is going to be quite valuable. I'd like to do a little experiment of my own. Would I be able to take a small vial of the formula with me?"

Dr. Obrial was taken by surprise. "Well, the serum has already been made available to a test group of farmers anyway. I see no reason why you cannot take a small amount, after signing the proper papers of course."

Newton smiled, "Thank you, Dr. Obrial. You'll never know how much this means to me."

He turned to Newton and placed a hand on his arm. Looking him straight in the eye he said, "Consider it a professional courtesy. But I must ask that you report your studies and findings to me. It's important that I know how the formula works for you and if you experience success or failure." Later Dr. Obrial would wonder why he hadn't asked Dr. Bennett more questions.

Newton agreed to the terms and watched as Dr. Obrial carefully secured the vial, placing it inside a second cushioned wrap for Newton to transport. Newton shook the doctor's hand while thanking him again. Then he patted the still attentive Mason on the head and cracked the door to leave. Mason edged past Newton, pushed the door wide open and bolted.

Dr. Obrial turned to the receptionist. "Amy, please call for Jake."

As Amy was speaking to Jake, Dr. Obrial stood in the doorway calling to the dog. If Newton didn't know better he would swear that the big dog was smiling. It was almost painful to watch as Jake attempted to put a lead on Mason. Mason stood very still until Jake almost had him and then he would dance out of range, turn and stand again, barking deeply. Newton's cab pulled up while this small drama was unfolding on the front lawn.

A distracted Dr. Obrial bid Newton goodbye, hinting, "Perhaps he will run inside on his own after you leave."

Newton understood that he should go quickly and walked over to the cab. As he opened the door, Mason zoomed past him and launched into the back seat. Jake saw his chance and quickly closed the gap in the open door, practically stepping on Newton's toes in the process. Jake fumbled around a bit and then finally snapped the lead onto the dog's collar. Newton hid a grin. He had been watching Mason the entire time and he was convinced that if a dog could roll its eyes and wink, Mason would have been doing just that. His body language demonstrated an impatient sort of tolerance as Jake tried to remove him from the cab. Jake was rather slight and Mason was not going anywhere. The dog looked at Newton and his tail wagged, thumping against the seat.

Newton said, "Jake, let me give it a try."

Jake, red in the face from exertion, was pleased to allow the doctor to intervene.

Newton backed away from the cab and whistled, "Mason! Come here, boy!"

Gone was the impish Mason, replaced by an obedient dog that jumped out of the cab and sat in front of Newton, looking up as if to say, "What now, hmmm?"

None of this had been lost on Dr. Obrial who rather impulsively said, "Dr. Bennett, how do you feel about taking this dog? It seems that he responds well to you."

Newton looked thoughtful as he patted Mason on the head. He couldn't help but think how much the big dog would love Pixieland. "Well, you see, I am going to be out of the country and what if his real owner turns up?"

Dr. Obrial spoke convincingly, "I'd be surprised if anyone calls. A number of weeks have already gone by. But perhaps if the owner does contact me, he would be willing to wait and collect the dog when you return." Dr. Obrial's voice trailed away, but his face looked hopeful.

Newton found himself saying, "To be honest, Dr. Obrial, I am not sure when I will be back, but I suppose I could take him along with me on a temporary basis. If the owner has not shown up by the time I send you my egg repair findings, I will consider the dog mine. You see, I travel extensively in remote areas and it will be difficult to reach me after I have concluded my business here."

A much relieved Dr. Obrial responded, "Very good, Dr. Bennett. He seems to enjoy being with you and I'm confident that he will be happy. A word to the wise, keep your shoes off of the floor." Dr. Obrial allowed himself a tiny smile as he gave Newton a conspiratorial wink.

The cab driver reminded them, "The meter is runnin'."

Newton said a final goodbye and climbed into the vehicle. Mason jumped up onto the seat beside him and Dr. Obrial waved as the cab pulled away.

The cab driver snorted, "I ought to charge you extra for that dog. He's a big one. Where to, Mac?"

"Take us to the airport, please," Newton responded. He had already planned to take a commercial flight to get as close as he possibly could to the Faerie Glen where he would meet Buddy and friends. He had thought to fly the rest of the way from there with his own two wings. But now there was Mason to consider.

Mason leaned heavily against him in the cab and licked his own lips with a popping sound. Newton scratched the dog's ears and Mason half closed his eyes as he relaxed against his new friend. Newton spoke in his ear, "You have made a reputation for yourself by eating shoes and barking when left alone, but you are going to have to be in a crate for this flight.   I am sure that you will behave, right, boy?"

Mason thumped his tail and looked at Newton quizzically. Newton gazed at the dog, glad that they were bonding.   He certainly would not like to be on Mason's bad side.   Again, he thought about the mysterious shadowy figure that had been in the room with them earlier.   Newton wondered if maybe someone was trying to spy on Dr. Obrial, perhaps to learn more about his research.   As the cab wound down the road toward the airport, Newton tried not to think about the other alternative.   He was not ready to admit that he himself might have been the target.

Newton regretted having to leave Mason in cargo, but the dog was simply too big to ride in the cabin of the airplane.   The doctor made his way to the main terminal and when it was time, filed onto the plane with the other passengers.   As was his custom, Newton fell asleep before the plane had finished its taxi down the runway.

As he slept, Newton felt something pawing at him.   He smiled and drawled, "Mason, quit that and stay in your own seat."

It was so nice that Mason was here with him.   He was fond of the dog and could tell that Mason liked him too.   Newton felt the dog's breath on his face, but it was cold, very cold, not the warm breath he would have expected.   He tried to move the dog's foot off of him, but it was so heavy and he was beginning to feel chilled.   His movements were sluggish as he tried once again with both hands to push the dog back.   "Mason, what do you want?"   Newton's voice sounded hollow to his own ears.

Then from far away he heard someone speaking. "Sir, sir, wake up."

Newton's eyes felt like lead as he cracked them open and squinted up at the flight attendant.

She looked and sounded apologetic. "I'm sorry to wake you, sir, but you must have been having a bad dream."

Newton struggled to wake up fully. He thanked the flight attendant and as soon as she turned away he instinctively reached inside his coat pocket to make sure the vial was still there. He didn't know why he felt the need to check. Maybe it was something about the dream. Satisfied that the serum was safe in his pocket, Newton sat back and looked out the window of the aircraft.

Fluffy white clouds floated past, looking like enormous cotton puffs. The very sight of them reminded Newton of the day when he had first arrived in Pixieland. He thought about how strange it had been to discover that he was a crow. Newton remembered meeting Buddy for the first time and the two of them laughing after he tried to shake hands with Victoria, presenting her with a wing instead of a hand. He recalled the scary feeling that swept over him when he first tested his new wings. And finally Newton remembered when the fear and uncertainty were replaced with the exhilaration of flying.

Since his arrival in Pixieland, Newton's sense of humor had emerged, having been somewhat buried under the load of responsibility he had placed on himself in his previous life. The retired doctor laughed more often now. He had formed close friendships in Pixieland.   Newton knew that he would do anything for each one of his friends and for Pixieland.   Whatever he had been called to do, he was ready.   He could not help but feel a bit proud. Newton had become, after all, a rather magnificent crow.   Out of habit Newton moved his shoulders as if ruffling his wings.

Chapter 7

As the plane landed, Newton smiled to himself. He wondered how Mason would react when he shifted back to crow form. Maybe he should remain human or take another form, just for ease of travel. Newton pulled himself out of his reverie and glanced around the cabin. He couldn't wait to see Mason again.

The Dogue De Bordeaux greeted Newton with anxious whimpers and a great thumping of his tail. After much snorting, snuffling and tongue popping, the large dog finally settled down. Newton snapped the leash on him and then hired a car to take them to the edge of town. He asked the cab to drop them off at a leasing office where a cabin in the woods could be rented. But Newton had no intention of actually renting a cabin. He skirted around the leasing office and entered the woods. He was anxious to join his friends and hoped that they had found the tiger hair needed for Buddy's elixir. They should be waiting for him in the camp where they had agreed to meet. He felt a sense of urgency. Now that Newton had obtained the repair serum, he was eager to return to Pixieland.

Mason stared up into Newton's face as if he could sense the man's concerns. For a moment it was almost as if he knew and understood Newton's thoughts and feelings.

But the moment was fleeting and as Newton did a double take, Mason looked like, well, just a dog.

The pair continued moving until they were at least a mile and a half away from areas where other humans were likely to be hiking or camping. "Now I'm going to remove your lead. You be a good boy and stick close." Newton knew that when he shifted into crow form, he would no longer be able to walk Mason on a lead. He hoped that when he shifted, the sight of his bird self would not cause Mason to think of him as prey. Newton was also concerned about prying eyes, especially after the incident with the shadowy figure. Since he did not want to reveal his ability to shift, he carefully checked the area to make sure they were alone relying heavily on Mason's instincts. When he was satisfied, Newton quickly changed forms. Surprisingly the dog never wavered and seemed to take it all in stride.

Newton was a good bit larger than the average crow and his wing span was every bit a match for his size. He adjusted his flight speed to accommodate Mason. The obedient dog followed him happily as he flew low to the ground. Newton stuck to a small foot path because he knew that Mason could move more quickly if he didn't have to fight the undergrowth that wound among the trees. Newton paused to check on the vial. He mentally thanked Buddy for making that small sling prior to the trip and attaching it to the ring that he always wore around his leg. Newton had secured the egg repair serum before shifting and it seemed to be holding well.

There was not much extra weight and the vial was well padded so everything seemed to be working just fine.   Newton watched Mason moving along on the path, pleased at how quickly the Mastiff could travel.

The pair made frequent stops so that Mason could rest and get a drink.   As the sun sank lower in the sky, the golden light that filtered through the trees turned orange.   After the sun dropped below the horizon, darkness descended on the travelers.   Newton could no longer see well enough to fly so he searched for shelter and found a small thicket several yards off of the path.   He thought about perching in a tree right over Mason's head, but Mason would have none of it.   The dog leaped into the air snapping his jaws and barking.

Newton stared down at him and rasped, "Ok, fella, have it your way."   The large crow settled on the ground right between the giant dog's two front paws.

Even so, Mason seemed restless.   He sat bolt upright listening to the woodland sounds.   Even inside the thicket the night air felt chilly.   Overhead, a few visible stars stood out in stark contrast to their velvety black backdrop.

Newton ruffled his feathers and murmured, "It's ok, boy, settle down now and get some rest.   We'll be on the trail again at first light."

But Mason did not settle down.   His entire body stiffened and a long, low growl emerged from him as he slowly stood.   The crow strained his eyes and ears, but could not see or hear anything out of the ordinary.   However, Mason behaved as if something was just on the other side of the thicket wall.   Newton would have liked to think that it was some ordinary animal that had aroused Mason's suspicion, but the uneasy feeling that swept over him hinted otherwise.

Newton's first impulse was to shift out of crow form, but he didn't know who or what was watching.   He flew up into a tall tree and peered down into the area just on the other side of the hedge. It was so dark that Newton could not quite make heads or tails of what he was seeing, but something was definitely there.   He moved to a branch that hung directly over the area of interest.   Mason's attention was now divided as he tried to keep one eye on Newton and the other on the hedge.   The dog had not fully decided to attack, but he had adopted an aggressive stance and stood watching and waiting.   Later, Newton thought that he really shouldn't have allowed himself the distraction of looking back at Mason right at that moment because it was then that he heard a whooshing noise followed by a burst of sharp pain.   The next sound was the crack of tree limbs giving way as Newton fell from the tree.

It was a crow who fell, but a man who landed on the forest floor.   Newton's eyes were closed and he did not move…even though there was something pulling at his legs.   Mason gathered himself for one tremendous leap through the hedge.   A loud and fierce roar reverberated through the trees.

Buddy sat straight up. The sound also woke Wildflower, Rosie and the others. Tango snuggled closer to Okikki and buried his face against her side.

Some distance away, Ernie and Skuba were also jolted from their sleep.

Ernie murmured, "Oh, no. Oh, no!" and looked as if he expected whatever made that noise to come for him immediately. He was shaking and it took Skuba some time to calm him.

Skuba had lived in these woods for many years, but never had he ever heard such a terrifying sound. He turned to the frightened mouse and in a soft voice said, "There is a small cave just ahead. I think maybe we had better sleep inside for the rest of the night."

Ernie nodded miserably and the two cautiously made their way to the cave.

Everyone in Buddy's camp looked to Morella for answers. They thought that since she was from this world she would be able to shed some light on what they had just heard. But Morella had no answers for them. Rosie sat quietly, looking out into the darkness. When nothing more happened, everyone else was finally able to get back to sleep. Still, Rosie continued to sit, watch and listen.

The morning sun peeked through the trees to find Skuba and Ernie already on the road. They were making good time, but Ernie was no longer talking and entertaining Skuba with his tall tales. The silence between them was heavy. The blue mouse was way too nervous for stories. He had not slept well the night before. Ernie knew that something was out there and he was afraid of who it might be and what it might do. He reminded himself of the importance of his mission and how the Dynasts, Sandrea and Summer, were depending on him. It was the only thing that kept Ernie from turning tail and running away. He still had the ghost fish oil and planned to use it on himself and Skuba too, if necessary. Ernie admired how cool and collected his new friend seemed and Skuba's presence helped put his own mind at ease. They should arrive at the camp soon and Ernie would be glad to finally get to deliver his message.

Rosie tossed and turned in those last dark hours before dawn. Just after sunrise something caught the restless faerie's attention. She listened carefully for several minutes, and then went to look for Buddy. She found the young elf nestled in the crook of two tree limbs and gently shook him awake.

Buddy squinted up at Rosie's worried face. "What is it, Rosie?"

Rosie glanced into the surrounding woods. "I think Newton is in trouble."

Buddy sat up rubbing his eyes. "What do you mean?"

Rosie looked a little uncertain. "I'm not sure. It started with that sound that we heard last night. Then, a little while ago, I heard a pair of doves calling to each other. You know how I can tell what the animals are saying?"

Buddy nodded.   Rosie had his full attention.

The faerie continued, "I could hear them plainly and they were repeating talk that had passed through the grapevine earlier this morning."   Rosie looked briefly at the woods and then back at Buddy.   "They spoke of a loud roar and a large crow that fell from a tree, then just disappeared."

Buddy tried to fight the fear that was growing in the pit of his stomach.   He shrugged and tentatively suggested, "There are other crows around here."   But his statement sounded more like a question to Rosie.

The faerie sadly shook her head.   "Buddy, they said the crow had something bright and shiny on its leg."

Buddy murmured, "The ring..."

Chapter 8

Rosie and Buddy wasted no time in rousing the others. When everyone heard what Rosie had to say they were anxious to get on the road.

JJ commented, "Well, there's only one way to find out. We have to go right down that trail until we find Newton or whatever made that noise last night or both." Then he cheered everyone by saying, "Likely as not, we will all be eaten by some dangerous monster, but never let it be said that we did not attempt to help a friend in distress."

JJ ruffled his feathers and flew onto Cookie's back. He grabbed a hunk of the little dog's fur with his birdie toes and settled in for the ride.

Buddy spoke to Wildflower. "Since we don't know what we're going to find up ahead, I'm thinking it might be a smart idea to dust Cookie, JJ, Okikki and Tango with some fairy dust. At least it will give them *some* protection."

The look on Buddy's face spoke volumes. Wildflower could tell that he was not convinced that they were dealing with anything ordinary. However, she did agree that the dust would afford partial protection, so she enlisted the help of Morella and Aline. The three faeries buzzed around their animal friends liberally dusting them all. JJ sneezed, but for once, he did not complain. When the two squirrels, Cookie and JJ sparkled and glistened and the camp was made to look as if there had never been anyone there, the group started down the trail that led in the direction of the sound heard the night before.

Cookie romped happily. The little dog was glad to be on the move. JJ grumped a little bit about the bumpy ride, but the others were mostly quiet and the general mood was somber. Buddy's ears twitched as he struggled to listen for anything that might sound out of place in the woods.

The group of friends had been on the trail for a while when Cookie's ears perked up and he began to growl.

From somewhere in the distance, a high pitched voice asked, "How much further to the camp?"

A softer more melodious voice responded and when Buddy heard that second voice, he began to smile.

Morella announced, "It's Skuba!" Then, in a quizzical tone she added, "Wonder what brings him here?"

Just as she spoke, Skuba and Ernie popped around the bend.

When JJ recognized Ernie, he fussed under his breath at Cookie, "So that's why you are growling. Now you be nice and don't even think about chasing that poor mouse again."

Cookie's tail wagged and he licked his own lips in what appeared to be a contrite manner. But JJ knew him well and he could tell that there was still tension in the little dog's body.

211

Everyone greeted Skuba and then the mountain elf introduced Ernie to the group.

Rosie stared at the blue mouse. "I remember you! You were at the last celebration party in Pixieland."

Ernie stared back at Rosie. "I'm sorry, but I don't remember you." Then the little mouse shuddered, "I was there alright. There were so many bears at that party! And I was chased by one of them!" Ernie's eyes grew larger and more fearful at the memory.

Cookie growled again and Ernie's attention shifted to the little dog.

"Oh, no," the mouse cried in dismay. "Not you again!"

Wildflower spoke firmly into Cookie's ear and placed a restraining hand on his muzzle. The little dog finally calmed down and JJ nodded his approval.

Skuba announced that Ernie had some important business with Newton and needed to see him right away. Ernie spoke up in his high-pitched voice, "Yes, indeed. Is the doctor among you?"

Buddy explained, "Newton had some business to conduct and separated from the group. We are expecting him to return, but we're afraid that he might have met some trouble on the way back. We're heading to his last known location to see if we can find him." Buddy tried to keep his voice even, but those who knew him could hear the worry in his tone. They all shared his concern.

Skuba said, "We are lucky to have crossed paths with you. If we had been any later, we might have missed you altogether."

Morella smiled, "You would have picked up our trail easily

enough."

The Papillon stood there looking completely innocent. They all knew that Cookie was like a little bulldozer in the woods, leaving such a trail that even a liberal sprinkling of pixie dust could not altogether hide his presence. There were several smiles as tolerant glances were cast at Cookie. JJ just ruffled his feathers and cleared his throat.

Buddy suggested that they get started again and Ernie and Skuba fell in with the group.

As they travelled along, Rosie sidled up to Ernie and confessed, "I was the bear who was following you at the party. I was not really chasing you. I just wanted to talk to you. But then you disappeared."

Ernie looked at her quizzically. "You were the bear? I have never heard of a faerie shape shifter."

Rosie giggled and the sound was like the tinkling of glass. "I drank Buddy's bear elixir."

Ernie nodded. "Ah, yes, I have heard stories of Buddy's famous elixirs, but being a seafaring mouse, I have never actually seen one." Ernie sounded wistful.

Rosie smiled at the cute blue mouse. "Well, if you stick around, I'm sure Buddy will put one in your hands eventually."

Ernie looked at Rosie's kind face and grinned. "I would like that very much. I have never known an elf who makes elixirs. Buddy is truly unique." Then the mouse asked, "I don't mean to be nosy, but what makes you think Newton is in trouble?"

Rosie studied Ernie's face for a minute. She liked what she read in his eyes, so she answered.

After hearing the story, Ernie swallowed hard past the lump in his throat that had sprung up suddenly. He turned to Rosie with a hint of awe in his eyes. "So, you are a Caller?"

Rosie simply nodded.

Ernie lapsed into silence for a moment. He knew about caller faeries. His grandmother used to tell stories about such a faerie and the many wonderful ways that she aided woodland creatures. Ernie appreciated how rare the Callers were and he had certainly never expected to meet one. This was an amazing group of Magicals, not least among them this rare faerie and the well-known elf who made interesting elixirs. And as if that weren't unusual enough, they just happened to be on the way to find a crow who was also a doctor. Ernie had lived long enough to know that deep magic was afoot. He also had a feeling that this small band of friends was headed for rough waves. The blue mouse just hoped that everyone would make it safely to port when all was said and done. Ernie asked the next question on his mind. "Why did Newton leave the group in the first place?" When the mouse noticed the surprised look on Rosie's face, he quickly added, "I mean to say, this is a strange world with many potential dangers. I would think that everyone would want to stay together."

Rosie could see no harm in answering to the best of her ability. "I know that he had some important Pixieland business here and the rest of us came along to find tiger hair for a special elixir, so we separated in order to accomplish both tasks more quickly. If you want to know anything else about Newton, you should ask Buddy."

The mouse was not to be deterred. "You mentioned a loud roar heard in the night."

Rosie nodded.

"Are you thinking it had something to do with Newton?"

Rosie sobered considerably. "I only heard the cry once, but I believe that it did have something to do with Newton, especially after I heard the doves talking this morning."

Skuba, who had been listening to their conversation, interjected, "Ernie and I also heard the roaring noise last night." Then he admitted, "It was frightening!"

Rosie looked as if she wanted to say something for a moment, but instead she kept quiet.

Ernie timidly asked, "Do you think we are going to run into whatever made that noise?" The blue mouse shook a little as he looked around to reassure himself that nothing was lurking nearby.

JJ had been busy doing his best to steer Cookie some distance away from Ernie, just in case the little dog had any bright ideas about playing chase with the mouse again. The small parrot joined the conversation with some words of comfort. "Like I said, we are all likely to be eaten by whatever it is. With a voice like that, it must be a horrible monster of some kind." Then JJ pulled himself up to his full height and added in a dramatic tone, "But it is our duty to stare danger boldly in the face and march right into what is bound to be a dismal and hopeless situation in order to rescue our friend." He punctuated his last remark with a chirping sound, for just then Cookie lunged for a bit of cheese that had fallen from Ernie's pocket, nearly unseating the little bird.

Cookie swallowed the cheese whole while the parrot fussed, "Was that YOUR cheese, Cookie?" JJ put his wings on his hips and tapped one foot for emphasis. "And what have I told you about chewing your food before swallowing?"

Ernie nervously eyed Cookie as the small dog sniffed all around his feet looking for any crumbs that might have escaped. The mouse was worried that Cookie might think that his feet were food morsels and take a bite out of him so he curled his tiny toes under his broad, flat feet just to be on the safe side. Then he reached into his pocket and pulled out some more small bits of cheese and offered them to the dog. Cookie gratefully gobbled the snack and then looked at Ernie with an animated face accompanied by a gleefully wagging tail.

The blue mouse dug around in his pocket and came up with one last bite of cheese. "That's it boy. I don't have any more." Just to prove it he pulled his pockets inside out. Cookie wistfully sniffed at the material. After swiping the fabric with his tongue to make sure there were no more crumbs he licked Ernie's hand and barked.

Wildflower smiled as she watched Ernie shyly petting the little dog with encouragement from JJ who spouted, "Watch out, Ernie! Cookie has sharp teeth! He might take a finger off!"

In spite of JJ's concerns, it seemed that Cookie and Ernie were becoming friends and the only friends that Cookie liked better than those who gave him feathers were those who gave him treats.

The group continued down the path, keeping their eyes and ears open for anything out of the ordinary. Several bright blue butterflies danced across the trail in front of them and the sun bore holes of yellow light through the leafy canopy above. Flowers nodded and rabbits bounced through the underbrush. A fox gazed curiously at the magical group as they hurried down the path. The buzzing sound of insects and the music of bright birdsong filled the air on that beautiful morning. But suddenly the temperature dropped and the woods fell quiet.

Chapter 9

Rosie stopped in her tracks. "Wait!" she spoke in a hushed voice. "See that tree up ahead? I think it's the tree we are looking for."

Everyone focused their attention on the tree in question, a very tall oak situated just off of the path on the left side. The trunk was huge and the spread of the tree quite expansive. Many of the limbs were as thick as most tree trunks and some of them overshadowed the trail.

It reminded Buddy of Newton's favorite tree in Pixieland. As the worried elf looked up into the branches he could almost imagine Newton sitting there looking down at him. He felt a lump in his throat and swallowed quickly.

Okikki examined the hedge along the other side of the path. She cautioned Tango to stay with the others while she squeezed through the bush. Cookie sniffed around the base of the tree and picked something up in his mouth. JJ noticed and warned, "Wildflower, Cookie has something."

Wildflower held up a pup treat and cajoled, "Cookie, trade it in. Trade it for a treat."

Cookie knew this game well since they played it often. He

loved to find things that were prized by Wildflower and trade them for something that he considered to be a more valuable treasure.

Cookie happily dropped what was in his mouth and grabbed the pup treat from Wildflower's fingers. Ernie bent down to pick up the discarded object. It was a small vial of thick clear liquid with a white label that gave the name and address of a Dr. Hammond Obrial. Buddy walked over and silently reached for the vial. Ernie handed it to him. The elf stared at it wordlessly for a moment before tucking it into his pouch for safe keeping. Wildflower and Rosie watched the play of expressions on the elf's face as he turned to Cookie in an attempt to mask his rising feeling of panic.

Buddy patted the small dog and said, "Thanks, Cookie. Good job!" To everyone else he announced, "Well, this confirms that we're in the right place. That vial belonged to Newton and without Cookie's sharp nose, it could have easily been overlooked."

Rosie studied the tree trying to put the puzzle pieces together. As she looked up through the center of the tree, she noticed some smaller broken branches. Her eye followed the trail left by them and she felt she was probably looking at the very spot where the crow fell. There was something different about this oak, but Rosie could not put her finger on it. The tree was certainly imposing and cast a large, deep shadow over the trail and even over the hedge and beyond.

Okikki called out, "Come and look everyone."

The squirrel pointed to a perfect footprint of a large bird etched in the soil. Morella, the best tracker among them, carefully examined the print, then confirmed that it was indeed that of a large crow.

Rosie looked up at the tree again. If the crow had flown at an angle straight into the tree from this spot, he would have landed just behind the broken branches. Rosie went right to the branch where she thought Newton must have been. Her eye followed the trail of broken limbs straight down. Rosie noticed that the position also afforded a nice view of the path.

The Caller returned to the group and asked, "JJ, where did Cookie find that vial?"

JJ pointed to a place further from the tree than she expected.

Rosie mumbled to herself, "Well, it could have rolled away..."

Buddy looked at Rosie curiously. "What are you thinking?"

Rosie carefully replied, "It looks like Newton was in that thicket last night. That footprint is too large to be any other crow. Then he must have flown into the tree. Maybe he heard something on the path. It might have been the same creature that made the roaring sound we all heard. If you'll notice, the view of the path is better right up there where you see the broken branches. I don't think that's a coincidence. By the trail of damage, it looks like he pretty much fell straight down. Something must have happened to cause him to fall. I would like to talk to some of the creatures who live around here and see what they know, but it is strangely quiet."

Everyone had noticed the lack of woodland sounds since they had arrived at the tree.

Buddy sat down and leaned his back against the trunk. He

asked himself, *What now?*

"Newton planned to meet us in the Faerie Glen, but Skuba and Ernie came from that direction and they didn't pass him on the way. He didn't come through our camp which he could have easily seen," Morella pointed out. "We know that he at least made it this far."

Buddy looked up at Morella, "You said that you had never before heard anything like the sound we heard last night, right?"

Morella answered quickly, "True." She shivered a bit as she recalled the loud roar. "Even the tiger Rashka never made such a noise."

Aline asked, "Why is it so quiet here? And the air feels funny."

Wildflower agreed, "The air does feel unusually chilly and strange."

Then Morella added, "It's sort of like when a big storm is on the way."

Rosie walked around the edge of the dense shadow that was cast by the large oak tree. She felt that something was not right about this small section of woods.

When Morella had finished talking, Rosie called to Buddy. "I'm going to find that fox we saw a while back. Foxes are clever and they pay attention. He may be able to help us."

Aline went with Rosie, but it was deemed best for the rest of the group to stay put. Too many unknown visitors might alarm the fox.

Buddy called to Rosie and Aline as they left, "Good luck!"

Near the entrance to the fox's den, Rosie told Aline.   "Just sit quietly beside me and I will do the talking.   Be sure that you don't look him straight in the eye.   We don't want him to feel threatened."

Aline understood and the two faeries sat outside the den a respectful distance away, but in plain view of the fox who lived within.   The faeries heard a short "yip yip" and then a beautiful red fox emerged.   His rusty colored fur was closely cropped against his muscular frame.   There did not appear to be one ounce of fat on the streamlined animal.   Dark fur on his feet extending part way up his legs gave the illusion that the cat-like canid was wearing boots.   In contrast, there was white fur on his underbelly and a white tip crowned his handsome plume of a tail.   The fox stood still for several minutes with only his ears moving, twitching back and forth as he took in his surroundings.   Finally he turned his yellow eyes toward Aline and Rosie.

Aline only looked out of the corner of her eye as Rosie had instructed, but it was what she heard next that surprised her.   Rosie was *barking* and she sounded just like the fox!   Although Aline couldn't understand them, she realized that the fox and Rosie were communicating.   Aline knew that Callers had unique gifts, but she had never before seen this type of faerie in action.

After their conversation, Rosie placed a small piece of fruit on the ground.   The fox sniffed it with interest and seemed satisfied. Rosie took Aline by the hand and they retraced their steps.   By the time they made it back to the main path, the fox had consumed the treat and disappeared into his den.

Aline exclaimed, "I didn't know foxes liked fruit!"

Rosie smiled, "Yes, they do and I wanted to give him a gift for being so helpful."

Aline quizzed, "Could he tell you anything at all about Newton?"

Rosie sobered.   "Yes, he saw the whole thing.   I can explain everything, but let's get back to the others so they can hear too."

Aline put a restraining hand on her friend.   "Just tell me one thing.   Does he know where we can find Newton?"

Rosie shook her head, "Sadly, no."

Chapter 10

Buddy stood up when Rosie and Aline returned. Everyone gathered around to hear the news and Rosie wasted no time.

"The fox saw what happened. He was foraging nearby when he noticed a large crow who was wearing something shiny on his leg."

Buddy interjected, "The ring."

Rosie nodded, "That's what I thought too. But, and this is really puzzling, there was a large dog with him. The fox didn't think that the dog meant the crow any harm because they seemed to be friendly toward each other. He didn't pay much attention to the pair, but he did sense something on the path that made his hackles rise. He told me that the air around the tree became inexplicably chilly, almost cold enough to see his own breath. The fox said that Newton flew up into the tree and that he appeared to be looking down on the path below. Following the crow's gaze, he saw a large shadow moving along the hedge. Then the path and hedge suddenly glazed over with ice. The fox said that the shadowy figure threw something at the crow. The crow was hit and fell, but here's where it gets strange. The fox saw a man lying on the ground, not a crow!"

Buddy's ears twitched at this last bit of information, but he remained quiet.

Rosie continued, "The shadowy figure appeared to be trying to drag the man away, but then a powerful wind came out of nowhere. It was so strong that it drew the ice up into swirls and crushed it into a fine powder. Then there was a roar so loud and intense that it hurt the fox's ears."

"I bet that was the same sound we all heard!" Ernie interrupted.

Rosie nodded and continued the story. "The fox saw a great beast jump over the hedge. He said that at first it looked like the force of the wind was pushing the beast toward the shadowy figure. But then he realized that the beast was trying to back the shadow away from the man. Eventually the shadow slid back along the hedge while the wind and the beast pushed against it until it disappeared. Now listen carefully. This next part is a little confusing."

All eyes were on Rosie.

"The beast blew warm air into the area which raised the temperature back to normal. The man stirred a little and in the next instant the crow was lying there instead of him. The tree's shadow just opened up and the wind spiraled down into it with a loud rushing noise. Then the beast picked up the crow in his jaws, leapt into the shadow after the wind and they were gone."

Rosie leaned forward as she finished her story. "The fox said that it was oddly quiet afterward. He wondered if that was because the ice or the wind or both chased everything out of the area. When he thought it was safe, he walked up to the tree and sniffed around a bit, but couldn't detect anything out of the ordinary. As unbelievable as his story sounds, he insists that it's exactly what he saw with his own two eyes!"

Morella, Skuba, and the other Pixieland friends were quiet for a minute after Rosie finished talking.

Buddy's ears twitched as he pondered aloud, "I wonder who took Newton."

Ernie cleared his throat and in a plaintive tone he cried, "But I was sent to find him!" Then he shook his head and sighed.

Buddy looked at the mouse's sad face. "Tell me, Ernie, just what is the nature of your business with Newton?" Before the mouse could respond, Buddy hastily added, "Ordinarily, I would not wish to pry, but right now we are looking for clues, any clues, that might help us figure out who has Newton and why."

Ernie looked uncomfortable. The group could see the wheels turning in his mind as he wrestled with the dilemma of whether or not to talk.

Skuba, who knew Ernie best, encouraged him. The mountain elf rested a hand on Ernie's shoulder and spoke persuasively into his ear. "We all want to help Newton. Your confidence will be in good hands and among friends. Please, share what you know. It might help us to find him and when we do you will be able to complete your mission."

The mouse stood erect with his chin up and his ears plastered back against his head.

As Ernie gazed into Buddy's eyes still uncertain, Skuba spoke again in a softer tone.   "You see, Newton was also on an important mission, sent here by Victoria, the Sentinal of the Main Portal."

This information came as no surprise to Ernie.   He already knew why Newton was here.   The words of the dynasts echoed in his ear.   They had told him that if he had trouble finding Newton, he should look for Buddy who would be able to lead him to the doctor. The blue mouse was not sure that anything he knew would help them now, but he decided to try, both for Newton's sake and for the sake of his task which he was honor bound to complete.

Ernie hesitated a moment and looked around at everyone. Skuba, his trusted friend, sat close by.   There was Wildflower with her beautiful multi-colored hair who smiled at him in an encouraging way.   Okikki and Tango sat together on the forest floor.   The youngster looked at Ernie with wide expectant eyes as if he were waiting to be told a bedtime story.   The mouse couldn't help but smile at the little squirrel.   Okikki patted Tango and gave Ernie a quick nod.   Aline and Rosie looked so serene seated side by side on a low branch of the large tree.   Buddy stepped back to give him more room.   Morella stretched and shook her wings sending a small amount of faerie dust swirling around the group.   Cookie was lying down with his head on his paws.   He turned his bright eyes on Ernie, sensing that the mouse was now the center of attention.

JJ walked up and down Cookie's back, foot over foot, but when he realized that Ernie was looking at him he adopted an air and waved his wings dramatically as he needlessly said, "Now everyone, get comfortable.   This is sure to be a long story or my name isn't JJ."

The small bird chuckled as he mumbled, "Well, my name isn't really JJ, now is it? But since I forgot my real name, my friends gave me a new name which is JJ.... um, well..." The green bird smiled sheepishly, "We might as well get settled in and ready to listen." The parrot finally closed his little beak and settled onto his favorite spot right behind Cookie's shoulders. He politely gestured with one wing, giving Ernie the floor.

"Well," said Ernie, "I was sent here with a message for Newton. But it's kind of complicated. I think you would understand it better if I told you something about myself and how this whole thing got started. And you're right, JJ, it's probably going to be a long story, but I'll try to keep it as short as possible." Ernie cleared his throat and began. "My people live on the other side of the Undula Ocean, you know, the one that borders Pixieland. A few of us have homes along the shoreline, but most live in houseboats. We love to sail about looking for adventure, but we don't have much luck with that and usually just end up right back where we started. However, my parents were determined sailors and they had heard of an island full of seashells, gold, gemstones, and lumber just lying around for the taking. The rumor was that a great and wise faun lived on the island as well. It was told that if you could find the faun, he would give you words of wisdom and guidance that rivaled any of the other treasures found there. One day my parents decided to look for the island. They scrubbed their tiny boat, loaded in supplies and last of all, brought me aboard. I was very young, but I still remember that journey."

Ernie's eyes held a dreamy, faraway look as he recalled the beautiful sight of water birds and rolling waves. The blue mouse continued, "To make a long story short, we ran into some trouble. Storms are rare, but after we had been at sea for a few days, my dad noticed some angry looking clouds along the horizon. We were already feeling a cool breeze and the water quickly became very choppy. The clouds rolled toward us and blocked the light of the sun. Right before the storm hit, my mother wrapped me in a large scarf and rolled it up like a cocoon. She tied it around herself so that I would be safe against her back while she helped my dad. They worked hard to steer to safety, but we could not outrun the giant waves. The wind was high and the boat rocked up and down as wave after briny wave lifted us and dropped us in turn. At some point I slipped out of the scarf and slid into the stormy seas."

Tango gasped in alarm.

"Don't worry, Tango," Ernie assured the young squirrel. "I was ok because there happened to be a floating plank of wood and I scrambled onto it. I cried out, but my parents couldn't hear me and the storm carried them far from me. I don't know how I was able to cling to that board, but cling I did. Finally the storm died down and all was calm again. By nighttime, I was hungry and sleepy in my wet, dark world. I called out to my parents hoping maybe they could hear me now, but it was not my parents who answered."

JJ helpfully volunteered, "Probably a huge dangerous shark, likely as not."

Ernie's eyes squinted and he smiled at JJ as he shook his head.

"No," he giggled, "It was a dolphin, actually several dolphins. They nudged my piece of wood, gently propelling me through the water." Ernie's eyes lit up at the memory of the beautiful animals. "I think maybe it was a game to them. This went on for a long time until finally, just before dawn, the dolphins started chattering back and forth. Then, one by one they abandoned me and swam away. I tried to stay awake, but the rising sun warmed my fur and I just couldn't keep my eyes open any longer." Ernie reminded everyone, "I was just a baby after all." Then he continued. "I don't know how long I slept before I fell off of that plank, but the cold, salty water woke me instantly and I struggled to the surface. I think it was my splashing about that first attracted their attention."

Ernie paused and JJ sagely nodded his head. "Ah, yes, splashing about in the ocean can be very dangerous. I have heard some scary stories about sharks. I am sure they came after you straight away." The small green bird snapped his beak and shook his wings at the thought.

Ernie laughed at JJ. "No, silly, not sharks. I never did see any sharks."

JJ looked disappointed that sharks were not a part of the adventure.

Ernie continued. "I tried to keep my head up, but before long I went under and when I did, they were right there." Ernie's eyes softened as he remembered.

Tango had moved away from Okikki and was now sitting right against Ernie's side. The young squirrel curiously eyed the mouse

230

and asked, "*Who* was there?"

Ernie looked at Tango and patting him on the head, he responded, "The mermaids. There were two of them. They took me by the paws and swam underwater. You see, I had floated into an estuary and it was not nearly as deep as the ocean. But it was plenty deep for me! I held my breath as long as I could until finally I had to breathe and when I did I found out that I could breathe water just like air."

Everyone in the group murmured their surprise as Ernie vigorously nodded his head in confirmation.

"As long as they were touching me, I was just fine. Even though they were still children themselves, they took good care of me. They could tell that I was tired from my ordeal, so they curled their tails around me and the three of us napped in a small underground cave. Later I woke up to the gently moving water and the most musical voice. My eyes opened and I looked into the face of one of the mermaids. She was every bit as beautiful as I remembered with long, glossy black hair and eyes just as dark. She said, 'Wake up, Little Fuzzy, wake up!' Then I heard another voice. 'I see his eyes are open. He's awake! Let's take him to Timna.' The second mermaid had long hair too, only it was bright yellow and her eyes were as blue as the bluest part of the ocean. The dark-haired mermaid took my paw and the next thing I knew we were gliding through the water at an incredible speed. It was so much fun! I found out that their names were Sandrea and Summer and even though they didn't look at all alike, they were twins."

Ernie remembered Summer giggling, "Look at his whiskers and his big ears, Sister."   Sandrea had added, "Yes, and his fur is so soft. He is such a cute little fuzzy."   He asked where they were taking him and Summer told him they were taking him to their guardian. "We're going to see if she will let us keep you."   Sandrea nodded in agreement and scratched the top of Ernie's head.   "You are such a cute fuzzy.   If Timna lets us keep you, we can play all the time and we will feed you and take good care of you."   Ernie was pretty small, but even so he was not sure he wanted to be *kept* no matter how much fun it was to swim with the mermaids.   He asked, "Is Timna your mother?"   Then his little face clouded up as he remembered that his own mother was lost.   But in the next minute, all of that was forgotten as his eyes fell on what looked to be a very large and very stern monster.

Chapter 11

Tango snapped Ernie out of his reverie. "So what happened next?"

Embarrassed that his thoughts had drifted, Ernie chuckled and continued his story. "I thought they were taking me to see their mother, but when we arrived, it looked more like a big monster to me!"

JJ hopefully asked, "Are you sure that monster wasn't a shark?"

Tango's eyes were practically pasted to Ernie's face as the blue mouse assured, "No, JJ, not a shark. As a matter of fact it was not even a monster at all. It was a sea dragon named Timna. I was plenty scared, you know? I just hoped she didn't decide that I might make a good snack! I did feel less afraid when Timna started laughing. She thought the whole thing was pretty funny. She told the mermaids between chuckles that they had found a baby mouse. She wanted to know where I came from so the twins told her how they found me. Then I spoke up and told them all how I had ended up in the water. After she sorted out everything we were saying, Timna called for a porpoise to go to the island, search for my parents and bring them back if they could be found."

Ernie paused again as he recalled the sea dragon saying to the mermaids. "Girls, this young mouse is a land animal and he belongs with his parents. I see no harm in you playing with him until his parents can be found, but he is his own little person and you must respect him and not treat him as a pet. He has fur and it does look a bit fuzzy under water, but his name is Ernie, as he has told us."

The girls obediently chimed, "Yes, Timna." Sandrea sounded excited as she turned to Ernie. "You can walk around on land? I want to see! Will you show me please?" The two of them grabbed Ernie by the paws and they were off again, headed for shore. As they swam away, Timna was still chuckling, probably at the girls' many questions.

"Do you walk on two legs or four? Can we still call you Fuzzy Ernie, oh, please? Can you run fast? Hey, you can run along the shore and we will swim and see which one of us is the fastest, ok, Ernie? You will still swim with us in the water sometimes, won't you?"

The mermaids rapidly fired their questions with barely enough time for Ernie to answer one before the next one was asked.

Ernie's eyes held a faraway look as he thought about the beauty of that underwater world. He recalled it as if it were yesterday. The water in the estuary was mostly greenish with ribbons of moving light that crisscrossed everywhere he looked. When he stuck his head out of the water, he could see that the emerald green of this secluded area shifted suddenly to the deep blue of the ocean in the distance. The cries of many birds filled the air throughout the day.   Eagles, ducks, falcons and black brants were all around.   Some of them dined on the sea grass that grew in profusion both on the estuary floor and along the sandy shore. Their long leaves and colorful flowers filled the underwater world. The smells of salt and water and wet sand were the welcome scents of home during those days.   Sand pipers ran along the shore as if late for an important meeting.   Dungeness crab and mud shrimp scuttled about in the soil beneath them.   River otters splashed and played both in and out of the water.   Puffer-type fish and large salmon also shared their home.

Ernie explained, "Timna watched over us and kept us safe. And though she was scary looking to me at first, she was actually gentle and very motherly."

JJ chirped, "What did she look like?   I bet she looked like a big 'ol shark."

Ernie's whiskers quivered as he tried not to laugh at JJ. "Well, she *was* huge!   Her head was large and there were these ridges over her eyes.   Her neck was long and thick and the front part of her body was wide and she had flipper-type arms.   Let me tell you, with that big tail Timna could move really fast!   She was feared by many and I wouldn't have wanted her for an enemy, but Timna was wonderful to us.   Anyway, my friendship with the girls grew stronger by the day.   They continued to call me Fuzzy Ernie when they thought Timna did not hear.   I always felt that she knew, but she could probably tell that I didn't mind.   The twins and I became inseparable.   Then, early one morning while we were playing, I saw a small speck way out on the ocean against the horizon. It was gradually getting bigger so I knew it was headed our way. We went straight to Timna and that's when I learned that my parents were coming. I felt a happiness that is difficult to describe. I really didn't think that I would ever see my mother and father again. The minute they landed my mother grabbed me and hugged me tight. My dad joined us and the three of us danced around in a circle, laughing and crying at the same time. Then we just stood there smiling and looking at each other. I had grown during the time we were separated, but my mother said she would have known me anywhere. The girls made an eel grass salad in honor of the occasion. As we were eating, my parents told us that they had landed on the island of treasures after the storm. They found the wise faun who gave them a choice. They could either take all of the treasures they could carry or they could receive his words of knowledge. My parents were so sad from losing me that they did not feel much like treasure hunting although the island held many beautiful and wonderful things. Instead, they decided to ask for the words of knowledge. The faun's gift was to tell them that their lost child had survived the storm and was safe. He also explained where they could find me. They were overjoyed and didn't have any regrets about giving up all those treasures."

Ernie grinned and then continued, "My parents wanted to leave as soon as they had rested from their voyage and the excitement of our reunion. It had been a long time since we had seen our home across the ocean and my mom and dad were ready for us to be on our way. They thanked Timna and my mermaid friends for all that they had done for me. I was happy to be with my parents again, but I was not eager to leave my friends. Before we left, Timna presented the three of us—the mermaids and me—with tiny, magical horns. She said that if we ever needed each other, we could blow our horns and magic would bring us together again. But she cautioned us not to use them lightly. I wore mine around my neck and Summer and Sandrea did the same. They hugged me one last time and Sandrea stroked my fur whispering, 'Farewell, Fuzzy Ernie.' They swam alongside our boat until we crossed over into the ocean. I looked to see Timna gliding silently behind them, ever protective, always watchful. I waved until I could no longer see them bobbing up and down in the water."

Ernie's eyes were a little misty as he fell silent and quickly blinked back a tear. Everyone was quiet for a minute, even JJ, after Ernie finished telling his story.

Buddy patted Ernie on the shoulder. The elf no longer doubted the mouse and everyone in the group understood Ernie's connection to the mermaids.

Skuba asked, "After you left the estuary, how much time passed before you saw the twins again?"

Ernie softly sighed as he recalled, "I *didn't* see them again...until after the trouble started."

Buddy's face mirrored his concern. "What trouble?"

JJ just shook his head and mournfully clucked, "I knew it!"

Wildflower hid a smile as she watched the little bird. He had struck such a dramatic pose, so full of himself.

JJ continued, "I knew there had to be big trouble out there somewhere..."

Rosie walked around the perimeter of the tree's shadow. She was still listening to Buddy, Ernie and JJ, but something was bothering her. It just felt different under this tree and she hoped to discover why.

Buddy noticed that Rosie seemed restless, but his main focus was still on Ernie. He asked a second time. "What trouble? Could it have something to do with Newton's disappearance?"

Ernie thought for a moment before responding to Buddy's question. "Well, let me go back for a little bit. I was saving Timna's magic, hoping one day we would all see each other again. At times I wondered if they even remembered me." Ernie reached up and ran a paw across the tiny horn dangling from cord around his neck as he spoke. "When word came that the twins had taken their rightful places as joint rulers of their kingdom, I was happy for them. I almost blew the horn right then and there. But I didn't. I remembered what Timna had told us and I waited. Many years passed, so many that I lost count. Then one day I was on my boat polishing and cleaning when the call came. My horn sounded and shook violently. The next thing I knew, my boat and I were on an inland waterway along the shore of Pixieland. I still had the polishing cloth in my paw. I knew right away that one or both of the sisters had called me." Ernie's ears flattened against his head as he continued. "They were all grown up and incredibly beautiful.

Their arms were decked with jeweled bracelets; their hair sparkled and shone in the sunlight. I could feel their strength and power and I was totally overwhelmed." Ernie looked at each member of the group. "Have you ever seen a mermaid?"

Buddy had seen one once, but he held his tongue. Everyone else said that they had not, at least not close up.

Ernie was satisfied with their responses and he continued. "Well, I can tell you that they are amazing. It was not the same as when we were young. I know they were glad to see me and I them, but they had become great rulers and I a simple mouse."

Buddy thought that Ernie was more than just a simple mouse, but again, he kept quiet. The mouse's story was fascinating, but Buddy did hope that Ernie would soon get to the part that might help their dear friend Newton.

Ernie's face looked serious as he motioned for everyone to move closer. The group closed in and the blue mouse spoke in a soft voice. "I am only telling you this because you are with Newton and are now involved." Ernie looked around to make sure no one was lurking nearby. He watched Rosie as she continued to walk around the tree. She turned suddenly and looked at the mouse. Something she read in his expression pulled her back into the group. When Ernie was certain that he had everyone's attention, he continued. "As you probably all know, the mermaids go through a leadership change every five hundred years."

JJ said, "Well, no, not really. I mean I don't know anything about mermaids."

Skuba shrugged and Morella shook her head.

Ernie sighed, "That's right some of you are not from Pixieland and wouldn't know. But the rest of us who live there understand the custom and we all know that in some mysterious way it's part of the balance that keeps Pixieland such a wonderful and peaceful place."

The Pixielanders nodded except for Buddy who never moved, nor did he speak.

Ernie continued. "When the Ladies Sandrea and Summer arrived, they greeted me warmly and it was an emotional meeting for the three of us—not only because we had not seen each other in such a long time, but also because there was trouble brewing under the sea and the ladies were very concerned for their own people and also for all of Pixieland."

Everyone's eyes were on Ernie's face now and even Tango did not fidget as Ernie continued, "We don't want to cause panic in Pixieland, so what I tell you must go no further. Will you give me your word?"

Buddy ran long fingers through his thick dark hair as he thought about what Ernie was asking. The young elf included everyone in his glance as he spoke to Ernie. "If any of us feels that someone back home needs to know what you share, then I believe we can all agree to first discuss it among ourselves and then decide to do only what we know will be right for our world."

Everyone agreed with Buddy.

Ernie studied each face. He would have preferred to have a

solid promise of silence, but after some thought he decided to proceed. "I believe that everyone here wants what is best, so that will have to do. Listen closely."

Chapter 12

Buddy held up a hand to interrupt Ernie. "Hold on a second, Ernie." The elf had been growing more worried about Newton by the hour and felt that this was not the time for secrets, at least not here among trusted friends. A few days ago he would not have considered sharing sensitive information. But now with Newton's disappearance, everything had changed and he no longer felt it was in Newton's best interest to remain silent.

"I do know something about Newton's mission here. The queen egg has arrived in the kingdom under the sea and it has been damaged. Newton was sent here to seek a certain specialist who has developed something that could maybe repair the egg." Buddy slid the vial out of his pouch and held it aloft. "I believe this is that very formula." Buddy's lips trembled as he tried hard not to think the worst about what could have separated his friend from this important egg repair and possibly caused his disappearance as well. Aloud he said, "We are lucky to have found this and we have Cookie to thank."

Wildflower proudly patted Cookie's silky head. The small dog grinned from ear to ear. He loved the attention even though he had no idea what was being discussed.

Buddy added, "Newton was sent here because he once lived in this world. He was human and worked as a doctor. Victoria and the queens hoped that with his background and experience he could persuade the specialist to part with some of the formula. From the vial here I would say that he was successful."

Skuba looked a bit confused as he injected a thought. "I have lived around humans for many years and I am wondering how a crow will be able to accomplish this? You said he used to be a man, but now he is a crow, right? Is he a shifter or something?"

Buddy thought to himself *or something* but aloud he only confirmed, "Newton can change forms."

JJ asked, "Are you saying that Newton can change into a man?"

Buddy nodded.

Morella thought out loud. "Well, it makes sense if you think about it. I mean, he used to be a man until he went to Pixieland. Now he's a crow. I guess the real questions are, why did he go to Pixieland in the first place and how did he become a crow?"

These questions were making Buddy uncomfortable and he fidgeted a bit. He knew it was not his place to discuss this, but he understood why the group would want to know. His ears quivered and he paced up and down under the tree. "That is a really good question, Morella, and one that Newton may answer for us when he is found. I apologize for interrupting you, Ernie. What can you add to what I have shared?"

Ernie responded, "You know that the egg is damaged and you

know why Newton was sent here.   Now I will tell you how the damage happened and why it might have something to do with what became of Newton."   Ernie lowered his voice, "The Ladies Sandrea and Summer could not have been more proud when the queen egg arrived.   There is only one such egg during the reign of a queen and when word spread that the egg was finally found resting there among all of the others in the incubation chambers there was much celebrating among the mermaids.   You see, the egg goes through several phases before hatching.   At first the egg has a thin shell. This is a very fragile time and the egg should not be touched or moved during this phase.   During the second phase the egg absorbs the thin outer shell and it becomes soft.   This is also a delicate phase, but during this time the egg may only be handled very carefully.   It is turned regularly in the warm sands of the chamber and just when it begins to harden, the queen egg is prepared for travel.   It is gently wrapped and placed snuggly in a cart.   Chosen mermaids accompany the egg to a secret location.   Timna, the water dragon I told you about, meets them and takes over from there. The queen is born away from home and is raised and tutored by Timna.   Then when the time is right, the new queen swims home alone.   When she arrives, the Guard announces her.   The people welcome her and there is feasting and celebrating for days ending with a beautiful coronation for a brand new queen."

Tango asked, "Why do they do that?   Wouldn't it be easier for the queen to be hatched right there, safe in her own home?" The young squirrel moved over and snuggled against Okikki as he thought about being away from the comforts of home.

Ernie smiled at Tango. "It is just as you said—it would be easier. However, the mermaids know that the young queen must be strong and independent and that she must develop her own special gifts. It's important that she be carefully taught, not just about the ways of the Mer people, but about the ways of others. She needs to be aware of so many things that go on in the world. When Timna has finished teaching the very last lesson, the queen must successfully complete her rite of passage before taking her place on the throne. It is the way of the mermaids." Ernie craned his neck and looked around. He didn't see anything suspicious in their surroundings so he continued, "The egg is now in the first phase. It is the thin shell that has been damaged. The queens told me that one night, Lady Summer woke suddenly from a sound sleep with an uneasy feeling that something was wrong. Her first instinct was to check on the queen egg. She found that the egg had rolled away from the others and worse than that, something shadowy appeared to be pushing it along. The shadow loomed larger and larger and the water in the chamber kept getting colder until ice began to form. Lady Summer cried for help. Lady Sandrea and several others rushed to her side."

Buddy listened closely to what Ernie was saying. "Did you say ice?" Before Ernie could answer, Buddy turned to Rosie. "Didn't the fox say that there was ice in the area after Newton fell and the shadowy figure was seen moving along the path beside the hedge here?"

Rosie sat up a little taller. "Yes, he most certainly did."

Chapter 13

Buddy's ears wiggled as he thought about what the mouse had said. He rubbed his chin with one hand and gazed at Ernie. "Please do continue, Ernie."

Ernie cleared his throat and resumed his story. "By the time everyone arrived, there was no sign of the shadowy figure. Lady Summer secured the egg with Sandrea's help and together they checked to see if all was well. They found a scratch on the surface of the egg which could threaten the baby within. None of them had an explanation for how the egg was damaged or why the water in the room had grown so cold. They wondered who had tampered with their precious egg and why. The Guard was called to the incubation chamber and commanded to watch at all times. The ladies hoped that the scratch would not prove to be too serious. But the next morning they could see that the scratch had gotten longer and deeper. The dynasts knew that they needed help and wanted to send someone they could trust to find Victoria." Ernie shrugged. "They thought of me and that's why I am here. It was around the time when you were having that big party, you know the one where Balor and his band played and so many bears attended?"

Rosie chuckled as she remembered drinking Buddy's elixir and turning into a bear. Then she cast a curious glance at Ernie. "Hey, how did you get away from me anyway? I was right behind you and then you just disappeared."

Ernie admitted, "I didn't really get away from you. It was ghost fish oil. It made me invisible so you couldn't see me even though I was right there."

Rosie's eyes widened and Morella, who loved all manner of herbs and natural remedies, asked, "Do you have some? How does it work?"

Ernie nodded. "Sure. I will give some to all of you. Before this is over, we may need to use it."

JJ ruffled his wings and wrapped them around his body protectively as he predicted. "No doubt we'll all have to use the oil and then we'll remain invisible. Who knows, maybe that shadow thing will still be able to see us, but no one else will ever see us again."

Ernie comforted JJ. "It's ok. I have tested it and you don't stay invisible forever. It has really helped at times when I have been in a jam or when I thought I was in trouble." Ernie gave Rosie an apologetic look as he said this last part for he now knew that she meant him no harm.

Ernie paused long enough to give everyone a small amount of ghost fish oil. After explaining how to apply it he said, "To get back to my story, the ladies told me to find Victoria. I didn't know anyone in Pixieland and wasn't even sure where to begin. I started down a trail that looked well-used and I came across your garden,

Okikki."

Taken by surprise, Okikki asked, "Was I there?"

Ernie nodded, "Yes, you were and a beautiful golden bear was standing right beside you. He was so bright and shiny that my eyes hurt to even look at him." Ernie's eyes looked a bit glassy as he recalled, "I have never seen anything like it. His fur was like pure gold."

Buddy smiled to himself as he remembered how his own bear elixir had turned him bright gold.

Okikki laughed and pointed at Buddy, but was laughing too hard to explain. Tears of mirth filled Okikki's eyes as she conjured up a picture of Buddy as a bear on the trail, sauntering along and whistling a tune with his face all rubbery looking. In spite of the serious concerns for Newton, Buddy flashed his famous smile as he too remembered his experience as a bear.

Ernie looked confused.

Okikki held her sides as she gulped air into her lungs. Then she explained in a breathless voice. "That big gold bear was Buddy. He drank his own elixir, but something went very wrong. It was so funny that we both collapsed on the ground laughing. But I don't remember seeing you, Ernie."

The blue mouse hung his head. "I was hiding. I was a little scared." Then Ernie turned to Buddy. "I must beg your pardon because I did something wrong that day."

Buddy questioned "What do you mean?"

If a blue mouse could turn red in the face then Ernie would

have blushed. He looked down at his feet as if they held the answer to Buddy's question. Ernie shuffled them nervously as he confessed his secret. "Well, I watched you and Okikki laughing so happily and I saw your golden tears falling like rain. I watched as Okikki scooped them into a bucket, put a lid on them and sat the pail in the bushes right next to that big tree. I wanted to take a closer look, so I waited until you both left. When I was certain that you were gone, I crept over to the bucket and lifted the lid. I could see a reflection of my own face in all of that gold. You left it behind and I kind of thought someone else might find it and I did love those gold tears, so I took the pail." Ernie cringed down, flattened his ears and squeezed his eyes to tiny slits as he anticipated a good scolding. There was nothing but silence. Ernie cracked one eye open and positioned it onto Buddy's face. Buddy was grinning at him so he found the courage to open his other eye. Everyone looked to Buddy for a response.

The elf surprised Ernie by saying, "Don't worry about that. I asked Okikki to save those tears thinking that they might come in handy for something or other since they were gold. But quite frankly, I forgot all about them and have never given them another thought."

Ernie relaxed visibly. "Buddy, I should have asked first. I know that, but I can return them to you and I will as soon as we get back home. It's just that I didn't know you at the time and they were so unusual."

Buddy put an arm around the mouse. Everyone else was

quiet and JJ pretended to be looking at something in a bush nearby.

"I won't argue with you about the fact that you should have asked. It's true. However, you are an honest mouse or you wouldn't have told me this and in front of everyone here too." Buddy gestured toward all of the friends. "I do remember that when you ran from the party you had a pail. I thought it looked familiar and now I know why." Buddy patted Ernie's furry shoulder. "You may keep the tears. Think of them as a gift from me. Now, put this from your mind and none of us will speak of it again, right everybody?"

Everyone nodded agreeably and the group gathered around Ernie to show their acceptance and support. Hugs were exchanged.

Ernie had never taken anything before and even though he told himself that Buddy had abandoned the pail of tears, he knew in his heart he shouldn't have helped himself to them. He decided then and there that he would do something very special and unselfish with those tears. That should help to make things right. Ernie's heart swelled with love for these dear new friends and he felt that he was becoming part of a truly wonderful extended family.

Buddy encouraged Ernie to return to his story. "Tell us, Ernie. After you left the party, did you find Victoria?"

Ernie replied, "Not right away, but when she left the party, she found me. I was cloaked in the ghost fish oil, but she could see me anyway and asked me what I was doing. I started to run from her, but she told me who she was and then I just felt relieved to have found her." Ernie continued, "I told her what had happened to the

250

dynasts and the queen egg.   She told me she would take care of it from there.   Victoria said that I should stay in Pixieland until further notice and that I might be needed again before long."   Ernie squinted and his face looked serious.   "We must find Newton.   In order to save the egg, he has to repair it before the outer shell is absorbed and I'm not sure how much time we have."

Buddy noticed that Ernie spoke as if he assumed that Newton was safe.   He hoped that the mouse's optimism would prove to be correct.

A thought suddenly occurred to Ernie and he turned to Buddy. "Do you have a recipe for elixir of mermaid?"

Buddy put his finger to his head.   "Right up here.   Why do you ask?"

Ernie explained, "Because Newton will probably need assistance when he goes to repair the egg and his helper will need to be able to swim and breathe under water."   While Buddy was considering that bit of information, Ernie asked, "Can you get most of the ingredients here?"

Buddy turned to Morella and quickly reeled off his list of ingredients from memory.

Morella nodded.   "Most of them can be easily obtained right here.   Well, except for the mermaid hair."

Ernie carefully opened the metal box given to him by the dynasts.   He gingerly plucked several black hairs out of the box and gave them to Buddy.   The hair glowed as if it had a life of its own.

Tango stared wide eyed.   "Wow!   Mermaid hair!"

Buddy carefully wrapped the hairs and placed them in his pack.

Ernie said, "The hairs came from Lady Summer herself. Somehow they knew about your elixirs."

The mouse and the elf exchanged glances and said in unison, "Victoria."

Ernie spoke again. "After I talked to Victoria I headed across the field and into the woods, well away from the party. I camped there and planned to spend the night. I was preparing my dinner when I heard a sudden bark." Ernie walked over to Cookie and patted him on the head. Cookie's tail thumped and he immediately begin sniffing Ernie's paws, looking for any hint of a treat. Ernie smiled fondly at Cookie before turning back to the others. "Before I knew it, this dog barged into my campsite. I was terrified and ran away, dousing myself with ghost fish oil as soon as I could. Thankfully it worked and he lost my trail." The blue mouse turned back to Cookie, smiling. "I am happy that we're finally friends." Ernie continued, "Like I said, time is important now and I should tell you that, after hearing what the fox had to say, I think I know who was after Newton and what might have become of him."

Chapter 14

Newton's eyes were still shut, but he felt and heard several things all at once. He was deliciously warm even though there was a breeze blowing. The moving air that fanned around him smelled like a sweet perfume. As if it were a game that he played, Newton tried to think what it could be without opening his eyes. Finally he began to stir and when his eyes opened, he looked out on a strange and beautiful place. He was lying under a large oak tree in some soft, spongy grass. His head rested on a root protruding from the loamy soil at the base of the tree. Newton slowly sat up and looked out on a very bright but flat countryside. An open field full of unfamiliar purple blooms spread out before him as far as the eye could see. The sweet scent that he had noticed came from the many flowers that bobbed in the gentle breeze, adding to the pleasing sound that reminded Newton of the very best of sleep machines.

There were billowing clouds overhead sailing swiftly across a low ceiling. Newton was surrounded by moving air and light. Here and there tiny funnel clouds dipped and swirled bobbing up and down across the flower-laden field. Newton stood and walked toward one of these tiny funnels. He reached out with his hands palms up and the small whirlwind moved up and down tickling his fingers in the process.   Newton rubbed his palms against his sides to rid them of the tingling sensation.   The tiny whirlwind that had skimmed his hands now dipped among the flowers flattening the grasses in its immediate vicinity before abruptly rising again into the sky and swirling away.

Newton heard the deep voices again.   The doctor caught sight of a reddish speck off in the distance moving toward him.   As it came closer, the size appeared to increase as well.   Recognition dawned on Newton and he smiled.

"Mason?"

But there was no answering bark.   When the animal drew close enough for Newton to see more detail, he realized that although this creature had the same color coat as Mason, it was much larger and had a huge mane as well.   *It couldn't be him*, thought Newton.   Was it a lion?   If so, it was the largest one Newton had ever seen.   The Shape Shifter stood with his back firmly braced against the large oak for he knew it would be useless to run.

The large animal slowed as it approached.   Newton watched in amazement and no small amount of fear as the lion creature walked right up to him.   The beast didn't look exactly like a lion.   He had a strong, thick jowl that more reminded Newton of Mason.   The animal closed his eyes and shook his mane.   As he did, small whirling funnels of air shot out from around his head and swirled away.   The lion-type creature's eyes twinkled with great familiarity and humor.

Newton spoke hesitantly, "Hello there.   My name is Newton.

Have you seen my dog?   He answers to the name of Mason."

The lion creature threw his head back and let out a roar of laughter.

Newton pushed back against the tree and stood stiffly while the creature's laughter boomed all around him.   He didn't know why the animal was laughing or what was so funny.   Newton tried to shift into crow form so he could fly away, but found that he was unable to do so.   He would have to deal with this creature as a human.   There would be no easy escape.

Newton waited until the laughter was spent and then he tried asking again.   "Have you seen a large dog recently?"

The Lion-ish nodded slowly and then spoke in a deep, rich voice.   "Yes, I most certainly have seen a dog recently."   Newton imagined that if Mason had a voice it would sound much like this. The Lion-ish showed his teeth, a move that startled Newton until he realized that the animal was grinning at him.   He tried to respond in kind, but his own smile was a bit weak.

Instinctively Newton blurted out, "Do I know you?"

The lion-ish answered, "You should!   It's me—Mason."

Newton carefully examined the face of the lion-ish.   "Mason? That's really you?"

The lion-ish confirmed with a nod of his head.

Newton flung himself at the beast, wrapping his arms as far around it as they would go.   A few tears gathered in his eyes as he hugged the great shaggy creature.   Mason blinked and held very still while the human expressed his affection and relief.

255

Newton cupped his hands around Mason's face.   "I'm so glad you're here.   But you are so different.   You look sort of like a lion. But you're not, are you?"

Mason shook his great head.

Newton stepped back to take it all in.   "What are you then?"

Mason replied, "I am a Shadow Dweller."

"Are you a shape shifter?"

Mason smiled, "Only on a very basic level.   I am able to alter my shape to look as I do now or as I did when I appeared to be a dog. The two looks are not so very far apart, as I'm sure you've noticed. It is shifting of a sort, but not in the way that you are able to shift, Newton.   Because I am a Shadow Dweller, I can also appear as a shadow, like the Shadow Dweller who was chasing you.   But, here in Shadow, everyone is who he is and that is that."

Newton suspected that he could not shape shift here for that very reason.   "So, this is more you than the dog that you were in Otherworld?"

Mason responded, "Yes.   But I appeared as a dog in Otherworld because I have heard that dog is man's best friend there. Those who inhabit Otherworld are not accustomed to seeing Shadow Dwellers such as me and I would have attracted unwanted attention." Mason smiled again.

Newton teased, "Well, you did attract the attention of Dr. Obrial when you ate a pair of his best shoes."

Mason hung his head.

Newton asked, "Why did you do that?"

256

Mason's eyes twinkled as he looked at Newton and teased. "Because that's what dogs do, right? More importantly, how else would I have gotten him to take me to his office so that I could meet you?"

Newton was puzzled. "Why would you want to meet me?"

"Victoria sent me as a protector of sorts. As we have just seen, your mission is very dangerous."

Newton glanced around at the shade of the tree under which he was standing. "You said you are a Shadow Dweller. Does that mean you live in a shadow?"

Mason explained, "This *is* Shadow. It is the name of this place. We are here, on the bright side of Shadow."

Newton recalled the events that led up to the fall. "Something was after me and then Mason—well, you. You intervened. You brought me here, right?"

Mason responded, "Yes, and as I said, this is the bright side of Shadow. But Shadow also has a dark side and the creature who was stalking you came from there."

Newton remembered. "I think it hit me somehow."

Mason's eyes looked sympathetic as he confirmed Newton's thoughts. "Yes, you were hit with an ice shard."

Newton's hand involuntarily went to his shoulder as he remembered the burst of pain. "An ice shard?"

Mason nodded. "Yes, the Dark Shadow Dwellers use ice in the same way that we, the bright Dwellers, use wind." Mason noticed Newton's look of confusion and tried to explain further.

"The wind is our friend while the Dark Shadow Dwellers are attuned to ice."

Newton asked, "Do you mean to say that you have command over wind?"

Mason grinned again. "No, not command. Wind helps us when we call."

"Are you suggesting that wind and ice are more than weather conditions?"

Mason's face was a picture of innocence. "Friend, I am not suggesting anything of the sort."

As they spoke a small funnel whirled over to them, hovered a bit and then swirled away again. Newton said, "You know I'm going to ask you about this again later."

Mason shot back, "I figured as much."

Newton spoke with some urgency. "Time is growing short and we need to get back to Otherworld. How far away are we, and how soon can we get back?"

Mason answered, "We are right on top of it, or to be more accurate it is right on top of us."

Newton's eyes narrowed as he tried to understand. "What are you saying?"

Mason explained, "You know that everything casts a shadow, right?" As Newton nodded, Mason added, "The oak tree that you fell from has a nice deep shadow and that's where we are right now, within the shadow of the oak." Mason said this as if he thought everyone should know all about shadows. "It's easiest to travel through them at night, but it can be done during daylight hours when the shadows are at their longest."

Newton remembered times when he had noticed long shadows at the end of day and he tried to imagine Shadow Dwellers coming and going. Mason seemed to read his thoughts.

"We only move about when times require it, such as now when the balance of Pixieland is at stake."

In a quiet tone, Newton asked, "Tell me why the Dark Shadow was after me."

Mason shook his heavy mane. Newton dodged the small funnels of air that scattered as a result of the movement.

"The answer to that is complicated," said Mason. "I realize that you do need to know more about it, but later. As you said, we need to be getting back to Otherworld. I sincerely hope that the vial has not fallen into the wrong hands."

Newton looked worried as he said, "It probably just got lost when I fell. It should be under that tree somewhere...at least I hope that's where it is. Lead the way back and I will follow."

Mason laughed. "I think not. You do not possess the ability to move between Shadow and Otherworld. It was easier to bring you here in your crow form. I simply picked you up in my mouth. Since you cannot shape shift while in Shadow, you will have to ride on my back."

Newton registered surprise at Mason's words, but he could see that Mason was indeed large enough for him to mount. He was actually much larger than a lion, closer in size to a small horse.

As Newton threw a leg over his back, Mason quipped, "Don't get used to this."

Newton smiled uneasily as he settled onto his friend's back.

The Shadow Dweller advised, "Hang on to my mane and don't let go."

Newton wrapped long locks of coarse mane around both hands and gripped tightly. He leaned forward and pressed against the back of Mason's head. The large beast sprinted around the tree and took a giant leap. Displaced air swirled around them more and more rapidly. Newton closed his eyes and held on for dear life.

Chapter 15

The Pixieland friends wondered who would want to hurt Newton and why. They were eager to hear what Ernie had to say about it.

"Those of you who are from Pixieland, you have heard of the Forest of Sighs, right?"

Okikki shuddered involuntarily and the other Pixielanders squirmed uncomfortably.

JJ spoke, "I don't know a thing about that place. What is it?"

Tango weighed in, "All I know is that I'm not ever supposed to go there." Then he murmured, "Like I would... it's dark and spooky in there."

Ernie informed them, "The shadowy creatures live there and it may be that they have taken Newton there too, but I don't understand the loud roar that we all heard that night." Ernie looked puzzled as he spoke. "That's not a sound ever heard from the shadowy ones."

Buddy asked, "Who are these shadowy creatures and what do they have to do with the mermaid egg and Newton?"

"I don't know everything there is to know about the Shadows, but..." The blue mouse was interrupted by a great wind that suddenly came out of nowhere.

Buddy reacted quickly. "This could mean trouble. Everyone group together and let's brace each other. Try to get as close to the tree as possible."

The group of friends clustered together with the smaller members, Cookie, JJ, Okikki and Tango in the middle. The sound of rushing wind was deafening to their ears. But then it stopped just as quickly as it had started. Buddy looked up to see Newton the human doctor seated on the back of a great lion-type beast. Buddy rubbed his eyes and when he opened his eyes he saw Newton the Crow sitting on the back of a very large dog.

Everyone could hardly believe their eyes. The big crow flapped over to the group and landed beside Buddy. They all rushed him, everyone speaking at the same time. There were greetings accompanied by laughter and tears. Ernie stood back a little, but the joy of the moment was contagious and he was smiling as he watched the reunion. The Pixieland friends were delighted with Newton's safe return and everyone had questions. More than one of them cast curious glances at Newton's companion.

The Crow answered as best he could and then raised his voice. "I would like to introduce you all to Mason. He is a Shadow Dweller and was sent by Victoria to help us." As if it would explain everything, Newton added, "He is from the bright side of Shadow."

Everyone welcomed Mason.

JJ hung upside down from the fur on Cookie's chest and peered up at the Mastiff's large mouth. He chirped loudly and then

262

asked, "How many teeth have you got there, big guy?"

When Mason curled back his lip to show a rather fearsome double row of teeth, everyone could hear JJ's sharp intake of breath. The green bird was thrilled. "That's pretty good—just as scary as a shark." JJ spoke with conviction as he declared, "I am sure you will be good help."

Wildflower hid her smile, but Ernie laughed right out loud. Crinkling his eyes, he exclaimed, "JJ, you are so funny!"

"What?" squawked JJ with an indignant tone, but it was difficult to take him seriously as he hung there with his tail straight up and his head pointing down.

Wanting to get everyone back on track, Newton redirected, "We must search for the vial. I was successful in obtaining a sample from Dr. Obrial, but must have lost it when the Dark Shadow came after me." Newton looked for the missing item among the roots of the large oak tree murmuring, "I really hope that it's around here somewhere."

Buddy removed the vial from his pouch and with one raised eyebrow asked, "Is this what you are searching for?"

When Newton realized that Buddy had the precious repair, he looked much relieved. "Where did you find it?"

Wildflower smiled. "Cookie and JJ found it."

JJ made no effort to hide his proud expression. He preened and held his head high as he half-heartedly chirped, "Really, it was nothing."

Newton thanked the green bird and Cookie warmly. "This

saves us so much time.   We should hurry back to Pixieland as quickly as possible."

Ernie stepped forward.   "Forgive me please, but I still need to complete my mission here." He produced a small metal box. Without saying anything further, the blue mouse handed it to Newton who accepted it and popped the latch to open the box.

Newton found a note inside which read "From Her Majesty Sandrea and Her Majesty Summer, reigning Dynasts of the Kingdom of the Sea/Pixieland to Dr. Newton M. Bennett/ The Crow/The Shape Shifter/Otherworld."

"It's from the dynasts," Newton informed the group.   "I will read it to you.   'We wish to inform you that the damage to our precious queen egg has increased since we first called on you for help.   Time is of the essence now as the egg will be entering Phase II within seven high tides or, as time passes in Pixieland, seven passings of the Sun.   We are worried that further damage may occur. Please obtain the cure as quickly as possible and return to us with all due haste that our royal daughter might be saved for the sake of all of Pixieland.   Most sincerely, the Twin Dynasts.'"

Chapter 16

Newton looked up from the note. "Let's go everyone. Mason, while we are on the trail, could you fill everyone in on the Dark Shadows?"

Mason responded, "Yes, and you need to understand a little bit more about what you are up against."

The group of friends started down the path, following Skuba and Morella as the pair of Earth Magicals led the way to the Faerie Glen.

As they travelled along, Mason told the story of the Dark Shadows. "As you know, there are portals between worlds and it takes a special being or a special event to open a portal and make travel possible between worlds."

Wildflower said, "That makes me think of how Cookie appeared in Pixieland and JJ too. No one knows how they came to be there."

Mason explained, "There are rare occasions when a portal opens for a short span of time and if someone or something is nearby, they may be pulled through the door and into another world. That could be what happened to your friends. The world where my story begins is a place of rare beauty, filled with golden oak trees growing tall and proud. Their trunks are wide and their branches reach out in all directions casting great shadows. This world is also home to a race of giants and the oaks consider it to be a great honor when the giants select a favored sapling to be transplanted into the King's garden. The chosen sapling is given a special place and a solution is poured over the roots as soon as it is planted. It is thought that this solution enables life to be sustained within the depth of the tree's shadow. A gardener is assigned to make sure that the young tree has the exact number of hours of light and dark along with vitamins for robust health. One day the giants walked among the trees and selected a fair sapling. The young tree's name was Wiloneomia. She was proud to be selected for the King's garden. The next day the gardener replanted her in a corner of the King's garden and the special solution was poured over her roots. But when the King came to look at the new sapling, he felt that she was a little small and would be seen better on a knoll a short distance away. The gardener lifted the tree and as he was making his way to the spot chosen by the King, a portal suddenly opened and the tree was snatched away. She landed in Pixieland. Although she survived, she was very sad and her beautiful golden leaves turned black. Even so, she grew and matured and from her seeds young trees were born. But they too had dark leaves and sad dispositions."

Tango cried out, "Is it the Forest of Sighs?"

Mason nodded. "That's how the Dark Wood was born."

Okikki said, "I often wondered about that. It's the only thing in Pixieland that is—well, you know the stories."

Wildflower added, "Everyone avoids the Forest of Sighs. They say those who go there never return."

Aline asked, "Have you ever known anyone who went in and didn't come back out?"

No one could recall ever really knowing of anyone who had disappeared.

Mason continued, "Well, in any case, it's not a good idea to go into the Dark Wood.   You have all done well to avoid it until now.   I know all about the place.   You see, that's where I am from." Everyone was quiet as Mason continued.   "Thanks to the special liquid that had been poured onto Wiloneomia's roots, her shadow provided a home for many of us dwellers.   However, she missed her own home and longed to be on that knoll in the King's garden.   The foreign soil did not please Wiloneomia, but most of all she mourned for the loss of her beautiful golden leaves.   Over time, her sadness turned to bitterness and anger.   You see, the oak had completely lost her joy.   She called us all forth and demanded that we do her bidding.   She said that she was queen of the Dark Wood and that we were her subjects.   She was unhappy and so she wanted to make others unhappy too.   It was her plan to disrupt the harmony of Pixieland.   When she demanded that we help her with her plot, fully half of us rebelled and refused.   Those who went along with her found her sorrow contagious and they turned dark just like her leaves.   The rest of us escaped into the deepest shadows of certain trees outside the Dark Wood.   We call it the bright side of Shadow, but those others who live in the dark do the bidding of Wiloneomia.

When Wiloneomia found out that the long awaited queen egg had arrived, she thought it the perfect opportunity for her to achieve her goal of disrupting Pixieland. She dispatched Dark Shadows to steal the egg from the unsuspecting mermaids, but they only succeeded in damaging the egg. It's important that we do what we can for the egg, but we must also find a way to stop the Angry Oak, for she will not rest until her goal is achieved."

Newton asked, "How did you find out about the plan to steal the egg?"

Mason tried to explain. "The Dark Shadows are my brothers. We are connected and they cannot hide their thoughts from me, nor I from them. Although we are enemies in thought and deed, the connection cannot be broken."

Newton asked, "Could they change their minds and choose the good path?"

Mason shook his head. "I don't know."

By the time Mason finished his tale, the group of friends had reached the Faerie Glen. Victoria was already there, standing beside Skuba's tree.

She addressed Mason. "You told them?"

Mason replied, "I did."

Victoria nodded and stretched her arms wide. As the portal appeared, a cooling wind accompanied it. Her white hair whipped around her face and each one of the Pixielanders entered the swirling disk as she called out their names. When only Ernie was left,

Victoria asked, "Shall I send you home to your parents now?"

Ernie blinked, then whispered into Victoria's ear.

She allowed herself a tiny smile, then turned away saying, "As you wish. Farewell, young mouse."

Ernie stepped into the portal.

Part Four:
Joy

Chapter 1

Buddy counted heads when everyone had landed in Pixieland. "Where's Ernie?" the elf asked Victoria.

The Portal Keeper smiled. "He made it through the portal just fine. I simply diverted him at his request."

Satisfied that the mouse was safe, Buddy turned his attention to Newton. "I want to go with you. I will meet you at the inlet as soon as the elixir is ready."

Newton nodded. He was not surprised. The crow knew that his best friend wouldn't want him to go alone.

In a firm voice Mason said, "I will be joining you too. I need to go along with you in case there is more trouble with my dark brothers." Lion-ish looked at Buddy quizzically. "I hope there will be enough elixir for me."

"There should be plenty," Buddy assured him. "I will go put it together and be back as soon as I can." Then the elf loped down the path toward his house.

Victoria spoke to the others. "You may all be needed before this is over, but for now it's fine to return to your homes and, as best you can, to your usual routines. Please take these orbs and keep them with you. They have straps so that you can wear them. If you are needed the orbs will glow at which time you should return quickly and meet me here."

Victoria solemnly passed the orbs around. She even gave one to Tango. He carefully placed it around his neck. His little heart swelled with pride having been chosen to help protect all of Pixieland. Okikki put an arm around him and smiled.

When Victoria handed an orb to JJ, he said with a dramatic gesture and a snap of his beak, "I will do what I can to help. We may all be marching down a very gloomy road indeed, but I will be there standing side by side with you, my friends, when the Dark Shadows come for us."

Wildflower thought that for once there might be some truth in the small bird's words of doom.

When she was alone with Newton and Mason, the Guardian of Portals placed a hand on the crow's shoulder and said, "You are a healer. I have confidence that you will be able to help the new queen. I will meet you on the outskirts of the Dark Wood after you have taken care of her egg."

Newton wished that he felt more confident. He said, "I will meet you there as soon as I can." While Buddy was busy making mermaid elixir in his cozy kitchen, Newton the Crow waded out into the inlet and shifted into Newton the Merman.

Mason stood nearby on the shore. While he shook his head, a transformation occurred. Beginning with his nose and ending at the tip of his tail, he grew larger and more cat-like. Small funnels of wind flew from his mane and disappeared into thin air. Mason stretched and yawned. Then he paced up and down along the shore keeping an eye on every shadow around them. Meanwhile, Newton practiced swimming, circling the inlet and taking in the sights and sounds of his new underwater world.

Buddy looked with satisfaction at the green liquid in the clear bottles. He placed them both securely in his pack and hurried down the path to the inlet. Buddy thought to himself that Pixieland seemed unnaturally quiet. When he arrived at his destination, the elf noticed a merman waving from the water. It was Newton and clearly the doctor was ready to get moving. Buddy waved back and called to Mason. Together they waded into the water.

Buddy warned, "Now remember, we only have twenty-four hours before the elixir will wear off." He pulled the bottles from his pack and he and Mason drank until the liquid was all gone.

Buddy made an interesting merman. His face looked much the same—handsome, with dark hair and eyes and ears that remained distinctively elf-like. The scales along his tail were olive green with electric blue tips that glistened. The fan of his tail was a rich plum color bordered by a splash of that same olive green. His fingers remained long and tapered.

Newton's face looked strong and wise. His hair was salt and pepper and his eyes were an intense bright blue. He had the sensitive hands of a surgeon (which indeed he was), but his Mer hands were slightly webbed—great for swimming, but not so good for healing. He studied them with concern while waiting for Mason to transform and decided that he would worry about how to use them effectively later.

Surprisingly, the elixir seemed to have no effect at all on Mason. However, he noticed that his air funnels were whirling madly, displacing the water that tried to hug his legs. The Shadow Dweller discovered that the funnels created a pocket of air around him which made it possible to breathe underwater.

When Buddy realized that Mason was not turning into a merman, he apologized. "I'm sorry, Mason. I don't know what could be wrong."

The great Lion-ish mused, "I can't say why the elixir didn't work for me, but my air funnels are working just fine. If the dark ones can move around below the water's surface, then I can too." Mason changed to his shadow form and dove under the water. He moved along rapidly, breathing easily as his ever present funnel clouds faithfully spun the water away from him.

Newton and Buddy were astounded to see that in this form Mason emitted a bright light which illuminated the water around him. He remembered Mason explaining that there were dark and light shadows, but he hadn't realized that his friend meant it so literally. Newton couldn't help but wonder what else he didn't know about Mason.

The Shape Shifter pulled his thoughts back to the task at hand and explained the first leg of their mission. "We are to swim straight out into the ocean proper where one of the Mer people will be watching for us and will escort us to the city."

Buddy and Newton swam side by side while Mason darted about freely always keeping Newton within sight. It was not Buddy's first time under the water, but it was his first time to be a merman. When he had first begun to swim, he moved powerfully and so rapidly that his stomach churned as if he had taken a steep hill too quickly. Buddy needed to learn how to control his movements since this streamlined body was built for speed. Both he and Newton soon adjusted and by the time the inlet had shrunk to just a speck in the distance they were swimming as if they had been mermen all of their lives.

The trio dipped and gradually descended toward the ocean floor. They leveled off at the edge of light where there were fewer fish. The water felt heavier, but their new bodies were made for this and they handled the changes in light and water pressure with ease.

Mason detected something in the distance moving toward them.

Chapter 2

Buddy and Newton strained to see what was headed their way while Mason, whose instincts told him that they were in danger, edged closer to Newton.   The air that normally swirled around Mason began to whirl faster and faster.   The force of the displaced water pushed Newton and Buddy back and away.   Mason's funnel clouds changed size and color and the formerly gentle swirls became angry tornadoes.   Where there had been many tiny funnels, there were now three large towers of circling wind that swirled around Mason with enormous strength and speed.

Buddy and Newton were locked away from Lion-ish by the gale force of the winds.   Mason hovered in the center where he shone like the sun and the dark winds continued to whirl in contrast to the bright shadow light.   Newton and Buddy had no idea what was going on.   Then they saw them—the Dark Shadows.   Buddy counted two and they were easily as large as Mason.   One of them positioned itself to confront Mason while the other skirted around the windy barrier in an attempt to reach Newton and Buddy.

The mermen drew as close to Mason as the wind would allow which unfortunately was not very close.   One enemy closed in on Newton hurling daggers of ice toward him.   The temperature dropped dramatically making it difficult for Newton and Buddy to swim in the suddenly slushy water. The mermen knew that they were in trouble and as the ocean around them began to freeze, Newton called to Mason for help. In response, Mason sent one of his large funnels which enveloped Newton and Buddy in a gentle cushion of air effectively protecting them from the harsh elements.

While Mason was distracted, the other combatant made his move, sending a wall of ice crashing toward Mason. Mason's two remaining funnels slammed into the ice breaking it apart and sending it flying in all directions.

The Dark Shadow who had attacked Newton and Buddy shifted gears when he realized that the two mermen were being protected. He redirected his attention to maneuver into a position behind Mason.

Newton watched the battle that raged between Mason and his foes. Wind and ice slammed together to create the storm of all storms. The area for several miles around them churned and writhed as the battle was waged. Seeing that his friend was outnumbered, Newton turned to Buddy and handed him the egg repair saying, "Keep this safe. When I shift, take hold of the topmost fin and hang on."

As Newton changed forms, a firm resolve settled over him. He was simply NOT going to allow anything to happen to Buddy and Mason. Nor was he going to permit the Dark Shadows to take the egg repair that was needed to help the baby mermaid queen. His new tail cut a large swath in the water and his enormous head and mouth would have struck fear into the boldest of the seafaring.

Momentarily stunned at Newton's transformation, Buddy scrambled onto the back of the giant megaladon, grabbing the fin and hanging on with his hands and his knees. The enormous shark circled around to face the enemy. Mason had been standing firm, but now the scales were tipping sharply in favor of the Pixielanders. Newton the Megaladon opened his huge mouth threatening the attackers with a row of sharp teeth, each one measuring twelve inches in length.

Newton's size was intimidating; he was twice as big as a bus. Wiloneomia's minions took one look into that gaping maw, turned tail and ran, taking their cold and ice with them. The angry winds that were whirling around Mason calmed immediately. Newton did not give chase although he could have quickly overtaken them and swallowed them whole. But Newton was a healer, not a warrior. Even though his appearance was frightening, he lived by the oath he had taken as a doctor to do no harm. As he watched the Dark Shadows flee, Newton wondered what they might try next. For now he had easily saved the day and with no harm done.

Buddy was quite excited about Newton's new look. "Good job, Newton. You look, well, really scary. What are you anyway?"

When Newton spoke his voice sounded loud and echoing. "I am a creature from Otherworld. I don't know if you have them here or not, but it is known as a megaladon. It's like a giant shark and the species is an ancient one, thought to have existed since prehistoric times."

Buddy swam around the giant shark.   He wasn't sure about prehistoric times, but he thought that Newton looked incredibly dangerous.   "Wait, Newton, I don't see your ring.   Where is it?"

"Come around to the front of me."

Buddy swam until he was even with Newton's nose.   The elf said, "Please don't accidentally swallow me."   He was very glad that this was just Newton and not a real shark.

Newton gazed cross-eyed down his nose at Buddy.   Keeping his teeth clamped together, Newton lifted his lips.   Staring at the fence-like row of long, sharp teeth Buddy saw the ring looped tightly around one of them.   The warm gold band stood out against the white tooth and the pearl gleamed softly from the nest that framed it.

It looked like such a tight fit that Buddy asked, "Is it stuck?"

Newton assured him that it wasn't.

Relieved, Buddy dropped the subject.   He wanted to know more about the wind and ice battle that had taken place so he asked, "Mason, I was wondering, how is it that the wind does your bidding?"

Mason laughed and the sound was contagious.   Mason replied. "The wind merely assists me.   The wind is my friend."

Buddy asked, "Do you talk to the wind?"

Mason replied, "Not in the same way that I am talking to you, but there is communication.   It's difficult to explain.   I can only tell you that from my birth, I have seen wind and it sees me.   Most don't see wind unless it takes certain forms and the wind doesn't see most of you either.   I have always been able to see the gentlest of breezes or the tiniest whisper of air just as clearly as you see the largest of funnel clouds."

Buddy quizzed. "Does the wind have eyes?"

Mason shook his head. "No, my friend, but you must remember that not everything is seen only with the eyes."

Buddy didn't understand, so he tried another question. "How is it that the Dark Shadows are able to use ice?"

Mason answered, "When they made the decision to follow the oak and turned dark, their hearts became cold and an affinity to ice was formed. For them it was a sort of replacement for the wind they had known before. You see, the wind turned away from the dark ones because when their hearts lost their light, the wind could no longer see them. They call upon ice whose chill relates to their own coldness while those of us who escaped the oak call upon wind."

Buddy scratched his head and asked one more question. "Are you saying that wind is good and ice is bad?"

Mason looked at Buddy with disbelief. "Certainly not!"

Buddy needed some time to ponder everything. He was pleased that the Shadow Dweller didn't seem to mind answering his questions. When this was over Buddy hoped that he would have the opportunity to spend some more time with him, getting to know him better and learning more about him. The idea of wind as a friend was fascinating to the elf.

Mason's rich voice sounded a warning. "Someone is approaching."

Chapter 3

Newton and Buddy scanned the murky water ahead, but neither could see anything.   There was not much marine life at this depth and the few fish seen were quite odd looking because they were especially equipped to survive so far below the ocean's surface. The water that stretched out before the travelers looked like a blank canvas.

Newton asked, "Can you tell if it's the Mer people?"

There were a few moments of tense silence as the trio waited to see what or who was approaching them.   They relaxed when Mason said, "It's the mermaids."

Newton was relieved that he had steered his group in the right direction.   They were soon surrounded by some of the most beautiful creatures they had ever seen.   Newton observed that there was much diversity in the group—different skin tones, hair and eye color.   But all of their scales were varying shades of green with splashes of other colors as if thrown in for good measure.

One of the mermaids spoke with a clear and bright voice. "Which one of you is the doctor?"

Newton identified himself.

The mermaid said to him, "Thank you for coming.   Just follow us.   We'll be taking the Queens' private entrance instead of entering through the main gate."

Newton said, "We hope to be able to help."

The mermaid added,   "I am forgetting my manners.   My name is Chantilee and I am Lead Ranger of the Guard."

Newton responded, "Pleased to meet you."   He then introduced his friends.

The three Pixielanders followed as the mermaids swam gracefully through the murky water, dipping sharply before leveling out again.

A mermaid named Deranga told them a little bit about what to expect.   "When we get closer, Chantilee will call out to the City Guards who will inform the Dynasts of our arrival.   We'll enter through the shaft which will take us to the Queen's private quarters. Then you will be escorted to the Incubation Chamber where the injured egg rests.   We need to hurry.   Soon the egg will enter Phase II."   Deranga pushed her long red hair out of her eyes.   The lovely tresses trailed like a banner behind her as she swam.   "We're almost there.   Chantilee will announce our arrival very soon.   All of our citizens are on high alert since the attack.   These are troubling times."

Newton thought that the mermaids should know about the recent encounter so he said, "I'm concerned as well.   We were attacked along the way and should be watching closely in case the Dark Shadows return."

Alarmed, Deranga quickly passed the information to Chantilee and the others.   Chantilee dropped back to swim alongside Newton. "How many of them accosted you?"

Several of the mermaids turned their heads in Mason's direction when he replied, "There were two."

Chantilee quizzed, "How did you defeat them?"

Newton looked at Mason for a long moment and then responded, "Mason stood against them."

Chantilee glanced at the Shadow Dweller.   "That's what I would have expected, but if he stood alone, then he was outnumbered."

Newton sighed then looked into Chantilee's violet eyes.   He knew that the time for secrets was over.   "I am the Shape Shifter."

As Lead Ranger of the Guard, Chantilee was strong and proud. Her face never revealed a thing, but the expression in her eyes flashed a mixture of wonder and relief as she looked at this Shape Shifter that she'd heard so much about.   Without another word to Newton, she announced to the group that it was time to notify the City Guard.   Chantilee called out in the fluid language of the Mer people, the piercing sound carrying far into the distance. Immediately there was an answering cry, then the ranger led the group in a sharp descent.

Newton could see something that looked like a very long wall in the distance, but the water wasn't clear and he couldn't quite make it out.   As he drew closer, the doctor could see what he supposed was the shaft looming just ahead.   A few more strokes and Chantilee led the group down the tunnel into one of the richest and most palatial rooms that the trio had ever seen.

It was brightly lit and the floor was covered with white sand. There were low tables here and there which were made of shiny tiles and anchored into the ground. The walls were covered with gold and inlaid jewels of various types and colors. The sandy floors were peppered with crushed gemstones. The whole effect was lavish and colorful. The Queens were waiting at the far end of the room.

Chantilee stood aside and gestured toward Newton, Buddy and Mason. "Lady Sandrea and Lady Summer, I am pleased to introduce you to our guests, Mason the Bright Shadow Dweller, Buddy the Forest Elf, and Dr. Newton Bennett the Shape Shifter."

After greetings, Sandrea said, "Dr. Bennett, the damage to our daughter's egg has increased over time."

Newton replied, "May I see the egg now? And, please, just call me Newton."

The three friends fell in line behind the dynasts as they moved down a long corridor and then into the room that housed the eggs. Lady Sandrea took them directly to the queen egg. It was larger than the others and distinguished by its rich blue color.

"Buddy, I need the repair please," Newton said.

Buddy felt inside his pack for the egg repair and handed it to Newton.

As he reached for it, Newton glanced at his own two hands. The skin was cool and the fingers slightly webbed. He knew that this wouldn't do so he closed his eyes and pictured his human hands. Could he just shift or alter one part of his body? The doctor pictured his strong capable, warm human hands in his mind's eye. The small group in the room watched in amazement as the hands of a merman shifted form and became the hands of a surgeon. Newton smiled at this success and accepted the vial from Buddy. The doctor turned to the Dynasts. "The movement of the water is going to be a problem. I need to be able to hold myself still while I work."

The ladies signaled and one of the guards swam into the room with a pole which she secured in a nearby stand. Lady Summer instructed, "Newton, wrap your tail around the pole. It will anchor you."

Newton stabilized himself and looked down at the egg. He could see the deep scratch that extended from the small end to a point about half way down the side.

"Buddy, please stand at the other end of the egg and very gently hold it as steady as possible."

There was silence in the room as the doctor began to work on the egg. Newton removed the stopper from the vial and exposed a tiny brush that was attached on the inside. He started at the top of the scratch and with a steady hand applied the thick repair onto the egg. He left wide margins on all sides of the damaged area and with even strokes he continuously applied the fluid until he was satisfied. Newton watched the egg carefully until he saw the binding effect of the liquid. Then he turned to the anxious dynasts and announced, "I have done everything that I can do. When will the egg enter Phase II?"

Summer said, "The sea dragon babies will come to warm the

water and the sands in this room which will trigger the egg to enter the second phase.   They should be here soon; we sent for them as soon as the guard announced your arrival."

Buddy asked, "Why is it the babies who come to warm the room?"

Summer smiled, "Because the adult dragons are too big to fit inside the chambers."

Newton carefully examined the egg again.   As far as he could tell, binding had taken place.   "This looks good.   How soon will you be able to tell if we have succeeded?"

Sandrea's voice shook as she replied.   "We will know shortly because if you have not saved her, she will not successfully enter Phase II."

Mason sat beside Newton and spoke softly.   "There is something that I haven't told you.   I didn't want to worry you before you helped the baby queen, but you need to know that the Dark Shadows were following at a distance.   They stayed just outside the mermaid radar."

Newton was sorry to hear this news, but he wasn't surprised. He didn't think that the Angry Oak would have given up so easily.

The Dynasts heard what was said and Summer informed them, "They will not get past the Guard.   When they came before, we weren't on alert."   She sounded sad as she continued, "Nothing like this has ever happened and we were not expecting any trouble.   But I assure you, we will never be caught unprepared again."

Sandrea nodded in agreement.   The Dynasts listened

carefully as Mason explained who the shadowy figures were and why they were trying to interfere with the egg.

Sandrea asked, "But why would they want to steal the egg?"

Newton mused, "My guess is that they were instructed to bring the baby queen back to Wiloneomia. If they had succeeded, then her fate would have rested in the hands of the Angry Oak."

Newton swam over to check on the egg. The repair had soaked in and the surface of the egg where the liquid had been applied was no longer shiny. The scratch looked properly sealed, but only time would tell for sure.

Chapter 4

As the group were talking they heard sounds in the distance. The Dynasts explained that the noise heralded the arrival of the baby sea dragons. Newton, Buddy and Mason listened to the echoing cries of the dragons as they called to each other. The calls grew louder and then the first of the babies burst into the room. They were quite boisterous and larger than Newton expected. The sea dragons sported rounded heads and big eyes which reminded Newton of baby seals. Their lips curved upward, like a permanent smile, and they were equipped with thick clawed flippers front and back. Dark red scales covered their wide black bodies and extended down the length of their long flat tails. Newton was reminded of a cross between a beaver, a seal and a dragon.

The babies flattened out across the floor of the room head to tail and began to hum. The sound was soft and almost hypnotic. Buddy blinked and rubbed his hands together. Mason stood quietly next to Newton and the three of them watched as the young bodies emitted a soft light. The light, which shone from underneath the dragons' bodies and flippers, cast an orange glow on the sandy floor. Gradually the sand and the water in the room warmed.

When the babies had completed their task they exited the

room, going as quickly as they had come. When most had departed, a very tiny baby swam over to the Dynasts and nudged both of them until they gave him a pat on the head and a soft word. Wiggling happily, he hurried out of the room calling to the others as he went.

Newton and Buddy exchanged glances. Buddy wondered about these baby sea dragons and their relationship with the Mer people.

Newton checked to see how the egg was faring. He asked the Dynasts, "How will we know if she enters Phase II?"

Summer answered, "The shell will disappear and the surface of the egg will become soft and pliable. If you touch the egg it should leave a slight impression. Touch carefully and it will do no damage. The imprint that you leave should disappear shortly."

Newton watched as the egg's surface started to change. When it seemed to be finished, the doctor re-wrapped his tail around the pole and gently touched the egg with his finger.

Summer and Sandrea were afraid to look, but look they must. They peeked over Newton's shoulder as he applied gentle pressure to the egg. Buddy didn't realize that he was holding his breath until he heard Newton say, "This is good news indeed!"

The mermaids sighed in relief and first hugged each other and then Newton. The impression of Newton's finger on the egg had completely disappeared before the Dynasts had finished hugging Buddy and Mason. Newton smiled broadly at no one in particular. The sense of happiness and relief was apparent as everyone congratulated the mermaids and thumped each other on the back.

Lady Sandrea announced, "Newton, we want to thank all three of you properly in due time, but right now the egg must be placed in the cart for travel to the Guardian."

As several mermaids entered the room and made preparations, Newton looked thoughtful. "I know that you feel confident that you could fend off an attack, but I should warn you that they use ice in battle."

Summer recalled, "It's true that the room was cold and icy when the shadow broke in. It was a good thing that all of the eggs were in Phase I at the time."

Newton looked at the lovely mermaid. "You see, that brings me to my question. What effect would chilled water and ice have on the egg should your people sustain an attack? Perhaps they can hold their own with the attackers, but what weapons will they bring to bear on the icy chill of the water around them?"

Summer was alarmed. "It would be dangerous for the egg to get chilled now that it is in Phase II."

Mason warned, "It's not just a matter of chilled water. The shadows will attack you with walls of ice. If the ice doesn't crush the egg, the water displaced by the ice might easily throw the egg from the cart. It's far too risky to send that baby out into the ocean right now."

There was a look of panic in Sandrea's eyes and she took hold of her sister's hand. "We have no choice. The baby must go. It is too important. She cannot rule as our queen if she doesn't go to meet the Guardian."

Mason informed the group. "My brothers who do the bidding of Wiloneomia know that the egg has been repaired and they wait for its transport. They will attempt to intercept it. "

Lady Summer asked, "How do they know that the repair is a success? We have only just realized it ourselves." The mermaid looked around as if she thought some of the Dark Shadows might be in the room with them.

Mason explained, "They are reading my thoughts. What I know, they know. It works both ways. I also know what they know."

Sandrea took the hint. "Chantilee, please show our friend Mason around. Perhaps a turn around the Great City would be nice."

Mason accompanied the ranger out of the room. When it was certain that he was not within earshot, Sandrea whispered to Newton and Buddy. "The less he knows the better."

Buddy said, "I have an idea that might work. The Queens' cart should be sent out in the traditional manner and with much pomp and circumstance. However, it will only be carrying a replica of the royal egg. After they are well away and we are certain that the shadows have followed them, Newton and I will escort the real egg to safety. One of the mermaids could show us the way to the estuary. Newton, you need to ask Mason to accompany the formal procession. He should not be told that the egg he accompanies is the wrong egg until he has reached the alternate location. Then, when we are finished escorting the real queen to the estuary, we can meet Mason in that little inlet where we first started out."

Newton asked, "What reason will we give for not going with the formal procession?"

Buddy answered, "My elixir does not last forever and I will soon need land and air. We can tell Mason that you don't want me to make the long trip back alone."

Newton considered Buddy's plan. "That sounds good, but I feel bad about lying to Mason."

Buddy agreed. "I do too, but he has warned us and we had better listen."

Newton knew that Mason wouldn't be happy about the separation. Besides, Lion-ish was very bright and wouldn't be fooled easily. When he voiced these fears, Buddy responded, "I think Mason wishes to be fooled. He doesn't want to reveal important information and thereby assist the Dark Shadows in their wicked plan."

Newton nodded. "True...true."

Summer spoke, "Buddy, your idea is a good one. However, we cannot mislead our sister mermaids and we will waste no time trying. They will keep the secret and while they and Mason combat our foes, you will have a very good chance at safe passage to the estuary where Timna waits."

Since no one could think of a better idea, they all agreed and Buddy's plan was set in motion. The mermaids constructed a duplicate egg with egg shells and dyes. It didn't exactly look real, but once wrapped and packed into the cart, everyone felt that it would do.   Then they prepared the true egg and carefully moved it into the dynasts' sleeping chamber.

When Chantilee and Mason returned, the Dynasts announced that the egg had been readied for travel.   With everyone in place, the group moved slowly out of the royal chambers and down the long halls that led to the Great City.

Newton spoke with Mason.   "Friend, will you accompany the egg and see to its safety?   Buddy's elixir will soon wear off and he will have to return to land.   I should go along with him for protection."

Mason hesitated.   Victoria had sent him to protect Newton from the Dark Shadows.   Everything in him wanted to stay by Newton's side, but then he thought, *The shadows are bound to be more interested in the egg than in Newton and Buddy.   Surely they will follow me.   It will be safer for Newton and Buddy if they return to Pixieland.* So Mason agreed.

After Newton explained where they should meet when the escort was complete, the two of them said their goodbyes.   Without even looking back, Mason churned his way to the center alongside the cart where he could watch both front and rear as the group began the procession through the city.

Newton and Buddy trailed behind.   A throng of Mer people lined the way.   They were cheering the egg, holding aloft everything from poles to giant seashells and some lifted Mer children over their heads as they added their blessings and well wishes to both the queen egg and the couriers.

The cart moved slowly down the streets and finally made its way outside the city gates. Sandrea and Summer were positioned one on either side of the gate and were the last ones to wave as the cart moved away from the city and toward its destination.

The mermaids in the front of the procession swam with great purpose. Those who carried the cart that held the egg did so carefully and with practiced skill. Mason was pleased to see that their foes stayed a good distance behind. As time went on, it became clear that there would not be an immediate confrontation. However, Mason sensed that their plan was to attack before the mermaids ever made it to Timna. They greatly feared the Guardian who they believed was waiting at the end of this journey. Mason didn't know that the egg he escorted was not the real baby and that was good. The dark ones who were following him would certainly have read the truth in his thoughts.

Eventually Mason and the mermaids reached a position just outside of a small inlet that led to a fresh water river. They swam to the bottom and sat the cart and egg on the sandy floor. Chantilee turned to him with something like an apologetic smile. That was the moment when Mason realized that the egg he had travelled with was not the baby queen.

"Deranga and your friends escorted the true queen egg," Chantilee confirmed. "Buddy and Newton should be waiting for you."

Mason was surrounded by a lively swirl of enchanting mermaids as each one said their goodbyes. One by one they slipped away into the deep.   Chantilee turned and gracefully waved one last time before joining her sisters for the long trip home.

Mason hoped the real queen egg was indeed safe.   He swam over to take a look in the cart at the egg made up of shell pieces glued together.   Sensing the anger of the Dark Shadows at being fooled, Mason turned and waited for them to arrive.   He didn't know how long he could hold them back, but felt that the least he could do for Newton and Buddy was to buy them a little bit more time.   As his brothers swiftly approached Mason's tornadoes grew and swelled around him.

Back in the Royal Chamber, several mermaids waited with the true queen egg.

Sandrea introduced the rangers, then she said, "Newton and Buddy, Deranga will escort you to the estuary."

Deranga was a strikingly beautiful mermaid.   Her hair was full and green.   Long bangs draped her face in jagged uneven lengths, her unusual golden eyes peeking through.   The mermaid's face was composed and serene.   She never smiled, but she was pleasant and helpful.

This time the egg was placed in a bag lined with soft grasses. More packing and grasses were placed on top and around the egg. Deranga took the lead position with Buddy and Newton behind her and the egg between them.   The trio moved up the old shaft allowing them to avoid the city and into the inky depths of the ocean toward the estuary where Timna was waiting.

Deranga moved at a staggering speed. Newton was glad that even with the egg, which was heavier than he imagined, both he and Buddy were able to keep up. Thankfully the egg was not nearly as fragile as it had been in Phase I.

At the speed they were travelling, they were making good progress and luckily there was no sign of the enemy. The Shape Shifter felt confident that the shadows had followed Mason and the others. Hopefully there wouldn't be a confrontation and the shadows would just follow the other group until they abandoned the cart and egg. With any luck at all, by the time the ruse was discovered the real baby queen would be safe with her guardian. This part of the journey wasn't over yet, but Newton had already begun to realize that the next step would be an even more difficult one. How would they finally deal with the Angry Oak? What was going to happen and how would it all end? Newton didn't have a clue, but he hoped with all of his heart for a happy ending.

Chapter 5

Victoria stood several yards away from the edge of the Forest of Sighs, Morella and Skuba right beside her. The petite white-haired lady spoke quietly to the two earth magicals. "Thank you for coming when I summoned. I know that your world needs you and I hope that you won't have to be away too long. I called you because the bond of friendship that you've formed with Newton, Buddy and the others who visited your world is strong. Things are worse than I feared and your presence here is much appreciated. Pixieland is in grave danger." Victoria paused, sadness evident on her face. "Right here, right now, we must do whatever is necessary to make things right."

Skuba responded loyally, "I am ready to do whatever I can to assist, Victoria. Just tell me what you would like for me to do." The elf stood proudly, awaiting further instructions.

Morella agreed. "I want to help too."

Victoria was deeply touched by their courage and loyalty. She knew that this was exactly the kind of bravery that was needed in order to emerge victorious.

In ones and twos the Pixielanders arrived. Wildflower flew in with JJ and Cookie. Okikki and Tango joined the crowd. Rosie and many others added to the numbers. They greeted one another with handshakes, hugs and soft words. As time wore on, the area outside of the Dark Wood began to fill. Barad the Elf King flew in on dragonback. He was accompanied by the most courageous elves in all of Pixieland. Forest faeries and night faeries flew in. There were dwarves, sprites and many talking animals of different species. Okikki greeted her cousins and their squirrel friends. Balor and Skittles found Cookie and JJ. Rosie hugged the large bear who had nearly eaten Buddy some time ago. Ever since Rosie had shown him that delicious honey, he considered her a friend. When she had asked for his help, he responded. Victoria watched as the courageous citizens of Pixieland assembled.

Out in the ocean, Deranga, Buddy and Newton began a steep upward swim. Strange-looking fish with gills pumping stared as the mermaid and the two mermen swam swiftly past with their precious cargo. Newton wished the circumstances were different. He found this vast underwater world fascinating and he would have liked to investigate it further. As the group moved into the upper reaches of the ocean, several different schools of fish darted to and fro. A herd of giant sea horses made a beeline for them. Buddy and Newton watched in fascination as the colorful creatures bobbed alongside for a moment before jetting away. Newton looked over his shoulder. No sign of the enemy. He thought to himself, *So far, so good.*

Then Newton spied what at first appeared to be a very large

fish off to his right. As if by magic, the small group was suddenly surrounded by friendly dolphins. Their soft beeps sounded like underwater music. Buddy and Newton listened as Deranga spoke to the newly arrived guests in a perfect imitation of both their high-pitched squeals and their melodious softer tones.

After a brief conversation, Deranga explained, "Timna has sent them. They will escort us the rest of the way to the estuary."

Newton thought that their mission was a well-kept secret so he asked, "How does Timna know that we are on the way?"

Deranga said, "The young queen is strong. Already she calls to the Guardian from within the egg."

Newton and Buddy were both glad to hear that the young queen was doing well. Newton glanced down at the bundled egg. He was puzzled about what Deranga had told him, for he had not heard any type of noise coming from within.

"The dolphins are saying that Timna has seen no sign of trouble in the estuary, but that doesn't surprise me. Our enemies should think long and hard before bringing trouble to her waters. Timna's power is legendary."

Newton thought about how the baby sea dragons had warmed the mermaids' incubation chamber. He wondered if the adult sea dragons warmed water in much the same way. Suddenly Newton heard a scream from one of the dolphins. When he turned to look, some icy shards narrowly missed him. A large wall of ice rushed toward them, pushed by several sinister and shadowy shapes. The attack was swift and had taken them by surprise. Buddy enlisted Deranga to help him carry the queen egg so that Newton's hands would be free.   The two egg bearers positioned their precious cargo between them.

Many of the dolphins swam around in confusion.   Their distress cries were deafening.   Deranga, speaking with a tone of authority, called out to one of them.   It swam over and stayed by their sides, shielding the egg with its body as the egg bearers tried to outrun the Dark Shadows.   Newton could only see a narrow way of escape for Buddy and Deranga.   The enemy surrounded them, adopting a clever pincer maneuver to close ranks and trap them. Newton anticipated what they were attempting and he was determined to stop them.   As the wall of ice drew closer, the water temperature dropped.   Newton knew that he would have to work fast because an extreme chill could end the life in the egg.   Deranga and Buddy swam in a zigzag pattern attempting to avoid being hit by the ice shards that whizzed past.   The chill of the water slowed Buddy's movement and he just hoped that Newton could buy the precious time needed for them to be able to escape.

Newton's primary concern was heating the water as quickly as possible.   In Newton's defense, he had never seen an adult sea dragon and part of the trick to a proper shift is familiarization with and being able to visualize what shape one is taking.   Newton's only experience with sea dragons had been the babies in the incubation chamber.   So Newton shifted into one very large baby sea dragon and started to warm the water.   Because of his great size, he was able to melt the ice so quickly that by the time the wall of ice reached him, it was nothing more than slush.

Buddy didn't have time to see what Newton was doing. He was concentrating on escaping with Deranga and the queen egg. He felt the change in water temperature almost immediately though and was greatly relieved. The wall of ice and even the icy shards melted and disappeared before their very eyes.

The shadows were intimidated by Newton. They had never seen such a creature and didn't know what it could or couldn't do. What they did know was that this giant beast had rendered their main weapon utterly useless. There was also some confusion about whether or not these Mer people even had the real baby queen. While the shadows hesitated, Buddy and Deranga made their way through the only route of escape and swam rapidly toward the estuary and safety. Newton decided to press his advantage. He adopted his best angry expression and swam straight toward the enemies. Without their ice, they backed down quickly and ran. He watched their retreat and when the last one churned out of sight, Newton the Giant Baby Sea Dragon turned and swam after his friends.

Timna heard a distress cry from the unborn baby queen. The sea dragon rose to her full height, bellowed loudly and rushed to aid the egg. An enraged Timna was one adversary that the shadows should not wish to meet. In a burst of speed, the large dragon covered the length of the estuary and entered the ocean. As she scanned the water ahead, her eyes performed telescopically, bringing everything from a distance into close-up view. She caught sight of a mermaid and a merman swimming toward her. Timna closely observed what they were carrying, identifying the bundle they held as the mermaid queen egg. But where were the dolphins she had sent? Only one accompanied them.

Timna closed the distance between them bellowing, "What has happened? "

After Deranga explained, Timna spoke abruptly, "Let's get the egg to safety."

The sea dragon swam straight to an area where a great deal of sand had been gathered into a pile. With Buddy's help, Deranga carefully unpacked the queen egg. In the brighter waters of the estuary, the sky blue color stood out boldly against the sand and the soft green sea. Timna gently took the egg from them and placed it in the center of the pile of sand. Her front flippers surrounded the shell and she emitted some soft bleats.

Timna told them, "She is alive, but she is silent. The temperature of the egg is slightly low. She will warm up soon and when she does, perhaps then she will speak." Timna commended Deranga and Buddy. "You have done well. You have escorted the young queen to safety and now you should return to the Great City.

Deranga hesitated. "I think you should know that when we were attacked by the shadows, the water became very cold. The Shape Shifter was with us and he warmed the water, but the egg had already been exposed."

Timna looked grave. "These are the shadows from the Dark

Wood, I presume.   Where are they now?"

Buddy answered, "We think that Newton, the Shape Shifter, frightened them away, but we don't know exactly what happened because we hurried to escape with the egg."   Buddy explained to Timna about Mason and the other group of mermaids transporting an empty egg in their ruse to distract and confuse their enemies.

Timna listened patiently and then responded, "I've heard stories over the years about travelers entering the Dark Wood and never returning.   But it's only been recently that the sinister ones have come out of the Forest of Sighs in what is apparently an attempt to taint our beautiful world.   Even if they pour out of those dismal trees by the thousands, the young queen is safe from further harm while she is here with me.   If they dare to enter my estuary, I will defeat them."

As Timna said this, she glowed softly.   Buddy and Deranga could feel the heat radiating off of her and moved a short distance away.   There was a faint beeping of dolphins in the distance.

"Newton must be with them," Buddy exclaimed as he swam toward the happy sound.   The dolphins stopped short at the entrance to the estuary, but a lone figure continued to swim toward Buddy.

Timna was right behind the elf/merman and her face registered stunned surprise.   "Well, what have we here?"

Newton, who was still in the form of a giant baby sea dragon, entered the estuary.

Timna laughed out loud as she stared openly at him.   "I have cared for difficult young in my day, but YOU would surely be a handful!"

"You must be Timna," Newton answered. "So THAT is what an adult sea dragon looks like! Well, at least this worked! I had to heat the water somehow."

Timna laughed a sound that filled the water around them with a special kind of music. "How very clever, Shape Shifter." Then she sobered. "Victoria waits for you outside the Forest of Sighs. It's time and past time to put an end to this threat once and for all." Timna looked at Buddy and Newton. "Thank you for all that you have done and good fortune to you both as you face the Angry Oak and her minions."

As the group departed, Buddy looked back to see Timna lightly covering the egg with warming sands. The elf paused to take a final look at the estuary. Underwater grasses gently waved. Colorful fish danced and splashed and beams of light sliced through the water, brightening everything in sight. Crustaceans scurried in and out of the rocks along the sandy bottom, kicking up dusty clouds in their wakes. The elf could hear the cries of birds and otters calling back and forth as they played and frolicked in the warm waters, an oasis of calm in a sea of trouble.

Chapter 6

Buddy and Newton swam several hundred yards out, but they kept the coastline in view.   The two were looking for the entrance to the inlet where it was expected that Mason would be waiting. Buddy squinted as he looked straight ahead.

"Newton, what is that?"

Newton strained to see through the murky water.   "It looks like some kind of disturbance or maybe there is a storm brewing."

The truth struck Buddy first.   "It's Mason!"

Alarmed, Newton cried out, "He's under attack!   When I shift, grab whatever you can and hold on tight."

Newton remembered reading somewhere that the dolphins were one of the swiftest animals in the sea.   He quickly turned into a dolphin and circled Buddy.   The elf grabbed the topmost fin and hung on.   Newton plowed through the water at great speed.   Using echolocation, he pinpointed each enemy.   His heart sank when he realized that there were way too many.   His echo also detected Mason.   Newton was relieved to know that his friend was still standing.

Newton told Buddy, "Mason is fighting alone against too many enemies."

307

Buddy needed both hands to hang on as the dolphin doubled his speed.   The elf just hoped that they would not be too late.

When Newton and Buddy arrived, the scene before them looked like the worst of cataclysmic storms.   Ice and wind slammed the area and rushed the coastline like a runaway locomotive.   Buddy cried out in Elven.   Newton had no idea what his friend was saying, but he could see that it wasn't going to be possible for the elf to swim through the gale force winds and dangerously cold, jagged ice, so Newton dropped him off on the outskirts of the storm.

He called loudly to be heard above the wind, "Wait here, Buddy."

For the second time, Newton changed into a megaladon and roared into battle.   He easily sliced through the ice and the chill of the water had little effect, but the wind buffeted and slowed him down.   As he pushed forward his eyes scanned the deep.   He knew that somewhere in the middle of all of those dark shapes was the bright and beautiful Mason.

Newton opened his great mouth and sucked in water, wind, ice, and shadows.   When his mouth was full he swam as close to shore as possible and spewed the contents onto the beach.   Then he returned to the fray and repeated the process.   The shark was careful not to bite down.   He did not plan to violate the doctor's oath that he had taken to do no harm.   It was not his wish to injure anyone, but he did want to help his friend and hoped that this would work.   Newton paused briefly to watch as the shadows scurried up the hill to the Dark Wood.   As they melted into the trees, Newton's spirits lifted. It *was* working. The scare alone had sent them packing.

After Newton scooped up the last of Wiloneomia's minions and deposited them on the beach, he returned to what had been the heart of the conflict. He observed that the wind had died down. When he was certain that all of the shadowy figures were gone, Newton shifted into a sea dragon and started to warm the waters. As the remaining ice melted and the waters calmed, Newton called for Mason. During this entire time, he had not seen his friend anywhere. Finally he swam back to where he had left Buddy, but the elf was no longer there. After looking around once more to make sure his friends were nowhere to be seen and not knowing what else to do, Newton changed back into a merman and swam toward the meeting place on the grassy shore of the inlet.

When Newton arrived, he made his way through the tall grasses near the water's edge. As he swam over the rocks along the silt-lined bottom and past a sunken log, a large water turtle was startled out of his hiding place. With flippers fanning, he swam past Newton on his way to the surface. The Shape Shifter also broke the surface. Wiping water from his eyes he looked to see Mason lying on the beach and Buddy sitting nearby. Curiously enough, there were two mini-dragons hovering nearby. One was brown and the other was gold. Much to Newton's surprise, standing just behind Buddy was the Grand Elf. Newton splashed toward the shoreline and as soon as the water was shallow enough he shifted into crow form and flew the rest of the way to Mason's side.

It didn't take medical training to know that something was very wrong with the Shadow Dweller. Newton could see that Mason's air funnels were missing and his eyes were closed, but he was breathing and appeared to be in a deep sleep. Newton shoved his personal feelings deep down inside and the doctor within him took charge. The crow reached for Mason and the change occurred with hardly any thought at all on his part. Right before the eyes of Buddy and the Grand Elf, crow became man and Dr. Newton Bennett bent over his patient with healing hands gently checking for wounds.

Newton knew that he needed to replace Mason's air funnels. He said, "Buddy, how fast can you reach Victoria? Ask her to send some of Mason's Bright Shadow brothers and please be quick."

Buddy called to the brown dragon and vaulted onto its back, swiftly flying away. Newton couldn't recall ever seeing Buddy ride a dragon, but he was thankful for the extra speed it would provide in this emergency. He did his best to make Mason comfortable and then turned to Barad with a question in his eyes.

The elf king looked directly at the human and in his silvery voice he replied to Newton's unasked question. "Buddy asked for my help and I came immediately. You see, Buddy is my youngest son."

Newton's look of surprise was met by Barad's steady gaze.

The elf king changed the subject. "I brought the Elven vessel of light. Before the last air funnel departed, Mason drank from it and now he rests."

The king looked regal in his gold and purple cape. He was

holding a slender staff which bore wings of gold on top with a jeweled crown resting lightly at the point where the wings curved and fanned outward. All of Pixieland loved Barad dearly. An elf of undetermined age, he was rarely seen out and about and passed most of his days in the Glimmering Glade among his sons and his brothers. There had been need for little else in such a beautiful world of harmony and happiness. Little need until now.

Buddy returned on the back of his brown mini. As he dismounted, the elf gently touched the face of his dragon and said, "Ellolui Malanam, Xanadree."

The dragon pressed his face against Buddy's hand and just for a moment, the elf closed his eyes. Newton was touched by the simple but beautiful gesture.

Buddy didn't have good news. "The Bright Shadows are trapped. The Angry Oak has extended her reign of fear and she now holds Mason's bright brothers as prisoners. It happened right after Victoria sent Mason to your aid in Otherworld. Victoria said that when Mason brought you back from Shadow, you had a lucky narrow escape. If the oak had seen where you were, you and Mason would also be prisoners right now." Buddy gave this time to sink in before continuing, "Victoria and most of Pixieland are assembled outside the Dark Wood. The Portal Keeper says that the time has come to right the wrong that has been done. She says that we are all needed at the gathering site and told me to tell you that she is waiting, but you must find your way."

When Buddy finished delivering Victoria's message, Barad

approached the sleeping Mason.   From his cape the King produced a vessel which shone more brightly than the day and lit the King's face dramatically.   He knelt down and spoke some soft words while lifting Mason's head.   Barad held the vessel close to Mason's face. At his direction, Buddy pulled the lion-ish lips up and the Elf King poured some of the liquid light through Mason's clinched teeth. Then Barad lowered Mason's head and regained his feet, the vessel of light disappearing again beneath his cape.

The king signaled for his golden mini dragon, but before he flew to join Victoria and the others he said, "Newton, I did all that I could for Mason.   His safety now lies in your hands and you must find your way."

Newton and Buddy exchanged puzzled glances.   What did Victoria and Barad mean when they said Newton would have to find his way?   Newton racked his brain for the answer.   Then it dawned on him.   Everything that had happened to him since he found *The Book of Crows* rushed toward this very moment.   He recognized that this was the time he was supposed to prove himself, show that he was worthy of being the chosen one, worthy of being *the* Shape Shifter.   He thought about the note that he found so many months ago in the secret compartment of the ancient tome, the book that had selected him from among all others and sent him to Pixieland. He struggled to remember the exact words.   Maybe they held the key.   As he concentrated, slowly the phrase returned to him.

"The strength of the elixir is guarded by the Shape Shifter. The power of the change is hidden within the ring."

Newton stood and paced back and forth beside Mason. He tried to apply the words to the circumstances. King Barad had just administered a powerful elixir and he, the Shape Shifter, was here standing guard. Maybe that was the first part. "The strength of the elixir is guarded by the Shape Shifter."

But what about the second part of the phrase? What did it mean? As Newton repeated the words, "The power of the change is hidden within the ring", it suddenly made sense. It had been there all along and the answer was really very simple. He had just been too worried to see it clearly before. Newton's expression brightened with hope and he turned to the elf. "Buddy, I know what I need to do."

Chapter 7

Newton carefully opened the ring's secret compartment and removed a generous amount of powder from within. He sprinkled it liberally over himself and Mason. Then he closed his eyes and conjured a vision of Mason at his very best. He pictured the mastiff as he had been in Dr Obrial's office—funny and stubborn. He pictured Mason as he had been on the trail, so protective. He recalled that Lion-ish had saved his life more than once along the way. Last of all he welcomed the fond thoughts of the bond they shared. In his mind, Newton held a perfect picture of Mason with his golden eyes shining and his air funnels whirling. The shift happened instantly and effortlessly. Newton became a Shadow Dweller complete with thousands of the much needed air funnels.

The shape of the Shadow Dweller was not an easy one to achieve. Even with the help of the ring dust, it was difficult to hold steady. He needed to work quickly. The Shape Shifter nudged Mason and called his name. At first nothing happened. Newton circled his friend and continued to nudge him. This action caused some of the ring dust to work its way down to Mason's skin. Newton was pleased to notice that one of his air funnels hopped off and landed on Mason. But almost immediately it slowed down and moved sluggishly. Newton thought that there might be a connection between the dust on Mason's skin and the jumping air funnel so he cried, "Buddy, hurry! Rub the powder into Mason's fur."

Newton continued to call Mason's name as Buddy rubbed the magic dust into lion-ish fur. One by one the bundles of moving air jumped to the unresponsive Shadow Dweller. As more funnels joined their fellows, they began to spin more normally and soon Mason stirred.

Newton called again, "Mason!"

He felt himself losing the shape. There were few funnels left on him and Newton was forced to shift back to his human form.

Buddy backed away from Mason. "I can no longer rub him, Newton. The funnels are forming a barrier."

Newton smiled in relief. "That's ok. Don't you see? That means they are working properly."

Newton looked down to see Mason's two golden eyes looking into his. Lion-ish slowly stood. Newton cupped his hands around the dear face. "How are you feeling?"

Mason answered, "I feel just fine thanks to you."

Buddy flashed his famous smile.

Newton asked, "Did you know that we were trying to help you?"

Mason replied, "I was aware. But I didn't know that you had the skill to save me." Mason said that last part as if he were disappointed in himself for not believing in his friend.

Newton placed a hand on Mason. "Don't feel badly. For a while there I wasn't so sure that I could help you either." Newton carefully studied the Shadow Dweller. "I need to know that you are completely well."

Mason nodded and said, "Yes, I am, thanks to you and Buddy. I must also thank King Barad."

Newton spoke with some urgency. "I am so glad that you are fully recovered. I wish there were more time to celebrate, but Victoria and the others wait for us just outside the Dark Wood." The Shape Shifter spoke softly, "Mason, everyone will understand if you choose not to join us. You have just come through a very difficult time and have already done more than your part to make us all safe."

But before Newton could finish his pretty speech Mason was already on the way to the meeting site. Lion-ish smiled broadly as he called back over his shoulder. "Hurry along you two. Let's not keep Victoria waiting."

Newton grinned at Buddy as they fell in behind Mason. Even if he was an elf prince, his best friend looked like the same Buddy Newton had known ever since he first entered Pixieland. He was indeed the same elf just as Newton was still the same crow. As circumstances had developed, it became clear that they both held some secrets.

But during these difficult times it had become necessary for the two of them to play all of their cards, so to speak, in an effort to protect their beloved Pixieland. Newton's eyes softened as he realized that he was beginning to think of Pixieland as his home.

The doctor thought back to those first days. Even though he knew that he had been sent here for a purpose, those had been carefree and wonderful days in this bright new world. Newton resolved that if there was anything he could do to help restore those times, for himself and for all of Pixieland, he would put his heart and soul into the task.

When the trio spotted Victoria and the others, Newton took a moment to change to his crow self. Buddy was surprised to see Skuba and Morella. Skuba waved in their direction and they waved in return.

Mason spoke out in his golden tones, "We will fight for our own homes and make a stand to defend our loved ones, but it takes special friends indeed to stand willingly beside us in defense of—what is to them—an unknown land."

Skuba said, "Pixieland is not a strange land to Morella and me. We know it well through the stories and experiences that you have shared. And besides, that's what friends do; friends look out for each other."

Victoria stood on a small rise, her white hair whipping around her. The Portal Keeper permitted herself a tiny smile as she noted that Mason had recovered.

"My brothers of light and I should be among the first to enter the Forest of Sighs," Mason declared to Victoria. "It is our best advantage because we will know the thoughts of our dark brothers."

Victoria replied, "I have no doubt that what you say is true." The petite lady's face softened as she delivered the bad news. "But the Angry Oak holds your brothers hostage in Shadow and because of this, they cannot enter our world."

As Mason instinctively moved toward a nearby shadow, Victoria hastily added, "Make no attempt to join them or you will be lost to us too."

Mason appeared to be undecided.

Victoria continued, "Your brothers are safe enough for now, but they cannot help us. You may choose to go to them, but you will not be able to break the bond that binds them. What we do here will help them more than anything you can do *there*."

Mason turned and stared at the outskirts of the Forest of Sighs. His air funnels buzzed excitedly in response to the nearness of his home trees. Mason trusted Victoria and knew that she spoke with wisdom. His final decision was a difficult one, but he believed it was for the best. "I will stay."

Victoria gave him a curt nod of appreciation. Turning toward the assembled group of Pixielanders, she raised her voice in order to be heard. "Those of you who are equipped with lights step forward please. "

A throng of magicals made up largely of faeries, elves and unicorns responded to Victoria's request. The Portal Keeper addressed one of the largest of the unicorns. "Destrea, I have heard that you once entered the Dark Wood."

The large pink unicorn's voice sounded like liquid silk as he answered, "I did. I was much younger and the trees were fewer in number."

Victoria asked, "You came face to face with Wiloneomia?"

The unicorn responded, "Yes, she was younger then too and not so angry, merely sad. She saved me from the Birch Binders."

Victoria said, "Much has changed since then. I do have an idea, one that I think might work. Since Wiloneomia knows you, she may permit you to pass through the trees unharmed. It is asking much, but will you lead this group?" Destrea did not even hesitate. "Of course I will," he neighed bravely. Victoria thanked him and then said, "See if the Angry Oak will grant us an audience and return to me with her answer." Addressing the light-bringing Magicals, Victoria explained her plan. "I will not send you all in at once so I will divide you into two groups. One group will remain here. As for those who do enter the Woods, I am hoping that the sum total of your lights will shine brightly enough to penetrate the darkness and gloom. Follow Destrea. Stay together and above all, be very careful. When you find Wiloneomia, just let Destrea do the talking."

Wildflower, Buddy, Skuba, Aline, and Morella were among those selected to follow Destrea into the woods.

Rosie waited beside the Portal Keeper. Because she was a caller faerie, Victoria had asked her to remain by her side and keep her informed of any important thoughts or impressions that she might gain from either side of the conflict. The Portal Keeper knew that such information could prove very useful and might help turn the tide in their favor.

The group with Destrea had been instructed to shine their lights as brightly as possible in order to penetrate the deep darkness of the Forest of Sighs. Destrea wore the amulet given to him by Wiloneomia many years ago. On that day, it had guaranteed him safe passage through the woods. He wasn't so sure that it would still be effective, but he would know very soon. As the group drew closer to the Forest of Sighs, Destrea kept a watchful eye on the amulet. If wearing it would still afford him protection, it should begin to glow brightly as soon as they entered the woods.

Faeries and elves as well as the horns of the unicorns glowed warmly. Victoria had decided against sending everyone in at one time. There were many Pixielanders who had been instructed to wait and see whether or not Destrea and his group would be successful. They organized themselves according to size and ability. The Portal Keeper thought that perhaps a relatively smaller group would be the best way to begin since they were seeking negotiation. Maybe it would be less threatening to the Angry Oak. Victoria didn't know what waited for them and although risks must be taken, she was not willing to risk an entire community all at once. The brightly lit group moved slowly toward the forbidding trees, Newton and Mason bringing up the rear. Newton was not luminous, but he wanted to be with his best friends, Buddy and Mason. The Lion-ish was in shadow form and as such glowed with his own special light.

As the Dark Wood closed around them, the horns on the unicorns shone with more intensity. The group was successful in lighting themselves beautifully which provided an awe-inspiring scene. However, in spite of the combined power of so many brave and noble magicals, the blackness of the woods stood like an impenetrable wall against them.

Destrea stumbled on the path as the amulet around his neck glowed with a white hot light and then exploded into a thousand powdery particles. The unicorn shook his head and reared up on his hind legs. His startled scream reached the ears of those who waited outside the woods.

Mason and Newton dashed forward as everyone's lights began to falter—everyone's, that is, except for Mason's. His funnels whirled madly at the close proximity to the familiar trees and his inner glow shone like a blazing sun within the forest. Dark Shadows emerged from the trees and like moths to a flame; they were drawn to their bright brother.

Newton sensed that the brave group of Pixielanders was in grave danger so he quickly shifted into a thick and prickly bush. The hedge spread out, growing rapidly until all of Newton's friends were surrounded by its protective thorns. The unicorns stood wide-eyed with arched necks and flaring nostrils. Their mystical horns thrummed with the struggle to maintain bright lights. The faeries and elves also concentrated on lighting the area, but their powers were diminishing.

Buddy had a flashback to the time when Newton had shifted into a much smaller thorn bush. It had saved his life then. He wondered if it would be enough to save everyone's life now. Mason stood like a beacon, waiting for the first shadow to penetrate their fortress.

Upon hearing Destrea scream, Victoria quickly went about the business of giving everyone else directions as to how to proceed. Rosie's face looked pained as she passed information to Victoria. The Caller had connected with one of the unicorns, a smoky grey named Silversong. Careful not to startle him, she had gathered his thoughts and impressions of the conflict taking place just inside the Dark Wood.

The Portal Keeper knew that her original plan had failed and that something must be done quickly to alter the confrontation taking place inside the Forest of Sighs. She instructed Rosie to tell Silversong to speak with Newton and the others and let them know that help was on the way.

Then she sent Rosie to join her friend the grizzly bear and signaled to one of the unicorns that had stayed behind. She whispered a few words into his ear and then he dropped down to his knee so that the petite lady could hop onto his back. Victoria's face looked determined as her unusual mount, Jax, galloped up and down in front of the remaining Pixielanders while the Portal Guardian motioned to them all. The message was clear—Victoria and Jax would lead them into the Forest of Sighs.

Chapter 8

Ernie arrived just in time to hear the unicorn scream. It made him very nervous and afraid. He had never heard such a distressed cry and it gave him pause. He grabbed his own tail and stroked it absentmindedly as he tried to make sense of what was happening. From his secluded viewpoint, he saw Victoria riding up and down the line of Pixielanders before motioning for them to follow her. He watched as the entire group was engulfed by the gloomy trees. The blue mouse was terrified when he could no longer see any of his friends and he wondered what was happening to them. The Forest of Sighs was more frightening than he could have imagined. He wanted to turn tail and run, but instead he took a deep breath and squeezed back the tears that were threatening.

Although the little mouse was shaking like a leaf, he pulled himself together as best he could. He had no light to shine. He was not big or brave or beautiful or strong, but he was a good listener. Ernie had paid attention when Mason told the story of the Angry Oak and it had given him an idea. As the scared mouse picked up his bundle and resolutely trudged toward the Forest of Sighs, he thought to himself that soon enough he would see whether or not his idea was a good one.

Ernie stopped again just outside the woods. The mouse expected to hear the sounds of a great battle being waged, but instead his ears were assailed by sorrowful sighs and heavy moans. From deep within the forest, there was the sound of bitter weeping which caused the fur along the back of Ernie's neck to rise. The crying spelled out a profound sadness. Ernie felt that the name "Forest of Sighs" described this place most accurately. The blue mouse's eyes widened with fright and his ample ears were pinned back against his head. He looped his long tail over one arm, took a deep breath, and plunged into the Dark Wood.

Fortunately for Ernie, the shadows were distracted. All attention was focused on the main body of Pixielanders who were attempting to enter the woods somewhere nearby.

The blue mouse blinked rapidly in the utter darkness as he struggled to find a path. Ernie ran in spurts. He couldn't see, but he followed the sound of the weeping. Sometimes he bumped into a tree or some dense brush. He stood very still and held his breath as a shadowy figure slid past only a few feet away. Ernie felt a sudden chill. When the mouse worked up the courage to do so, he slowly turned his head to see where the shadow was going. In the distance, he saw the flickering of his friends' lights and was afraid that every enemy in these woods was probably on the way there. Ernie blinked back tears and shook violently. He was every bit as scared for his friends as he was for himself.

Ernie repeatedly started and stopped. He fell over a root

and froze to the spot as its tree creaked loudly. Carefully, he regained his footing and continued toward the weeping sound. Deeper and deeper into the woods he went. From time to time he looked back at the lights of his friends. They winked at him through the dimness, but seemed to be fading. Ernie was not sure if this was because he was getting further away or because they were growing weaker. He started to second guess himself. Maybe this was not a good idea after all or maybe the stories he had heard were true and he was doomed to wander around lost in these woods forever. The darkness felt heavy like a cloak and Ernie couldn't even see his paw in front of his face. The blue mouse looked straight up in hope of finding some relief, perhaps a blanket of stars in the sky, but the canopy of inky leaves prevented any view of that which would have been familiar.

Ernie dared not make any more noise than necessary. He blinked frequently and each time he hoped that he would be able to see a little bit better, but all was black around him. However, Ernie had good ears and he used them to pinpoint the proper direction as he followed the sound of crying. He could no longer see the lights of his friends when he looked back over his shoulder and this scared him most of all. He also noticed that the forest was growing colder. At some point, icy water started dripping off of the trees. Ernie trembled part from fear and part from the chilly water that was soaking his fur.

The blue mouse left the path, following the bitter sounds. This turned out to be a very good decision, for right afterward several shadowy figures crept past him.   If he had still been on the trail they would most certainly have seen him.   Ernie stood very still and hardly breathed as he watched them go by.   He was having difficulty making out the dense shapes in the utter darkness.   No doubt that was why the blue mouse didn't see that one of the shadows stopped and waited.   As Ernie moved again, the dark figure turned and then fell in behind him.   It hugged the trees as it moved along in Ernie's wake.   The blue mouse was beginning to feel very cold and his feet slipped on the icy forest floor which slowed his progress even more.

Ernie was unaware that he had attracted a shadow because he had been concentrating on working his way through the ice without falling.   He was also growing tired and maybe a little of the forest's sadness was rubbing off on him.   Ernie thought about giving up. He had no way of knowing if his friends were ok or if he would ever see any of them again and he no longer felt up to this task.   Ernie wondered if he should have told Victoria or Newton about his idea. They would have known who to send in his stead.   After all, he was just a simple mouse.   While these thoughts plagued Ernie, his feet moved as if all on their own toward the sound of bitter weeping.

Ernie felt that this was the lowest point of his entire life.   The sobbing sounded louder and as the blue mouse paused to make sure he was still headed in the right direction, the Dark Shadow that was following decided to make its move.   Under the inky blackness of its home trees the shadow took shape and form for the first time.   It threw back its shaggy head and howled.   From all over the woods there were answering cries.   Ernie stumbled backward and fell against a tree root. He could tell that one of the creatures was nearby and from the sounds he heard, it was clear that many others were on their way. Ernie clutched his bundle to his chest as if it could protect him from the sinister ones who were approaching. As he blinked against a darkness that was blacker than night, the blue mouse could not see his enemies, but he felt certain that they knew exactly where *he* stood.

Ernie looked in the direction of the bitter weeping. He thought about making a run for it. Ernie needed to reach the Angry Oak in order to put his idea into action, but he could tell that the shadows had him surrounded. He was wet and cold and if that wasn't enough, his own fear threatened to consume him. Ernie believed that he was living his final moments and he thought about his dear parents. He remembered that when he was a very young mouse and feeling afraid, his mother would sing to him. Ernie didn't know how to fight his fears or these enemies, but as he recalled the familiar refrain, the blue mouse opened his mouth and sang. With a voice both sweet and bright, the mouse penetrated the night with the simple melody and his mother's wise words of comfort and cheer. At first his voice wavered, but as he continued to sing it became stronger and more certain. The sinister ones who surrounded him stopped to listen.

They were not the only ones listening. From deep in the heart of the woods, a giant tree paused in her weeping. In all of the years that Wiloneomia had been growing in this place, she had never heard such singing. Something stirred deep within her. Her whispered command flowed out to her subjects, "Bring it to me. I would see the one who fills my woods with such song."

One by one the Dark Shadows took form. As they closed in around the mouse, he stopped singing and shut his eyes tight. He knew they had approached, for he could hear them well and all else was quiet in the woods. Even the sighing and moaning had ceased. One nudged him forward. He took two steps and stopped. The shadow nudged him again. Finally Ernie realized that he was being pushed forward, so he started walking.

Ernie was so tired that he barely noticed that the leaves of the trees had stopped dripping icy water. When his escorts stopped moving, Ernie stopped too. He held his bundle tightly as he awaited his fate. When he heard her voice for the very first time he needed no introduction even though he could not see the Angry Oak. He tried to control his quaking with little success. He had anticipated harshness, but Wiloneomia's voice was surprisingly rich and mellow.

"Who are you and why do you trespass among my sisters?"

The mouse's voice trembled, "I am Ernie. I am only a mouse."

The tree spoke again. "Ernie Only a Mouse, how did you manage to find a path in my woods past both my sisters and my shadows? You do not look powerful enough to have accomplished such a task."

Ernie answered, "I don't know, but perhaps they did not notice me right away because I am small."

Ernie wished that he could see the tree, but the complete

darkness made that impossible.

"You are not the first to try to enter my woods tonight. I have only just turned away quite a large group."

Ernie was afraid to ask just how she had accomplished that. He only hoped that his friends were safe. The leaves of the surrounding trees rustled and the Shadow Dwellers pressed against him. Ernie felt very small as he stood facing the powerful tree in the heart of the Forest of Sighs.

Wiloneomia asked, "Why do you seek me? Everyone knows the stories and I am certain that you have heard that I would never allow you to return."

Ernie could hear sadness in the tree's voice. He stared up into the night. "I have not been through what you have experienced and I have no idea how much you suffer. I am only a mouse, but when I was a baby I did become separated from my parents. I was alone and frightened. Fortunately I was found or I might not have survived. Even though I was treated well, I missed my mom and dad. There's nothing like being with your own family. My parents finally found me. I had a happy ending because I had new friends AND my family, but I do understand how it feels to be separated from your home and all that you once knew and loved." Ernie paused for breath. The leaves of the oak rustled ominously. Then Ernie said, "Everyone says you are angry, but you really seem mostly sad to me."

The oak snapped, "What do you know about me and my troubles?"

Ernie blinked into the blackness. "Mason told me about what happened to you. He told me that you were snatched from your world and all that you knew and from the King's garden where you longed to be..."

The oak sobbed and then spoke harshly. "You waste my time with idle conversation. I only brought you here because of the song. Where did you get it?"

Ernie felt fuzzy-headed and more than a little bit confused. "Where did I get it?"

The tree creaked and groaned. "THE SONG! WHERE DID YOU GET THAT SONG?"

Ernie was shaking in earnest. The tree was yelling and the Dark Shadows were pressing him on all sides. His voice squeaked as he answered, "My mother used to sing it to me when I was a child and frightened. I learned it from her. It came from her heart."

Wiloneomia really looked at the mouse for the first time. He didn't seem like someone who could waltz right into her woods. She had not allowed a living thing to enter for many, many years. Only the shadows who had stayed with her and her sister trees were permitted here. ALL was sadness. ALL was sorrow until finally ALL mourning was replaced by a burning anger.

Ernie tentatively opened the bundle that he had been carrying and slowly pried the lid from the small pail. As he looked down into the puddle of golden tears he could see his own bedraggled reflection in the shiny surface. This was the first thing he had seen with his eyes since he entered these woods. He moved forward dragging the pail and felt with one paw until he located Wiloneomia's roots.

Wiloneomia felt the tiny paw and something about it touched her heart. Then before she could respond, Ernie poured the contents of the small pail over her roots and said, "These golden tears belonged to my friend Buddy. One day when he was sharing a happy moment with his good friend Okikki they laughed so hard that they cried. These are his tears of joy. They saved them in this pail,but...I took them. Later Buddy told me I could keep them as a gift. I wanted to do something really special with the tears and then I heard your story. I don't think you are mean. I think you just lost your joy. I am giving the golden tears of happiness to you because I think they will make you feel better. And the song can be yours too. Mother's song always made me feel happy when I was sad or afraid." Then Ernie sang to Wiloneomia the simple lullaby that his mother had sung to him.

When you're very small
The world can seem so scary
You may feel afraid,
But you must find your way.

When you're just a babe
I'll hold you in my arms
I'll see you through each day
But you must find your way.

When you've grown up tall
I'll hold you in my heart
I'll watch you as you play
But you must find your way.

When you're old and grey
My love will not depart
You'll keep it in your heart
But you must find your way.

If the world grows cold
And you feel all alone
Just remember what I say
That you must find your way
You must find your way.

Chapter 9

Newton had worked hard to both protect his friends and keep the Dark Shadows out, but Shadow Dwellers are very good at slipping through any sort of vegetation and the Shape Shifter was growing tired. The unnatural darkness that existed in the Forest of Sighs threatened to rob them all of both their hope and strength.

Jax reared up time and again, but Victoria held her seat upon his back in a way that would have won admiration from the most expert of riders. It was clear to the Portal Keeper that this plan was not working. There might be a way to penetrate the Dark Wood, but this was not it. She spoke quietly to Newton and then to the others.

"We must retreat. The Shape Shifter is beginning to lose the form of the hedge and we need to back out of the woods, regroup and decide what to do next."

As the group began the slow backward exit from the trees, Victoria leaned down and stroked the unicorn's neck. This seemed to calm him, but just a small amount as the heavy, cloying woods took their toll on this most sensitive creature of light. The Pixielanders moved carefully out of the trees. As the last magical retreated, Victoria and Jax paused for a moment. The Portal Keeper rubbed her hand down the length of his glowing horn and held up her arm. The palm of her hand shone brightly with the reflected light. In a firm voice she cried, "We are not finished here!" Then she turned Jax and retreated. The petite lady was followed by Newton the Crow who had finally lost the shape of the hedge and had been forced to take to wing. Several Dark Shadows gave chase, but turned back at the edge of the woods.

The Pixielanders milled around talking among themselves. They turned to watch as Victoria and Newton emerged from the trees. The unicorns nickered at Jax. The young stallion rolled his eyes and shook his mane as if trying to rid himself of the dismal sadness of that place. Victoria rode through the crowd speaking with first one and then another, making sure that no one was injured in any way. When she had satisfied herself that (although everyone was concerned and many were frightened) no real harm had been done, the Portal Keeper drew aside to think. She did not want to use stronger measures, but she knew that the Angry Oak must be stopped.

Victoria stood for a few minutes gazing into the trees. Something at the edge of the forest caught her eye. Jax danced nervously as she coaxed him to once again move closer to the trees. Victoria rested a hand on the stallion's shoulder as she spoke into his ear. The unicorn's skin quivered beneath her fingers as he moved with flared nostrils, arched neck and small prancing steps. It was apparent that Jax wished to be anywhere else but here. Victoria kept him moving smoothly along the outer edge of the wood until she reached the unusual item, a small flap of material. Victoria asked Jax to pick it up with the tip of his horn which he did. Then the unicorn turned his head toward his rider while she leaned to reach the fabric.

Victoria looked closely at the small piece of material. She knew immediately what it was. The crisp white fabric was the same as that of Ernie's sailor suit. Victoria looked at the ground and noticed a round indention where something heavy had been. She looked thoughtful as she directed Jax back to the other Pixielanders. By the time she reached them lines of worry were etched around her mouth and eyes. With a concerned tone, she announced, "I believe the young mouse Ernie has entered the woods on his own. It appears as though he is carrying something."

Buddy interjected, "My bucket of tears."

Victoria squinted at him. "Your what?"

Buddy tried to explain, "He carries them around sometimes."

Victoria persisted, "Tell me again what it is that he carries?"

Buddy pointed to his eyes with both index fingers as he answered, "My tears, the ones I cried the day Okikki and I were laughing."

At the mention of her name, the red squirrel stepped forward. Young Tango snuggled next to her and Okikki cuddled him as she spoke wistfully, "It *was* the most wonderful day. Buddy came to my garden to invite me to join him on a new adventure." The squirrel cast an affectionate glance at her elf friend as she continued, "Buddy made a bear elixir and had the strangest reaction to his." Okikki's eyes grew large as she recalled, "He turned into a big, bright gold bear and it hurt my eyes to look at him! His face was all rubbery and he was whistling." Okikki had a sudden urge to grin as she retold the story. "It was really funny and we laughed until we cried. But we were surprised that Buddy's tears were golden! He wanted to save them so I scooped them up in a pail."

Buddy interrupted, "Truthfully, we forgot all about them. After we left, Ernie found them. He felt badly about taking them, but I told him that I hadn't even missed them and to keep them as a gift from me. He did promise to do something special with them someday."

Victoria nodded as it dawned on her just what the little blue mouse was attempting. The Portal Keeper turned to Rosie. "Can you sense him?"

Rosie responded, "I will try." Then she flew as close to the Forest of Sighs as she dared and searched mentally for the small thread that would provide the way to the thoughts and impressions of the mouse. Rosie tried to penetrate the woods with her bright, sharp mind, but even her special gifts couldn't slice through that gloom. The sadness and despair that soaked the trees was more than she could bear and she looked helplessly at Victoria. "There is such sorrow. It blinds me to anything else. If Ernie is there, I cannot see him. I see nothing living in those woods except trees and Dark Shadows." When Rosie noticed the look on Victoria's face, she hastened to add, "That doesn't mean he's not ok. I just couldn't connect with him."

Victoria nodded. "It is as I feared, but we had to make the attempt." Victoria dismounted from Jax and selected a few Pixielanders to accompany her. "Newton, Skuba, Morella, Wildflower, Okikki, Buddy, Aline and Rosie, let us try to enter the woods at the last known spot where Ernie was. Perhaps if he found a way inside we can too."

As they headed to the Forest of Sighs, Buddy felt thankful to be surrounded by his friends. He fell in beside Skuba. "I am so glad you and Morella are here." Buddy glanced at the morel faerie, including her in the conversation.

Skuba spoke for the earthling magicals. "We wouldn't have it any other way. I must say, I have never seen anything in nature that compares to this. Tell me, what's been done in the past to try to help these trees?"

The question was phrased innocently enough, but it hung heavily in the air. Victoria stopped and turned. It was as if a light switched on for all of them as Buddy shuffled uneasily and Wildflower shook her head.

Okikki said, "The squirrels have avoided the trees here. The stories kept us out. We heard that those who enter never return."

Wildflower added, "A few faeries tried to go into the woods, but the sounds of sighing struck fear in their hearts and they changed their minds."

Buddy weighed in, "Elves do not go here."

Victoria finished the story, "So we have an unhappy tree that was left alone year after year until, from her seeds, a great forest of sorrow developed and spread across this land. This went on until her sadness turned to anger. And we are only just now addressing the problem, when the actions of the Angry Oak have begun to affect us all and ignoring the woods is no longer enough of a solution."

Buddy said, "When you put it that way, it sounds so unkind and no one in Pixieland meant to be unkind."

Victoria responded, "I am aware that no one meant to be thoughtless or unkind. But we have made assumptions based on what we were seeing here and simply reacted to our own fears".

As the group approached the place where the fabric had been found, Victoria pointed out, "He entered right here."

Buddy made a move forward, but Victoria put out an arm to stop him. "I think I know why Ernie was able to enter the woods. It is a matter of attitude."

Okikki parroted, "Attitude?"

Everyone's eyes were on Victoria as she explained. "We tried to enter Wiloneomia's woods in order to help the mermaids and defend our land from the threat of the Dark Shadows. I'm pretty sure that our friend Ernie entered to try to *help* the Angry Oak." Victoria turned her penetrating eyes onto the group. "We should go back and tell the others."

Newton asked, "But what about Ernie?"

Victoria looked past the crow into the trees. "What indeed."

Everyone took notice as the trees rustled. A small, bright voice drifted out from the woods, carried to them by the very leaves of the trees.

Rosie smiled in recognition.   "It's Ernie and he's singing!"

Upon hearing the faint notes, everyone stood quietly.   From somewhere in the blackness, the mouse continued to sing, "If you're very small, the world can seem so scary.   You may feel afraid, but you must find your way."

Chapter 10

As Ernie sang each succeeding verse to Wiloneomia, his words of encouragement and love bounced from the Angry Oak across the trees and out to the waiting ears of his friends. As Wiloneomia felt the gift of golden tears trickling down to her roots, she listened to the words of Ernie's song and started to feel something that was neither sadness nor anger.

From the tips of her roots way below the surface of the earth and up through her trunk to her heart, Wiloneomia felt a spontaneous burst of happiness. From the topmost leaf to the lowest branch on the tree, a transformation was taking place. Like a veil gradually lifting, the darkness disappeared from the woods. The branches and leaves of Wiloneomia were black no more. It looked as if someone had loaded a brush with liquid gold and painted the Forest of Sighs. As the bright gold of her leaves slowly returned one by one, her sisters' leaves changed as well. For the first time, light slanted down into the woods and the shiny trees welcomed it.

Ernie blinked up at the bright, golden tree. He stopped singing and stared. "You're beautiful!" he blurted. "You're not scary anymore!"

The Dark Shadows that had been pressing in on him began to

change.   They brightened one by one until he was surrounded by creatures who looked much like his friend Mason.   He giggled as a couple of their tiny air funnels spun along his fur, drying and warming him as he stood before the golden oak.

Wiloneomia looked out at her branches.   The sight of her restored beauty reinforced the happiness and joy that she was feeling.   The gentle rustling of her leaves sounded like beautiful music.   Soon her sisters took up the melody and the transformation was complete.

In a loud voice, Wiloneomia proclaimed, "There will be no more sighing and moaning.   The days of weeping are over.   From this day forward we will be known as the Forest of Song.   There will be music here and respite for the weary soul.   Those who come in will go out with a lightness of step and a song in their hearts."   Then Wiloneomia the Golden Oak called out to her sons.   "Join us, Dwellers of Light Shadow.   Your brothers and I welcome you to return to your home trees."

From deep shadows all over Pixieland, the Bright Shadows once imprisoned by the Angry Oak were now set free.   They entered the Forest of Song from all sides.   There was a great reunion as brother greeted brother and all was restored.

Mason watched the transformation from outside the Forest of Song.   His funnels spun a bit faster and his red-gold coat shone brighter.   Mason gently nudged Newton and the crow understood that it was time for his friend to go.   He cupped his wings around Mason's face and looked into those dancing eyes.   "Goodbye, dear friend.   I will never forget you," rasped Newton.

Mason spoke gruffly, "Nor I, you"

Newton attempted to lighten the mood.   "If you find a pair of expensive shoes lying about among those trees one of these days, you will know that it's a gift from your old friend."

Mason threw his head back and laughed such an infectious laugh that those around them smiled in response.   The rest of the friends said their goodbyes to Lion-ish who then bounded away to meet his long lost brothers and to seek the comfort of Shadow.   Just before he entered the Forest of Song, Mason turned once more as Newton waved a final farewell.   Then the Shadow Dweller disappeared into the waiting golden trees.

Wiloneomia looked at the blue mouse who stood gazing up at her.   The tree's roots wiggled slightly, drinking in every single joyous tear.

"I want to do something special to thank you properly for what you have done for me."

Ernie smiled up at Wiloneomia revealing his two prominent front teeth.   "Just knowing that you are happy again is enough for me.   I am a simple sea-faring mouse and my needs are few."

Ernie impulsively hugged the tree.   His arms were short and could not begin to surround the wide girth of Wiloneomia, but he did his best and pressed his furry face against her too.   The tree felt his hug and her heart melted.

"I know just the thing, Ernie Only a Mouse!   Your home is on the ocean, correct?"

Ernie nodded.   "I love the sea and I have a boat too."   Ernie hastened to add, "But no living tree was harmed in its making."

Wiloneomia laughed aloud.   "I would have known that you could not harm a living thing, Ernie Only a Mouse!   Tell me though—do you have a home in Pixieland?"

Ernie answered, "No, my home is on the other side of the ocean."

Wiloneomia shook her branches and as her request went out to her sisters, they stepped this way and that until a wide path opened up.   As Ernie gazed down the newly formed path, he could now see the top of the hill that led to the beach and beyond that, glinting in the sun, a wide expanse of beautiful bright blue water. His eyes filled with tears which he quickly brushed away.

The tree spoke with some humor, "Do you mean THAT ocean?"

She smiled as the mouse mutely nodded and then revealed a large gap between two of her sizeable roots.

"I myself will make a place for you within my own trunk for when you are visiting Pixieland.   You will be the first of many who may find shelter and comfort waiting in these woods."

Ernie curiously peeked into the dark entrance.   "You mean...this is for me?"

The tree rustled gently.   "If you like it, it is yours.   When you are not on the sea or with your people, this will be your home away from home."

The small mouse was wide-eyed. "Then I will be like you because you are away from home too. Pixieland is your home away from home, right?"

Ernie flashed a smile that the tree couldn't help but return.

Victoria's own smile was a beautiful sight to see. The lines of concern around her eyes faded and she turned to the citizens of Pixieland.

Newton asked, "What just happened?"

Victoria responded, "You will all know more in time, but suffice it to say that Ernie found a way to help the Angry Oak and she is no longer angry. But Ernie is not the only hero here today. Each one of you is a hero. You all worked together for the peace of Pixieland. While you waited here for the right moment to deal with the Angry Oak, Newton, Buddy and Mason rescued the mermaid queen egg. Everything we did was important, but Ernie found a way to go straight to the heart of the matter."

Ernie couldn't wait to see everyone again and introduce them to Wiloneomia, so he scampered to the edge of the beautiful woods. As soon as he was spotted, his friends surrounded him. Hugs were exchanged and questions asked. Ernie explained what he had done to help the tree.

Buddy put an arm around the blue mouse. "I am so glad that you had those tears. I would never have thought to use them to help the Angry Oak."

Skuba said, "I heard you singing." Noticing Ernie's

embarrassment the mountain elf added, "I liked your song."

Morella grinned and said, "Obviously Wiloneomia liked it too."

Ernie smiled shyly and offered a tiny, "Thank you." Then he pulled Skuba toward the trees. "Come on everybody. Come and meet her. Wait 'til you see. She is so beautiful!" The blue mouse chattered excitedly as he led his friends into the Forest of Song to meet Wiloneomia the Golden Oak.

Meanwhile in the estuary, Timna noticed that the bright blue egg was rocking slightly in its sandy bed. This was good news indeed. The egg had not moved since it had arrived and she had been concerned that the extremely cold temperatures may have harmed the life within.

Timna drew close. "Yes, little one?"

The sea dragon gently wrapped the egg in her front flippers as she listened to the voice of the unborn Mer Queen. Since it was not yet time for the hatching she returned the egg to its place in the sand, signaling to one of her dolphin friends.

"Swim to the Mer City and find the Dynasts. Tell them that the new queen is doing just fine and that she has already chosen her name. She wishes to be known as Joy."

Victoria smiled as she looked out over the beautiful Forest of Song. Gone forever was the blight that had been the Dark Wood. All of Pixieland was bright and beautiful, as it was meant to be. Strong friendships had been forged and valuable lessons learned.

The Portal Keeper planned to stay long enough to see Morella and Skuba safely home.   She also needed to have a word with Newton. Afterward she would return to her library of beloved books, those ancient volumes, the gateways to other worlds.

About the Author

MaryBeth Hewes, a native Memphian, enjoys life with her husband who is also her best friend. They are surrounded by their "fur kids," including Cookie, the Papillion who appears in her stories. Mary is a mother of four children and a grandmother of nine. Her writing background is in poetry but in more recent years she began to tell stories about faeries, elves, and other magical creatures.
**Follow the author at
www.marybethhewes.com**